The PLAYER

CLAIRE CONTRERAS

"What do you base your happiness around?
Material, women and large paper?

That means you're inferior. Not major."

-Nas

Prologue

Reporter: "Your one constant has always remained that soccer is the number-one love of your life. That you'd never trade it for anything or anyone. Does that still stand?"

I inhaled a heavy breath when I heard the question. I set down my fork and knife and walked over to the television. I'd promised myself I wouldn't. I'd promised myself I wasn't going to look at him, listen to him, talk to him, have absolutely anything to do with him once he left. Yet there I was, like I was sure countless of other females were, waiting on bated breath for his answer. When he came into the screen, my breath left me altogether. God. I missed him. I hated him. Couldn't stand him. But seeing him on the screen, the way he sat back on the seat with his ankle crossed over his knee, looking completely relaxed as he was being drilled with questions . . . the way his chiseled jaw moved when he gave the reporter that lopsided smile that hinted at legions of pleasure that would make any sane woman blush furiously, those arms, roped in muscle and etched in art that I'd touched, clung to during so many sleepless nights . . .

"Of course it still stands. What do you think?" he asked,

tilting his head, green eyes twinkling in flirtation.

Reporter: "So the rumors about a woman you left behind in the US during the holiday—"

"I think we both know how many rumors are spread about me." He tore his gaze away from her and looked directly into the camera. Directly at me. "If there was a woman that special, I would never leave her behind."

Reporter: "So you would be willing to make your career number two for the right woman?"

He continued to look at the camera, his face sobering, all traces of flirtation gone. "I'd give up my career to chase moments with the right woman."

I leaned back in my couch, fighting back the tears that threatened.

I hated him.

Chapter
ONE

Sometimes I closed my eyes and tried to remember what it felt like to live in luxury. To have the cold silk sheets beneath my fingertips, the warm air on cool winter days, and the cold air on hot summer nights. All things I once had (albeit, for a short time) and now could just barely imagine. I was happy, though. Most of the time. And that was more than I could say for many of us. I didn't have much other than a roof over my head. Not a big one, or one I owned, but it was one I'd called home for the past three years, until my landlord slapped me with an eviction notice that said I needed to be out by the end of the month.

"By the end of the month? How can they do that?" my sister Vanessa asked, her voice a whisper before she raised it and looked at her husband. "Can they do that? Is that legal?"

"They own the building," Adam said from the other side of the room.

He walked over to where we were sitting in front of the marble fireplace and plucked the paper out of Vanessa's hand. We both looked at him as his eyes scanned the page, breaths held, waiting, hoping that maybe somehow he could find a loophole in the plethora of legal terms written on the page. When his eyes stopped moving and he shot a regretful look our way, my shoulders sagged once more. I let myself have a pity party for a few more seconds before getting up from the couch.

"It's fine. I'll just have to start looking for a new apartment."

"You can always stay with us," Adam offered. "We have more than enough room."

Unlike my studio apartment in Washington Heights, they lived in a sprawling Brooklyn brownstone, with three bedrooms and two and a half baths. They even had a small backyard with patio furniture and a grill. I could move in with them for a while, but I wouldn't. Help wasn't something I accepted easily, even when it came from my sister and her gracious husband. I psychoanalyzed myself regularly enough to know that the issues I had with my dad were the reason I couldn't accept help.

"At least until you get back on your feet," Vanessa added softly as she reached for my hand.

I looked at her hand over mine. Her pale skin over my olive complexion. Dainty pink manicure over bloodshed red. Growing up, I studied and mimicked her every move until I realized she and I weren't as alike as I once thought. Although we were similar enough to finish each other's sentences and find humor in the same things. She was outspoken and kind. Her voice was marked with reverie, but never obnoxious. She was the kind of person who was always heard. I was the type to hide behind my silence. I'd been stumbling through life since I was sixteen, trying to find my footing and failing at every turn. Not much had changed. The only thing I could say had possibly changed was my defiance—my need to do things for myself—and I had my neighborhood to thank for that. Their drive was infectious. I met my sister's brown eyes and smiled.

"I can't," I said.

"Camila, please. You guys just buried your grandfather. The light of your life, as you said in your eulogy. The last thing you need is to worry about finding a new apartment," Adam argued.

His words sliced through me. Abuelo had been the light of my life. He'd picked me up so many times I'd lost count. Picked us all up. If my mother was the patchwork our family was made of, my grandfather had been the thread used to piece us together. But he was gone now, and I knew he wouldn't have wanted me to live my life in a perpetual state of mourning, so I compartmentalized my pain and shelved it.

"I love you both, but no. I need to do this myself."

I left their place determined to make that happen, and when I got to Charlie's bar and saw the frustration in his face, I knew something needed to be done. Charlie lived in the same building and owned the bar across the street. It was a family bar passed down for generations, and had been there for so long, it might as well have been a landmark. He'd inherited it from his father when he passed away last year, and though he was only six years my senior, he seemed to know how to handle the stress that came with being a business owner.

"I'm sorry," I said as I settled into one of the barstools across from him.

"You're sorry?" He shook his head and let out a heavy sigh. "You just buried your grandfather, Camila."

I blinked away from him to the glass of water in my hands. I wished people would stop bringing that up today. The burial had taken place three days ago.

"You need anything?" he asked, his voice soft, beckoning my gaze.

I hated seeing sympathy in his brown eyes. If I'd been through five struggles in the past ten years, Charlie had been through ten. He'd lost his dad, his mom was so ill he had to transfer her to a facility, his wife left him, his brother had a gambling habit and seemed to owe money to everybody in New York, he was getting kicked out of his apartment and business, and yet he still somehow found a way to be sympathetic toward me. It wasn't that I didn't care about the loss of my grandfather, I just didn't want to accept the loss. Not yet. I wanted to do it on my terms, but once that casket was lowered to the ground and I understood that I'd never see his light brown eyes or touch his soft hands again, I realized death doesn't wait until you're ready for it. I put my elbows on the bar and pressed my forehead into the heels of my hands.

"I don't want to talk about it," I said finally.

He was quiet for a beat before clearing his throat. "Can we talk about the eviction? These rich fucks make me sick. They don't care about us or what we think. A month's warning? It's bullshit."

It was bullshit. I looked at him again and took a sip of water, waiting for his rant to continue, and sure enough it did.

"Everybody is freaking out, but the people on this strip are the worst. We can look for new apartments, but how are we gonna survive if they close down our businesses?"

I sighed. It wasn't surprising that they'd moved up to where we were since they'd already taken over the rest of the area. Still, it was sad that so many of the things we knew and loved were being demolished. Luckily, the bar, unlike the yoga and nail salon beside it, was a standalone building.

"They can't close down your bar, though." I grabbed a handful of peanuts from the small plate he'd put between us. "Don't you own this?"

"I used to own it. I sold it to Belmonte when I needed to get my idiot brother out of one of his jams."

My fingers froze on the shell of the peanut I was unraveling. "Shit, Charlie."

"They're holding a meeting for us. I don't know why since they've already decided what they're doing," Charlie said. My head snapped up.

"When?"

"Thursday morning at the Belmonte building in the city."

"They're letting us into the Belmonte building?"

Charlie chuckled, clearly amused by my surprise, though he shouldn't have been. Not only was Belmonte the biggest, most successful real estate and investment company, it was also the first owned by a minority, with Javier Belmonte as the founder and front man. Not to mention, the mecca of modern day New York. It was the thing people could point to and say, "And that was when Brooklyn became Brooklyn." It wasn't Sex and the City. It wasn't the Nets or The Notorious BIG, or Jay Z. It was Belmonte. They made living in Brooklyn hip by giving it a more accessible look.

They made it desirable for every person with a story to tell (or edit or publish) to live. Celebrities quickly followed and flocked to Brooklyn to walk around with the hipsters and pretend to be normal citizens. And Belmonte's nice buildings and pretty storefronts were the reason. Now they wanted to move all of that to Harlem, and while I was all for improvement when they first proposed it, I was beginning to hate the way they were changing our makeup.

"At what time is this meeting?"

Charlie raised an eyebrow, brown eyes twinkling. "You gonna go fight?"

His response made me smile. I had a reason to fight, but the idea of me doing it was laughable. I never spoke out of turn, never raised my voice, and tried hard to not argue unless I absolutely felt I needed to. My apparent damsel in distress vibe was what earned me the nickname Peach in the first place. When we were kids, Mario Bros. was all the rage, and as baby of the family, I'd always been coddled. If I climbed a tree, my brother would climb up right after me. If I scraped my knee, Vanessa was instantly beside me to help me up. It was probably why when our family lost it all, I'd taken it the hardest. I no longer had people doing my laundry for me, or feeding me. I no longer had the comfort of going to a small private school. I'd been thrown out into the world. The real world, where you had to fend for yourself and hope that at the end of the day you were still in one piece. That thought made my decision easy. I couldn't let this happen without putting up a fight. Especially because it involved Belmonte Investments.

Chapter
TWO

Warren

I was standing in the middle of the pitch when I got a call from my brother asking me to come home. *Home*, he'd said. I laughed into the phone line. I hadn't called New York home since I left when I was fourteen years old.

"You'll regret it if you don't, War," he said. "You can take a look at your investments while you're here."

Sadly, that last bit was what got my attention. The financial advisor in charge of my investments had been taking too many liberties with my money before I decided to get rid of him a few months back. I had a few weeks off before the season started and had planned on working out and catching up on local investments anyway. I figured I'd make some appearances I promised my sponsors and schedule photo shoots I'd put off, but I knew if I didn't go back to New York now I'd have to wait months before doing so, and between the investment and that little voice inside my head that told me I should go see my family, I decided to book my flight.

The last few times I'd traveled to the US had been because I had football matches, and none of those trips made visiting New York possible. I'd gone to Los Angeles, Portland, Orlando, Miami, but skipped New York. Even the one trip I had enough time to fly up, I didn't. My teammates always said that if you came to the US and didn't visit New York, you might as well not say you went at all. I would agree with that sentiment if the memories I had here didn't haunt me as much as they did, but being here only reminded me who I was and where I came from. And while for some people that may be a humbling experience, for me it was anything but. Yet here I was, back where it all started and hating every minute of it.

My brother made fun of me for that. He called me a fake New Yorker, and because it was the only thing he was right about, I let him take the jab every time. I was fourteen when I left for Spain and like every other child from a wealthy family, I could have traveled back whenever I wanted, but chose not to. I'd booked my flight a few times, and much to my father's dismay, never got on the plane. In my defense, I was a teenager whose life revolved around dribbling a football and trying to get a new girl in my bed any chance I got.

For the last ten years, my holidays had consisted of football practice for different clubs, photo shoots and appearances for different sponsors, and figuring out where I could continue to make investments. My first day back in New York I decided I'd only be here for one week, but when Thomas Belmonte called and told me that things needed to be taken care of while Javier Belmonte wasn't in the office, I knew it was in my best interest to be there.

My second day going by the office had been a lot of "sign here" "sign there" "we need you in this meeting". By the third day, I was tired of it all. I had half a mind to sell my shares to the majority owner and get it over with, but when new construction was mentioned, I felt inclined to stay yet again. I had a group of men working on construction in Barcelona and I figured being in on this meeting may help me learn a thing or two.

I was sitting in the office, scrolling through files on the computer, when I found the cameras, and I was trying to click my way out of the program when I saw her. A leggy woman with the most incredible olive complexion, and short, wavy dark hair. Normally, long hair caught my attention. The longer, the better so I could run my hands through and tug on it. Her sculpted legs, sweet tits, and small waist caught my attention, but the scowl on her face held it. She looked ready to climb in a ring and knock somebody out, and when she turned that glare straight to the camera, effectively looking directly into my eyes, my breath stopped.

I needed to see the exact floor she exited so I could follow her and get a closer look. When the elevator stopped, she dropped her phone into her bag and looked at the man standing beside her, which gave me an excellent vantage point. She looked to be at least five foot five, with hips and an ass that would make any person's mouth water. I looked at the elevator doors when they opened and my heart sped up. *She* was on my floor. I stood up, grabbed my jacket, and left the office.

Chapter
THREE

Camila

"I hate wearing ties," Charlie said beside me.

"You look fine."

"This shouldn't take too long, right?"

I looked over at him. "No idea."

"You sure you're comfortable doing this?" he asked, concern filling his eyes.

"I'm here, aren't I?"

He nodded and let out a breath. "Is my hair still intact?"

"I think your hair was intact for all of five minutes. You're not supposed to fiddle so much with it if you want to keep a style."

I'd never seen him with his hair brushed back or wearing a suit. His daily repertoire of leathers and flannel was a mix between a biker who'd been kicked out of an MC club and a farmer from Wisconsin. As his dark hair was too short to put up into a ponytail but too long and curly to tame without using hair products, it was normally left wild.

"You've dealt with people like this before," he said, waving a hand around the large, cool space. "Right?"

I tore my eyes away from his and stood up to get away from his nervous vibe. I made my way over to the large windows on the side of the room. It was a sunny summer day. Hot as hell, I'd said on the way over. From the conference room, with the beautiful view of the city, it didn't feel unbearable, though. I wondered what the people who worked this high up thought of it all. If I squinted hard enough, I could probably spot the building I grew up in. If I closed my eyes long enough, I could still remember how it felt to walk along those streets. Oftentimes at night, I wondered what it would be like to still live there.

Especially nights like the recent ones, with no working air conditioning and the insufficient wind that blew into my cracked windows. All I had to do was screw my eyes shut and remember the smell of the foods our housekeeper made for us, and the sound of my dad's keys jingling when he got home after a long day of work. I could practically hear my parents laughing in the other room, because it was what you did when everything was going right with the world. The hard times always made me wonder what our lives would have been like if things hadn't come tumbling down on us; if my family had made better decisions, used better judgment.

Vanessa said it was a dumb thing to think about. Johnny said I needed to stop living in the past and focus on my future. But it was hard for me. They'd been older. They were already out of the house. Vanessa in college; Johnny off doing

11

God knows what. I couldn't relate to them or to Charlie, who'd been working since he was sixteen. I had gotten a late start on that aspect of life.

The opening and shutting of the door behind us jarred me out of my thoughts. Again, more people from the neighborhood. This time, the elderly lady who lived on the first floor, who always came into Charlie's bar on Friday nights with homemade goods because she couldn't accept the fact that the bar didn't sell food. I smiled and walked back down when she took a seat behind us.

"Did they offer coffee yet?" she asked.

"The receptionist did," Charlie said. "I don't think she'll be coming around though."

"Figures. This is why the world is the way it is," she responded.

"Because of the lack of coffee?" I asked. The look she shot me made me smother my smile and sit up straighter.

"Because of the lack of decency," she said, raising her voice. "People don't know how to treat guests anymore."

"This isn't a housewarming party, Doris," Charlie said.

"I suppose it's not," she said, her face twisting at the thought before she started to look around. "What kind of cutlery do you think they have in their homes?"

I closed my eyes. This was going to be a disaster. For the tenth time since I agreed to do this, my sister's words rang through my head, but as long as I could gather the courage to speak loudly and project my voice across the room, I'd be fine. Once the meeting was over, I could go back to being shy Camila, who didn't raise her voice at anybody. Until then, I was going to channel my sister's outgoing personality. I was wearing her clothes, so it shouldn't be too hard to do.

As the door behind us opened again, the three of us

swiveled in our seats and my heart leaped as two men in dark suits walked in. They were both older, at least older than me, probably closer to their mid-thirties and forties. I turned around in my seat, my gaze following them as they walked to the front of the room. The man who walked in next made my eyes widen, mainly because he was so . . . unexpected. So unlike the previous two.

This one was younger, and walked as if he knew all eyes would be on him. He had an easy way about him that made it hard to imagine him being weighed down by anything, and was the kind of good-looking that made you pause mid-sentence and forget what it was you were talking about. With poised posture, a square jaw, and a tan that made me want to hide my pale arms under the just-in-case cardigan I'd stuffed in my bag this morning.

He was definitely not the kind of man I'd normally find attractive, but something about him held me captive. Maybe it was the gloomy expression on his face that spoke *don't fuck with me*. Or the way his broad shoulders moved with each step, as if they were heavy and he needed that extra push to take the next step forward. His eyes swept the room, stopping on each person, as if he wanted to make sure they were looking at him. When they reached mine they held. I tore my gaze away from his quickly and turned my attention back to the front of the room.

The three of them took a seat behind the desk in front of the podium. It reminded me of the year I'd gone to New York Comic Con with my brother and we listened to one of the Spider-Man panels. The cast had sat behind a table with white linen just like it. Name tags had been set in front of the actors. That's the only thing these people were missing: name tags. They introduced themselves as Thomas Belmonte

13

(COO of the company), Carson Bradley (CFO), and Warren Silva, majority shareholder for this project. *Warren Silva.*

"It is my understanding, from speaking to the people in the community, that the residents feel they're being shut out of this project," Thomas said.

I swallowed, waiting for somebody behind me to lash out at his words, and when nobody spoke up and Charlie cleared his throat, I took a deep breath and kept my eyes on Thomas as I spoke.

"It is our understanding that you want to tear down our streets in order to rebuild a newer strip mall as well as new apartment buildings."

"That is what we're proposing," he responded.

"That means we'd have to move out of our work places, and some of us, our homes." I paused. "Where exactly do you expect us to go?"

"There have been a lot of changes in the neighborhood in the last five years. I'm sure you'll understand why it's important we strike now."

"So that you can get ahead of the other development companies," I said. His expression remained blank, so I continued to speak. "And where do you expect us to go? Don't you care that many of us will be out of a place to live? With no compensation or timeline as to when you'll be finished. Furthermore, no promise to let us come back to our homes if we decide to stay in the neighborhood."

"As you're probably aware, most of the people you're referring to wouldn't want to stay in the neighborhood. It's becoming inundated with young families and young professionals," he shot back.

I gaped at him. "And as you're probably aware, many of them have been living there since before Cameron Giles became Cam'ron."

There was a deep chuckle from Warren that beckoned all of our attention.

"What do you suggest we do, Miss . . . ?" Warren asked, his gaze dead on mine.

He had a slight British accent that took me aback, and I stayed silent, just staring for a beat until I was able to get over it and swallow down my awkwardness.

"Avila," I said. "Camila Avila."

"Camila," he said.

A shiver rolled through me with the way he said my name, with a slight husk in his voice. I tried to suppress it. Move past it. Ignore it. This wasn't the time or place for my body to decide to wake up and take notice of the opposite sex. Warren's green eyes twinkled as if he noticed. I blinked and soldiered on with my argument.

"Give us a little time and compensation for those who need to find other places to live."

"Do you reside in that building, Miss. Avila?" he asked.

"Yes."

"Fair enough. I also want to point out that the new residents who will live there, will certainly bring great business to Mr. Ferguson's bar, which will be able to open back up shortly."

"Do your papers make mention of Charlie's two-bedroom that you'll tear down with the renovation? Where is he supposed to go when he loses not only his business, but also his home?"

"Our company reinvigorates. We tear down ugly things and make them beautiful again. This is something we know can improve a lot of things in these areas. We don't look for alternatives for people, but we do give them enough time to make arrangements," Thomas said clasping his hands in front of him on the table.

"With no compensation," I said, closing mine into a fist to keep them from shaking. Charlie placed one of his over mine and offered a reassuring squeeze.

"We just want to make sure we're taken care of at least to some extent before we're thrown out of our apartments," Charlie offered.

"How many units are there in this residential building?" Warren asked looking at Thomas, who was trying to convey some kind of warning with his gaze.

Thomas jotted something down and slid the sheet of paper toward Warren. His eyes flashed as soon as he read whatever it said.

"And we're not offering them anything? Just kicking them to the curb?" The firmness in his voice caught me off guard, and when he looked over at me and our gazes met again, the ferocity I found in them made my heart lurch.

"We own the buildings, War," Thomas said.

"But you don't own our lives," I said. "You want to take away things we've worked for. Most of these people work their asses off to afford to live there, and you don't want to give them an opportunity to come back and move into the building because you have a different vision for your project," I said using air quotes. I took a breath to take control of my shaky voice. I could imagine what my face and neck looked like, all red and blotchy, the way it did when I let my emotions get the best of me. I lowered my voice when I spoke again. "It's not your job to decide whether or not they're worthy of the neighborhood you're trying to build."

The room was silent as the three of them looked at me. Thomas just stared, Carson looked contrite in his chair, and

Warren sat back slightly, crossing his arms against his chest as he looked at me with a serious look in his eyes.

"If that was true, Donald Trump would be living in a ditch," Thomas said finally.

"I highly doubt that somebody who started out with a one-million-dollar loan from his father would ever be living in a ditch," I said. "All we're asking is for you to please reconsider what you're doing. I'm not telling you not to rebuild. I just ask that you do it responsibly and in sections. The businesses, for one, don't have to close if you're only doing outside work."

Thomas and Carson shared a look before he looked over at me. "I'll speak to the architect. If he thinks we can work around them, the businesses can stay open. The apartments are a different story. That's a tear-down job."

I hated my building, and I knew I wasn't the only one to share that sentiment. But it was mine, despite the water pressure issues, the power going out, the leaks and smell of the hallways, and the fact that the walls seemed to be made out of thin paper. It was where I rested my head and moved in with a boy for the first time, and then broke up with that boy and managed to stay despite the heartache. I'd picked up pieces of myself in that apartment. I'd grieved and loved and lived. I sighed.

"When do you plan on starting?" Charlie asked.

"A month."

I gasped. Charlie exhaled loudly. I could only imagine what he was thinking. Where would we go? What would he do?

"A month?"

"A month is more than enough time to get sorted out," Thomas pointed out.

"We'll see what we can do," Warren said before he finished the sentiment.

"When can we expect a more solid answer?" I asked.

"Give us a week," Thomas said looking around the room. "Any other questions or concerns?"

"One more. What will happen to the land right behind the building? It's been zoned for a park. Construction is supposed to start soon, but I'm assuming Belmonte owns it as well," I said.

"I'll have to look into that. As of now, I think it will stay empty."

We all let out a collective breath. I stood first, and everybody else followed suit. After thanking them for their time, I made my way outside and fished my phone out of my purse to make sure I hadn't missed any calls. My head snapped up from my screen when the door opened again. I expected to see Charlie, but Warren was the one who walked out. He was so much taller than I'd anticipated, and even more gorgeous up close. And when he stopped directly in front of me, his cologne was divine. It was the kind of smell that welcomed you to bury your nose in. I had to blink a few times to make sure my mind didn't run free with thoughts of me doing that to him.

"You made a lot of good points back there," he said, looking back over his shoulder briefly before his dark green eyes flicked back to mine.

I wasn't sure what kind of answer his statement required, so I went with polite. Polite seemed to always be a good idea.

"Thank you."

"I should probably formally introduce myself," he said, offering me his hand, which I took. "Warren."

"Camila."

"Have I seen you before, Camila?"

The way he said my name did things to me. I dropped my gaze to his navy blue tie, but all I could do was wonder how he looked under that suit, and it was a bad idea all around. Where could I look and not feel enticed by him? I tried the floor, which was the worst option of all. Looking at the floor spoke lack of confidence, and I'd always been taught to pretend, even in the most mundane situations like this one. I couldn't help it, though. Warren made me uncomfortable, and when I tore my eyes from the floor and looked at him again, I felt it and I could swear he could too. It wasn't just discomfort because he was good-looking. It wasn't discomfort because he was definitely rich and if he had any involvement in Belmonte, inarguably powerful. It was because he looked at me with an intensity I could feel from the inside, as if no part of me was left untraced.

"I don't think so. I think I would remember seeing you," I said, and instantly regretted the way it sounded.

He chuckled. "I'm experiencing the same thing."

"That's not what I meant." I frowned. "I mean, that's not how I meant it."

"How did you mean it?"

He was still grinning as he cocked his head and searched my eyes. It was unnerving. The grin, the tilt of his head, the way he was looking at me. I tried to shrug nonchalantly, but wasn't sure my shoulders moved much.

"I don't know. I've been told I have a familiar face."

"If everybody looked like you . . ." his eyes scanned my face slowly, and he chuckled, a deep, velvety sound that sent a shiver down my spine, "I'd be in trouble."

The compliment made my cheeks burn. I looked over his shoulder, at Charlie, who was finally exiting the room.

Warren's gaze followed mine over his shoulder.

"Well," I said, "I look forward to hearing what conclusion you come up with."

"Do you work at the bar?" he asked.

My eyes flickered to his again. They were so dark and green, like a forest. One you could get lost in if you weren't careful enough to watch where you were going. He seemed genuinely interested in an answer, so I shook my head.

"Sometimes."

"And you live in the apartment building," he confirmed as I started to step away.

"Uh-huh."

His eyes trailed over my features once more, his eyes narrowing slightly. For a horrid second I thought he was going to keep asking questions, but instead he nodded once and began to walk away.

"It was nice meeting you, Camila."

I nodded, unable to find my voice to respond. Charlie and I left and rode the elevator in silence. It wasn't until we reached the sidewalk that he spoke.

"Do you know who that was?"

I shook my head slowly, trying to play it cool even though my heart was still beating wildly at the entire encounter. Or maybe it was the adrenaline still rushing through me for the way I'd spoken up. Charlie's brows rose.

"Warren Silva. European soccer star? Youngest player to ever receive the FIFA Ballon d'Or?" he said as if those things would ring a bell. It didn't, so Charlie shook his head, putting a cigarette between his lips and lit it the moment we stepped outside.

"Wonder what percentage of this he owns."

I shrugged. I didn't know what the heck a Ballon d'

whatever was and I'd never heard of a Warren on the board. Not that I'd done extensive research on the board. My interest with Belmonte began and ended with Javier Belmonte.

"He seems tall for a soccer player."

Charlie stopped walking and started laughing. "You really don't know who he is?"

I shook my head. Unless your name was Derek Jeter, you weren't really on my radar, and since he'd retired and gotten married, nobody was on my radar.

"He's one of the best. I'm telling you," Charlie said.

The only time I'd ever seen FIFA was on the shirt of the Dominican owner of the tiny corner store I frequented, and I was sure he didn't even know what he was wearing until the day Charlie went in there with me and commented on his shirt. Charlie loved to speak in hyperbole, especially when it came to sports like soccer and rugby, which were his favorites. At the bar, people complained that both televisions shouldn't be playing soccer when most Americans preferred to keep up with American sports. "This is an Irish bar," Charlie would say to them. And when that excuse failed, he would remind them that it was his bar. There was no arguing that.

"Why would a soccer player invest in Belmonte?" I asked.

Charlie shrugged as we stood in the landing waiting for the train. "Why would he not? Belmonte is a fast-growing company. I'd invest there if I had that kind of money. And he's from here, so maybe he feels like it's the smart thing to do."

"He has a pretty heavy British accent to be a New Yorker."

He shrugged in response to that.

"Why'd you take so long in there after I walked out?" I asked, stopping at the cross light.

"I was inviting them to the bar on Friday," he said and

21

then shrugged at the look on my face. "I figured maybe if they see how it is, they won't want to tear it down."

"I don't think a little kumbaya is going to go a long way with those people," I said quietly.

"Yeah. They've been known to tear shit down with no notice," he said.

"Don't I know it," I muttered under my breath.

"The upside is that if Warren Silva shows up, I can have him sign a spot on the bar," he said. I laughed.

"If he's as popular as you say he is I wouldn't bet on him showing up."

"Maybe he will. I saw the way he was looking at you when you were talking."

I didn't believe it, but my cheeks burned nonetheless. "Popular sports guys usually date the model types. Look at Jeter."

"There are more athletes out there aside from Jeter, you know?"

"Okay," I said, smiling. "Look at Robinson Cano."

Charlie chuckled. "They play baseball. It's different."

"Doesn't matter. I'm not about that life."

"What life? The rich and lavish life?" he asked, laughing at the scowl on my face as we walked into the train. "It sounds pretty fantastic to me."

I scoffed. It sounded fantastic. Until you lost it all. I knew better than to put any emphasis on materialistic things, and I definitely knew better than to get involved with a man like Warren Silva. No matter how hot he was or how it felt when he looked at me.

Chapter FOUR

Warren

"I want her."

Thomas laughed loudly. "You can get any woman in the world and *that's* the one you want?"

"What's that supposed to mean?"

"You know what it means." He shook his head as he got out of his chair with the stack of papers. "What do you have planned for the day?"

"Absolutely nothing," I said.

I'd canceled my appearance at the sneaker company to be here as well as everything else my agent had lined up for me while visiting New York. I told him I wasn't here on football business and he needed to respect that. It was also the only three weeks of the entire year I had to myself.

"That's your problem," Thomas said as I stood up and joined him in walking out of the conference room. "You're not used to not being busy. Go find yourself a woman to fuck while you're here. Preferably one that owns an apartment a little bigger than the guest room closet in yours."

He turned and went back to his office before I could answer him, and I headed downstairs with that thought in mind. Of course he expected me to find a woman to fuck while I was here. It was what I did. Well, what I used to do. I liked to think I wasn't that guy anymore, but the only thing I wanted to do was proposition Camila. It's not like she would say no.

"This isn't the Harlem I remember," I said quietly.

"When was the last time you were in town?" Antoine asked.

Never was on the tip of my tongue, but I couldn't even bring myself to say it. The only time I'd ever seen these streets was on music videos and movies, and other places no real New Yorker would ever attest to. Yet there I was, seventeen years after moving out of the country. In Harlem. One of the things I wanted to do when I got to New York, was take an Uber, for the mere reason that I could never do something like that back home. Also, it made me feel more like a New Yorker. Although, the few times I'd visited since moving away I realized that true New Yorkers would never accept me as one of their own.

I couldn't blame them. I didn't know what trains to take where, and even if I did get the hang of that, I had drivers at my disposal. I'd told my brother to hold off on the drivers this time around. I wanted to experience the real New York. The only problem was I wasn't the kind of person who could walk around the city and go unnoticed for too long, as Antoine the Uber driver proved by noticing me and calling me by my moniker, *War Zone*, as soon as I slid into his town car. The last time I'd been here, nobody recognized me. In the States, American football players, baseball players, hockey players, basketball players, even the damn golf players were the gods. Football players (the *real* football) were just a bunch of guys chasing after a ball for ninety minutes. This trip, I'd already received a lot more recognition than I'd imagined or hoped for.

"Your season starts soon, right?" he asked on our drive.

"Yes. Practice begins in a few weeks."

"Do you miss it when you're not playing? You keep busy?"

During our drive I learned that Antoine had gone to college on an American football scholarship and had dreams of making it big. According to him, he wasn't good enough for the NFL right off the bat, so he came back home.

"I don't really know what to do with myself when I'm not playing," I said, looking out the window. "Do you miss playing?"

"I do, but it is what it is."

We were quiet until we came to a complete stop in front of a strip mall.

"I heard they want to tear down this whole neighborhood," he said. I blinked away from the storefronts and looked at him.

"Just this block I think," I said. "I'm sure the apartment building will look better once the builders are done with it."

He sucked his teeth, his disapproving eyes meeting mine in the rearview. "That's what they said about twenty-first, and look at how that's coming along."

I didn't know what he was talking about. I didn't care, either. "How much would I have to pay you to wait for me?"

Antoine smiled. "How long will you be?"

I glanced away, back toward the strip. Groups of people were continuously walking along the sidewalk. Some entered Scully's bar at the end, which I knew belonged to Charlie Ferguson. Others walked into the cupcake shop beside it. Most of them strolled past the strip altogether. A light switching off caught my attention. The door swung open and shut shortly after and my heart gave two quick, strong pounds, some sort of adrenaline building up inside me as I looked at her, before going back to normal speed. It was *her*. Camila. The brunette with the most determined eyes I'd ever seen. Her short hair was all messy waves, the kind that invited you to grab a handful of. She looked different in a pair of tight black exercise pants and equally tight black shirt. Different in the best way, since I could see every fucking curve on her body, and she definitely had a hell of a body on her. The thought of gripping her small waist and grabbing her large ass made my blood heat.

"A few hours," I said, clearing my throat. "Probably around midnight."

"You can rent the car for the evening for three hundred dollars," he said.

"That's perfect," I said, getting out of the car.

From the outside, the bar was exactly what you'd expect a hole in the wall to look like, with a rusty wooden door and a handle I would've replaced twenty years ago. On the inside, though, it was an entirely different story. It was narrow, but deep, with an ambiance of people talking and bobbing their heads to the live band's sped-up rendition of *Santeria* by Sublime.

My gaze scanned the bar, taking in the colorful art that provided pops of color in the otherwise stark space, and finally landing on Camila, who was staring at me with a confused look on her face from the other side of the bar.

She'd changed into a short tie-dye shirt that had hues of purples and blues with the word *Scully's* written across the length of her chest. It made her look like she belonged on the wall along with the rest of the collection. I hadn't planned on walking up to her from the get-go, but my feet carried me that way nonetheless. Our eyes locked as I sat in the empty corner barstool across from where she was standing.

"Hi," she said, her cheeks turning a deep shade of pink.

I knew the affect I had on women, but I could count on one hand the times I was actually delighted over it. Camila was definitely on that hand.

"So you do work here?" I asked, unable to keep my eyes from exploring her features.

Her almond-shaped eyes, her high cheek bones, the tiny specks of freckles on the tip of her small upturned nose. I tried to keep my gaze on her face, mainly because I didn't want her to feel uncomfortable, even though it was difficult not to let my eyes roam down, where I could see her bare midriff. I was sure I could make out every curve of her ass and thighs in those tight workout pants she was wearing, too.

"I don't." She paused. "Well, technically I don't. I help out once in a while, and since this doesn't interfere with my nine-to-five job, I do it."

"What's your nine-to-five job?"

"A non-for-profit."

"What kind?"

"The good kind." Her eyes stayed on mine for a few beats

before she turned around.

"You have the loveliest eyes," I said, leaning in a little closer when she walked back over.

She smiled, and it made her nose scrunch up a little, bringing attention again to the freckles on her nose. They made me want to reach out and connect the dots. I wondered what it would feel like to touch her, to run my thumb along her cheek and down her neck. I cleared my throat, but it did very little to help me smother the lust I felt. She looked so familiar. Being around her felt familiar, which was what shook me the most in the office.

"Brown eyes are pretty common."

"Not like yours." They were the color of warm honey. I could almost taste them.

"Are you here to see Charlie?" she asked, her eyes sweeping along the bar momentarily. "He stepped out, but I'm sure he'll be back soon."

I wasn't there to see Charlie. I was there for her. I liked that she didn't pay attention to me as if I wasn't one of the most successful football players in the world, the top-paid endorsement model for three different brands, and lastly, *War Zone*, a god on the field. I had a reputation for bedding different women in different cities. It was a piece of information somehow leaked to the press by one of the girls, and shrugged off as a rumor by me because I didn't want to confirm that I was that kind of man. I didn't want to fuck any New York woman who was going to look at me like I was their personal piggy bank. I wanted to fuck this woman. I wanted to command *her* attention.

"I'm just here to satisfy a curiosity," I said.

She examined my face for a long moment. "Would you like something to drink while you figure out if your curiosity is satisfied?"

I felt myself smile. "Sure."

"You want to start a tab?" she asked after I asked for a Stella and began to pour it in front of me.

"Is there normally a band here?" I asked.

"Friday nights," she said just as the music started up again and a woman from the other side of the bar waved for her attention. "I have to . . ." she said, nodding over there. I smiled.

"I'm not going anywhere."

She nodded and walked to the other side of the bar, her hips swaying, not in that exaggerated way women walked when they knew men were watching them walk away, but in a natural unassuming way. When she got there she laughed at something the man sitting there told her and brushed a flyaway hair back into her ponytail. Soon she'd served four different people drinks and I realized I'd been so captivated by her in that time that I hadn't even touched my cellphone. She moved with grace and smiled with confidence, as if she was born to entertain a crowd. And my objective became reading the unspoken language in the way she moved her hands when she was talking and smiled differently at the patrons. She seemed extra friendly with the females, something I hadn't seen in a barmaid. She listened to their stories intently, and reached her hand over more than a few times to place over theirs. She was completely hypnotizing to watch.

I took a sip of beer, and almost spit it out in a cough when I heard her laugh. I could only make out the way her full lips moved as she spoke to one of the women sitting on the other side of the bar. The woman caught my gaze for a millisecond before I tore my eyes away from her and looked at Camila who was singing along to Bohemian Rhapsody as if she was in some lip-sync showdown.

"Make sure to leave Camila a good tip," the singer shouted out in the middle of the song, pointing toward the bar.

People hooted and clapped, and Camila buried her face in her hands briefly. When she dropped them, she was still laughing. Her face transformed when she laughed unabashed like that, and to my disappointment, I realized she'd been giving me fake smiles all along. I hadn't really paid attention to the band, but I turned in my seat to look at them now. There were four guys, and if the name hadn't been taken, they should have called themselves The Misfits: half of them with their tattoos, piercings, and weird haircuts, and the other two looking a lot like the guys I played with—preppy and in shape with parted hairstyles. The lead singer was one of them. His eyes seemed to still be on Camila. I looked back at her and felt oddly satisfied, my chest letting go of the earlier squeeze when I realized she was no longer looking at him.

"I've never met a shy barmaid before," I said when she picked up my glass and refilled it with the tap beside us. Her cheeks heated again. Her eyes were on the glass when she set it down in front of me, and I felt my lips pull into a smile. Normally, I wasn't one to buy into that act, but it worked for Camila, and it made me want to find out how loud she could be.

"They're called mixologists now, or bartenders. Barmaid is very . . . archaic," she said, her voice almost a whisper, but my eyes were on her lips and I could read them clearly.

"Noted," I whispered, matching her tone.

"So, what brings you all the way here?"

"Charlie invited me," I said.

"Are you waiting for your colleagues?"

I almost laughed, but caught myself before I did. I didn't

want her to know that my *colleagues* thought they were above visiting a small bar in this neighborhood. If it weren't for her, I'd probably be having drinks with Tom in Chelsea.

"They had other things already planned for the night."

She gave me a look that told me she wasn't buying that excuse, but let it go. When she came back over, she put her elbows on the bar across from me and let out a long, deep breath.

"Tired?"

"Yeah, the day is catching up to me," she said, moving her neck side to side as if to relieve herself of some of the exhaustion.

"Want a massage?"

Her eyes widened, and she shook her head, but not before glancing down at my hands quickly before looking away, her skin flushing once more. I wondered what she was thinking. Everything inside me tightened at all the possibilities. My fingers on her back, her neck, her ass, inside her . . .

"Charlie thinks you're some sort of star soccer player," she said so suddenly I almost choked on my beer.

"What? I don't look the part?"

Her gaze trickled down my chest slowly, then to my arms. I felt my pulse quicken at the way she licked her lips. I hated when she looked away quickly again, so I spoke, because I wanted her to look at me again. I wanted to tell all the patrons of the damn bar to leave so that she had no choice but to look at me.

"Well?"

"I'm not sure what soccer players are supposed to look like."

I smiled. She didn't know who I was and didn't know what football players looked like. I wasn't sure why any of it thrilled me, but it did. Camila walked off once more and when she came back, she gave me a folded-up napkin. My eyes met hers. People still did this?

"You wouldn't prefer to type it into my phone?" I asked with a smirk.

Camila frowned. "What?"

"Your phone number. Writing it on a napkin seems so . . . archaic."

"Oh," she said, still looking serious for a beat, and then her lips started to bloom into a smile. "You think I'm giving you my phone number?"

My smile dropped. What the hell?

"It's from her," she said, signaling at the other end of the bar with a nod.

I glanced over and saw the busty blonde that had been eye-fucking me earlier. She was giving me the same look now. It wasn't a look I shied away from, but it was one I didn't appreciate when I was getting it from the wrong woman.

"The usual?" Camila asked, beckoning my attention once more. She was talking to the guy standing beside me. I recognized him as the lead singer of the band.

"Unless you're going to let me take shots off that body," he responded, reaching over the bar.

I gripped the mug in my hand and let it go quickly. It hadn't occurred to me that she might have a boyfriend. Fuck. If that was the case, I definitely stood no chance.

"Definitely not," she said, slapping his hand away playfully. She made her way toward the middle of the bar to serve three beers. I took the moment to size up the guy again. He didn't seem like her type. Not that I knew her type, but he was the complete opposite of me.

The guy noticed me looking and his face snapped toward

me, eyes wide. "You look just like Warren Silva." He paused to smile at Camila when she handed him his beer before looking back at me. "Anybody ever tell you that?"

My heart stopped beating. In an effort to be normal, I came up with different answers: I get that all the time. *Who is Warren Silva? I have no idea what you mean.* In the end, my response was to shrug. I didn't mind attention when I was out in the street with the rest of my club, but when I was on my own I preferred to stay under the radar. I wore a baseball cap for that very reason.

"He has a familiar face," Camila said, smiling at me as she spoke to the guy.

The guy's smile broadened as he turned to give her his complete attention. "I'd like to get real familiar with your face again."

Again. He'd said again. They were definitely something.

"I'll make sure I tell Kayla you said that when she comes in," she said, winking as she walked away again.

"Not with Kayla anymore," he shouted, and she shook her head without looking back to acknowledge that she heard him.

They went back to the stage and I continued to fiddle with the napkin, and finally opened it. The name Erika written across the Scully's Bar napkin followed by a seven-one-eight area code phone number and the words: *I can be your NY girl.* I glanced up from the napkin and looked at the blonde on the other side of the bar. It was obvious that Erika had heard rumors about me and wanted to find out whether or not they were true. Unfortunately for her, the only woman I was interested in fucking in New York was the one standing on the other side of the bar.

"I think she wants you to buy her a drink," Camila said

as she walked over again.

I leaned into the bar, closer to her. She was fiddling with the drink mixer, but when she realized how close I was, she put it down and looked at me.

"I'm a lot more interested in what you want," I said, fully aware of the way my voice sounded and what my tone was implying.

Her mouth popped open, and I wished I could hear it from where I was sitting. I wished I could hear it in another setting. I was glad my mates weren't with me tonight, because they would either have a laugh at me or would have made their move on her by now. I blamed Elena for this. The bloody bitch broke me. Before her, I would have never waited this long to make a move. Change was good, though. She cleared her throat.

"I'm not sure what you mean," she said, her voice so quiet I could barely hear it.

"I think you know exactly what I mean," I said, leaning in a little closer.

Her eyes met mine briefly again and even with the dim lights, I could tell she was blushing. There was a plea in those big beautiful eyes of hers when she looked at me once more and I couldn't figure out if she wanted me to stop or keep going.

"You're not my type," she said, finally.

All I could do was stare at her. Stare at her after she said the words and walked away to serve another drink. Stare at her as she nodded and spoke to a patron as they paid their bill, and stare at her as she spoke to a woman who came behind the counter and seemingly took over her shift. Camila walked past where I was sitting and through the back door. The last thing I saw before it shut behind her was her pulling the apron thing over her head and tossing it aside.

"Is she done for the night?" I asked the woman behind the bar.

She was an older woman, about my mother's age, maybe older. The frown on her face in response to my question only deepened her wrinkles.

"Cami?"

I nodded.

"She's about to head out. You a friend of hers?" she asked, sizing me up.

"Yes." No. I wanted to be more than that. Much more than that.

The old lady scrutinized me again once more before going back to the register and printing out a receipt for me, which she brought over with my card. I felt her eyes on me as I signed it and gave it back to her. Before I asked her any further questions, the back door opened and Camila came back wearing her previous black shirt and a slouchy green bag over her shoulder.

"Do you need a ride?" I asked, getting up and sending the driver a quick text telling him to come back.

Camila frowned as she walked around the bar, toward me. I hadn't stood beside her until now, and she was much shorter than I'd envisioned without her heels.

"I live a block away. Technically, not even a block a way."

"How do you get there when you leave?" I asked.

"I walk."

My eyes widened as I looked at my watch. "At twelve thirty? By yourself?"

"Yeah. Unless Quinn walks me."

I looked over my shoulder. The band was on a break, talking to a couple girls sitting near the stage. Twice while

35

I was looking the lead singer glanced our way. I looked at Camila again.

"The lead singer?"

"Yeah," she said, giving me a weird look.

"Are you together?"

She laughed. "Definitely not."

"But your faces have been acquainted," I said, knowing damn well I sounded bitter.

Camila didn't look fazed by my words or the way I said them. She only shrugged, which was the worst kind of answer. The thought of them together made an unsettling feeling develop in the pit of my stomach. *Back away. Back the hell away.* I told myself that, but I knew it would be difficult to listen to the warning. I'd pursued Elena hard in the beginning, until she fell, and for what? I needed to listen to my brother or best friend for once. I needed to let things develop on their own and not force them. But it was all I knew. I admitted it. I was a brat. Always had been.

"Let me take you home and we can talk about the development," I said. I had no real news about the damn development, but it was all I could think to say.

"Okay."

I watched as she walked ahead of me and waved around at the people she knew. Something about her captivated me. One could argue I needed to get laid and this was the first woman I'd met in a long time that had no idea, or didn't care, who I was. But it wasn't just that. It was the way she smiled at the people all night as she was serving, as if she was genuinely happy to be there talking to them. Maybe she was. It had been a long time since I'd met anybody who looked genuinely happy to be anywhere.

"You have a car," she commented followed by a whispered,

"of course you have a car."

"If it makes you feel any better, it's not my car," I said, though I wasn't sure why that would make her feel better. The sarcastic laugh that escaped her made it clear it didn't.

"You have a car and a driver," she said when Antoine got out of the driver's seat and walked around the vehicle.

I had never felt ashamed for having money. It was all I knew. By the time I was five, my father had already made enough investments that would secure my children's futures. I'd never been ashamed of any of the perks that came with it, and when I started getting paid for playing football, it was intensified. I was used to driving the hottest cars and being seeing with equally hot women. The glitz and glamour was part of the game and something I relished. But with the way Camila looked at me beside the town car, I felt like taking it all and hiding it. I'd taken Elena on our first date in my Bugatti, and the only comments I got were compliments. Camila was looking at the town car like it was the flashiest thing she'd ever seen. I sighed. It's not like I could change my lifestyle. It's not like she should want me to. But there it was, that little nagging feeling inside me that nudged me not to lose my shot with this girl.

"Would you prefer it if I walked you home instead?"

She took a step back, eyes wide, and blinked slowly up at me for a moment before tearing her gaze away and looking up and down the street. I wondered what she was thinking. I wondered if she was trying to figure out whether or not I could cut it.

"Whatever you prefer, Camila. Just let me take you home," I added. My heart held while I waited for the consensus.

"It's literally right over there," she said, pointing at the building down the block.

"Lead the way."

We started walking side by side, and suddenly I didn't know what I wanted to say. I just knew I needed to say something. Anything, to let her know I was interested.

"Where are you from originally?" she asked, tilting her face to look at me.

"Here." I said. "Manhattan. I moved to Europe when I was fourteen to live with my family in Spain."

"Do your parents live over there?" she asked.

"No. They never moved."

Camila stopped walking suddenly and turned to me. "You moved to another country when you were fourteen . . . by yourself?"

"For football," I said, shrugging. "I know guys that moved there that had moved from all over the world when they were nine, so in a sense I came in late."

"Wow." She shook her head and continued walking. It took me a second to follow behind her.

"You don't approve?" I asked, amused by her reaction.

She shrugged. "I'm not a mother. To each his own."

"I take it your parents wouldn't have let you do it."

She laughed, looking over at me. "My parents didn't let me participate in sleepovers until . . ." Her smile faded and she looked away as she shook her head slowly.

"Until?"

"Doesn't matter. So, what's going on with the development?"

"It's going. I should have real news soon. Do you have somewhere to move in the meantime?"

She stopped walking again suddenly, and I stopped with her, facing her as we stood in the middle of the dark sidewalk.

"That's my building," she said pointing behind me. "Not

that I have to point it out since you're the one tearing it down."

Her words stabbed at me. Belmonte had torn down and rebuilt countless buildings, but this one bothered me. Camila made me feel like I was shredding everything from her. I looked at the glass door in the front, which was slightly unhinged from the top. I'd seen pictures at the meetings in Belmonte, but hadn't really paid attention. I'd been on my phone answering emails from my agent and sponsors. I hadn't really cared enough to look at how bad the building looked. Seeing it now and knowing somebody like Camila lived in there . . . I looked back at her.

"How safe is this area?"

She laughed. "For me? Very. For you? Not so much."

I wasn't sure what to do with that answer, but I didn't like it. What was I supposed to say though? *I don't want you living here? I don't like the thought of you being in this neighborhood? You're too gorgeous? Too kind? Too quiet? Too small?* I didn't know her well enough to impose those kinds of thoughts about her. I swallowed down all of those thoughts.

"I want to see you again," I said, finally.

She took a quick step back, eyes wide. "What?"

I repeated myself.

"Why?" she asked, frowning.

"Do I need a reason?"

"I think so," she replied, though it sounded more like a question.

"Why's that?"

"I don't know. You're—" she glanced away momentarily, "you're kicking me out of my apartment."

Her voice, although soft, held a bitterness in it that I hadn't experienced. She was small and quiet, but the way she was glaring at me made me sink into the shadows of the building behind us.

"I'm not kicking you out," I reminded her. "I would never do that."

"Your company is."

"Not my company," I clarified.

She let out a harsh breath and crossed her arms. "Whatever."

"I went to the bar for you tonight," I said, hoping that the gravity I held in my gaze would be enough to appease her.

"Why?"

"I think you know why, Camila."

Her lips parted slightly, as if she was going to say something, but then she shut them again and looked around. I wondered what she was looking for. There was loud Hispanic music coming from the corner and some guys sitting around a domino table, but aside from that the street was empty.

"Let me take you out," I said, earning another surprised look from her.

"I don't think it's a good idea."

"What?"

"I. Don't. Think. It's. A. Good. Idea," she said, enunciating each word slowly. I crossed my arms.

"Why the hell not?"

"Because I don't think it's a good idea and I'm sure you have better things to do while you're here, Mr. Hotshot Soccer Player."

I uncrossed my arms and took a step toward her again, forcing her to tilt her face to look me in the eyes. "It's football, and I have a lot of things to do, one of which will be you."

She blinked. "Yeah, no. Not going to happen."

"Why not?"

"I gave you two good reasons, if you need me to give you

more, I will."

"Are you always this much of a peach?"

She seemed startled for a second before she started to smile. "That's what my family calls me."

"What? Peach?"

She nodded, licking her lips.

"Because of your poor attitude?"

Heat spread over her face. "Most people say that I'm a very nice person. Too nice. Doormat nice."

"Maybe most people don't see the real you," I said, trying to keep myself from smiling at her obvious discomfort. "So they call you Peach because you're doormat nice?"

"No." She laughed. "Because of Mario Bros."

"Princess Peach. I get it." I chuckled and then put my hands up in fists. "I personally think Rocky suits you better."

"You have a real future in comedy, you know? Maybe if that soccer thing doesn't work out you can try that next."

I laughed. A real, honest-to-God laugh, and she joined soon after. When we both stopped laughing, we stared at each other for another long moment, and I felt like if I didn't at least kiss her by the end of the night, I would explode with need. When her lips parted again, my attention was fully on them, on the perfect way they curved when she spoke. I was so enthralled by them and her tongue, which she used to lick them, that her words didn't register until it was too late.

"Thanks for walking me home."

And just like that, she walked into the building. Right before she shut the door, she tucked her head out and added, "I hope your curiosity was satisfied," and went right back inside.

I was too shell-shocked to move. Had that really just happened? I stared at the glass door for a second, two, three, four, just blinking and trying to figure out what the hell had just occurred.

Did she really turn me down? Did I really let her? This couldn't be. I definitely wasn't just going to let it end here. I'd been mildly curious before, but now Camila had my full attention.

Chapter
FIVE

Camila

On principle alone, I was supposed to hate Warren Silva. On principle alone, we should have never met. He should have never offered to walk me home and I never should have let him. Yet here I was, a day later, standing in line at the corner store still thinking about him. *Him.* And his dark green eyes and the way they glimmered when he flirted with me. Men like him didn't notice girls like me. And I had never wanted them to.

"Is this all you're taking? Want your usual card?" Pedro, the clerk asked.

My usual card meaning the calling card I bought so I could call my brother in the Dominican Republic. My brother, who was probably living the life over there, with a driver, a maid and a cook, while I was over here jumping through hoops to hear his voice for just a second. I sighed. I tried not to be upset at Johnny. I loved him to death and I loved that he was doing well, but sometimes the thought made me want to punch him.

"Please," I said, smiling at Pedro.

"Any plans to visit your mom's?"

"I'll probably go in a couple of weeks."

"Still not considering moving in with her while this housing situation gets sorted out?"

I pursed my lips. "You trying to get rid of me?"

"Never, Rubia," he said, laughing. I smiled when he called me that. It was such a Dominican thing. I wasn't blonde at all, but anybody who was pale and had light eyes was automatically nicknamed blonde. "You thought about moving in with your sister?"

"Definitely not."

He threw his head back in laughter. "You can always stay with us. Mayra would love it, especially if you're available for babysitting."

"Ha. Your kids will really drive me out of this neighborhood," I said, turning toward the door. "See you next week."

Pedro was still laughing as I left the store. Thinking about all the things I had to do was making me anxious, and amongst them was calling my grandmother in the Dominican Republic. Every week I bought a calling card for the long-distance call, and each time I held it in my hand and debated whether or not I would actually use it. My grandmother didn't have a cellphone. She refused to own one because she heard they cause cancer, so this was my way of calling her landline and not paying a fortune for the fifteen minutes we spoke.

As of late, more often than not, I gave it to Elisa across the hall so she could call her family in Puerto Rico. It wasn't that I didn't want to talk to my grandmother. I loved talking to her, but since my grandfather died, hearing her voice made the ache in my chest worsen. I'd always preferred holding the calling card more than actually using it. It reminded me of my childhood, before we had it all, when my mom still used one to keep in touch with our family.

It made me think of laughter and all of us sitting around in the kitchen as we waited for our food to be served. Of my brother sneaking up on my mom while she fried food just to steal a slice of fried plantain, and my sister's endless gossip about the boys in school. It reminded me of my dad coming home from work, his face filled with exhaustion as he set down his briefcase, and how it cleared and became jubilant the moment we kissed him on the cheek. It reminded me of the kind of love we used to have before.

Before.

Before.

Before.

It was all I thought about these days, especially after the funeral, and clutching the calling card in my hands made the nostalgia worsen. As I reached the corner of my building, I noticed a few men in suits standing in front of it and stopped dead in my tracks when I spotted *him* standing off to the side. Unlike the others, he wasn't wearing a suit, but jeans and a collared shirt with two buttons. His free hand was moving animatedly as he spoke on the phone. The sun glistening on the different works of art etched over his arms with each movement. I resumed walking, intent on ignoring him, but the thrumming of my heart worked its way up to my ears until I felt a whooshing sensation with each step. Our eyes met the moment I reached my door and in a slow, deliberate movement, he ended his call and tucked the phone into the front pocket of his jeans. He began to walk over to me with an expression so serious, it made the hairs on the back of my neck stand up. I cupped my hand and brought it up to shield my eyes from the sun as he reached me.

"Hey, Rocky," he said, looking very amused at his own joke.

I resisted the urge to roll my eyes, even though the way he looked at me when he said it set me ablaze on the inside. His eyes swept over my face before locking with mine.

"You in a rush?"

"I have to be at work soon," I said squinting at the sun on my face. Warren moved an inch to the left to block it. I smiled in gratitude.

"Is it far from here?"

"Brooklyn," I said. "I need to leave here in about thirty-five minutes to make it on time."

"This is for your other job?"

I cracked a smile. "I only have one job. I already told you, I don't work at the bar."

"Right." He smiled. "The non-for-profit you won't tell me about."

"The Winsor Foundation," I said. "We work with troubled kids, mainly teenagers. Offer them counseling, housing, places to spend time after school. Stuff like that."

"Sounds important," he said, raising his eyebrows as if impressed.

"Definitely the most important thing I've done thus far."

His eyes hadn't left mine for a second, and I was starting to feel uncomfortable with the attention. The look he was giving me making me want to back away and run up the stairs to my apartment where I was safe and away from the pull I felt between us, so I fidgeted with the calling card in my hand, clutching it a little tighter.

"Let me take you out," he said.

My heart did a little flip at the unexpectedness of it. I didn't respond because I wasn't sure what to say, and when one of the men in suits called out his name and he looked over his shoulder, I was relieved I didn't have to answer at all. I studied his profile as he listened to the man, his thin nose, his defined jaw and the shadow of the beard that covered it, the tiny hole in his ear, his brushed-back dark hair, his tanned neck, which was seemingly the only place he didn't have tattoos. I wondered what the suits thought of a man like him. I wondered if they judged him. He was untamed perfection. That was what every inch of him screamed. And I was not about to be the one trying to tame him. I'd been there before. Last time I tried to tame a player, I got burned. And the player I tried to tame was nowhere near Warren Silva's stature.

I turned toward the door and unlocked it, holding it open with the side of my foot as I waited for Warren to stop talking to the man. I didn't want to be rude, but I also didn't want to be late for work, and when Warren turned his body and fully faced the guy he was talking to, I dashed inside and took the stairs two at a time to my apartment and started to undress as soon as the door shut behind me, kicking off my flip-flops before peeling off my shirt. My jean shorts came off as I rushed into the bathroom. Most of the time when I was on my way to work I wished I had a uniform and today was no exception. Luckily, I was encouraged to dress casually. I thought by the time I made it back downstairs Warren would be gone, but again the shock of seeing him made me stop dead in my tracks as I neared the door.

And again, his eyes found mine as I got closer to him. When he did stop looking into my eyes, it was to let them roam over me in a slow movement that made my skin prickle. It made it difficult for me to pull the door open and not have that space between us. It made it difficult for me not to want to find out if we shared anything in common.

"Have you figured out your living situation?" he asked as I stepped outside, and just like that he reminded me of what it was we did share.

"No, but don't worry. I'll be out of your hair soon enough."

He flinched. "I never said you were—"

"You didn't have to," I said, interrupting him. I turned and started to walk away. "I'll catch you later."

"How do you get to Brooklyn?" he asked, catching up to me easily. I stopped walking so that he wouldn't chase me down to the subway.

"A train."

He nodded once and looked around, at the men who were still standing there, down the sidewalk at the guys setting up the domino table outside of the corner store, and back at me.

"I'm supposed to head to Brooklyn for a football match with some kids tomorrow. I can give you a lift."

Either the guy couldn't get a clue or he was just that used to getting his way. That was probably what bothered me most. The thought that every woman before and after me was quick to drop her panties for him and he was so willing to accept them.

"No, thank you," I said.

"I have a place, that's why I was asking you if you'd figured out your living situation," he said suddenly. He must have seen the confusion in my face, because he continued quickly. "Not my place, but a building. A building for you and the others to move into if you choose."

"Why would we do that?"

"Belmonte wants to offer you a temporary place to live."

I narrowed my eyes on his. "Why would Belmonte offer that?"

He studied me for a beat. "You really have a thing against them, don't you? Is it the company or the owners?"

"The owners."

"So we're clear," he said, his voice dropping as he stepped a little closer. I took a breath and stepped back, but he completely invaded my space. "I'm not them, so stop treating me like I'm the enemy."

"Okay," I whispered.

"But, I spoke to some people there and they decided that this would be the perfect solution. That way we fill up the building and you guys have a place to live. It's a win-win. Give me your phone number so I can send you the information. I'm sending it to everybody who lives here right now. It'll be a good price. Comparable to what you pay here, it won't be far, and best of all you'll have the same neighbors."

"Oooookay." I took the phone he handed me and reluctantly typed in my name and number. "Only because it'll save me a lot of time."

He smiled as he took the phone back. "Of course. Want me to drive you to Brooklyn?"

"Again with the car thing?"

"It'll be faster, won't it?"

I laughed. "When did you say the last time you were here was?"

"Too long ago," he responded, his eyes hinting at

amusement.

"The train is definitely faster than a car, especially at this time, but thanks for the offer."

"What if I want to ride the train?"

My eyes widened. He was really doing this. All my life I'd been surrounded by bullshitting men. The ones who drive a hard bargain to get you in their bed and fuck it all up once they have you there. It wasn't a foreign concept to me. I was Dominican, for God's sake. But when a man like Warren Silva paid attention to me . . . damn, he made it difficult to remember that I didn't trust men. His eyes were searing into mine again. I was trying to figure out ways to say no, but the longer we looked at each other the more difficult it proved to be.

"And you're going to come back all by yourself?" I asked.

"Tomorrow I will," he said, then thought better of it. "I may have someone with me."

I shook my head and tried to smother a smile as I looked at the exercise watch on my wrist and read the time. Shit. If I made it to the train in the next ten minutes I would be ten minutes late to work.

"Oh crap. I have to go. Let's just take a rain check."

Warren started walking beside me, keeping up with my rushed steps. "I have never met a woman more intent on getting away from me."

"I know this is hard for a man like you to believe, but not everything is about you. I'm not trying to get away from you. Just trying to get to work. There's a difference."

"Very well. Prove it. Go out with me then."

His words made me come to a full stop. I was amazed and thankful my heart hadn't tumbled out of my chest and onto the concrete in front of me. Why did this man insist on seeing me again? I turned to face him.

"We have nothing in common. You know that, right?"

He raised an eyebrow. "You're sure about this?"

"Uh, yeah."

"How?"

"I just know. You're all . . . high class and Belmontey and I'm all . . . broke Dominican girl from Washington Heights. It's just not a match made in heaven."

Warren chuckled. "You say this as if you're a hoodlum."

That made me pause and frown. I looked around the corner we were on, across the street, where Pedro was outside smoking a cigarette. We waved at each other. Him, with a frown on his face as he assessed Warren; me with a smile that assured him I was fine. Unlike most of the people here, I hadn't lived here since I was born. I hadn't been to District Six or P.S. IS 187. When I'd arrived at George Washington, I was the quiet new kid and I came to learn that there were a lot of quiet new kids. We weren't shunned for being different like we would've been in the private school I'd been to for most of my life. We weren't judged by what we wore or what we looked like. It felt more home to me than a lot of places I'd lived in before then.

And I wouldn't consider myself, a straight-A honor student who was paid by a great University to attend based on grades a hoodlum, but I knew a lot of people who were considered hoodlums. I worked with many kids who were seen in that light and I hated that they were put in that box to begin with. I looked up at Warren again. At least the guy had good manners, unlike ninety percent of the rich people I'd met. Still, nothing in common. Nothing.

"The fact you'd even say that proves we're not compatible."

He looked crestfallen. "I didn't mean any harm by it."

I shook my head. "People like you never do."

"What does that mean? 'People like me'?" he asked, following me down the stairs to the train.

"People who don't know any better."

"So teach me," he said. I turned to face him again. The honesty in his eyes made my heart skip a beat.

"Teach you what?"

He smiled. "Teach me how to understand."

We looked at each other for so long, I didn't know what to say next, so I went with the first thing that popped into my head.

"What kind of music do you listen to?"

He frowned for a beat before a smile began tugging at his lips. "Are you going to quiz me to see if we're compatible?"

"Maybe." I was startled by my phone ringing in my purse. "Shit. Work. Look, I really need to go. If you want to walk me to work tomorrow, you're more than welcome to."

I turned around and swiped my card to get to the platform and stopped when I heard him shout my name. He was on the other side of the bars, his hands holding on to the fence, looking like he was trying to get out of a cage. I walked back toward him and stood on the other side of it, looking up. He moved closer to the links of the fence, and on instinct, I moved closer as well, enjoying a whiff of his cologne, preparing myself for what he would do next, knowing he couldn't do much with a fence between us. His fingers brushed over my own as he looked at me, or more accurately, what felt like *into me*.

"Have a good day at work," he said. "Just so you know, I won't stop until I get that date."

I couldn't even manage to form a response as he dropped his hands and retreated, walking backward first, and then fully turning around. I let myself check him out for a moment; his back was perfection. He wasn't overly muscular, but every inch of him looked hard. Hard. I blushed furiously at the thought and turned around just in time to hear the train's tires squealing as it approached. For the rest of the day, I tried to focus on the kids and setting up our next networking event, but all I could do was think about Warren and seeing him again.

Chapter
SIX

Warren

ntoine and I were waiting outside Camila's building. I didn't want to bring him, but my publicist threatened to call the media if I didn't walk around with at least one of my security detail. It didn't matter to me. It's not like Antoine looked any different than any of my friends, and with as much as we'd been hanging out after I hired him, he was quickly becoming a friend. He pushed himself off the wall beside me and stood up straight when Camila showed up. She was wearing a blouse with thin straps that made me wonder if she wore a bra beneath it (not that I could tell. The shirt was covered in a flower pattern). Her hair looked damp and she wore very little makeup, if any. I could make out the freckles on her nose. She looked beautiful. In fact, the only thing I would change about the scenario was that she wouldn't be looking at Antoine, but at me instead.

"You went to Washington, right?" she asked frowning slightly.

Antoine nodded slowly, clearly checking her out in a way I didn't appreciate. From experience, I knew what he was doing, trying to figure out if he'd fucked her in the past. I waited on bated breath for his answer, and when he smiled and chuckled a bit, I instantly knew he hadn't.

"That's right," he said slowly drawing out the word. "Johnny's kid sister. Damn you've grown up. I almost didn't recognize you."

That, I didn't appreciate.

Camila smiled. "Years will do that to ya. Are you still driving an Uber?"

"I was, but Mr. Silva gave me a better opportunity," he explained, nodding toward me.

Camila's eyes flew to mine. "No shit."

"Shit," I said, confirming it. I walked up to her and put my arm around her to embrace her in a half hug. I wasn't going to push it yet, but even if it was just that, I needed to feel her against me. "You two obviously know each other . . . "

"We sort of grew up together," Camila explained.

"I went to school with her older brother and sister," Antoine offered before turning his attention back to Camila. "I heard Vanessa married some rich guy."

"Remember Adam?"

Antoine frowned, but it quickly went from confusion to complete shock. "The rich Jewish kid?" Camila laughed at his reaction, and Antoine continued. "Scrawny, nerdy Adam?"

Camila laughed harder. "Yup. No longer scrawny. Still nerdy."

Her laughter made me smile, though I felt conflicted because I hadn't made her laugh like that. Yet. She gave me an opportunity, and now I was regretting bringing Antoine along.

"She's happy," Camila added.

"Shit. I'd be really happy too if I had all those funds in my bank account," Antoine responded with a chuckle. "Good for her. Is she still teaching?"

"Yeah. That's how they met."

"No shit."

"Shit," Camila said, smiling up at me with a twinkle in her eye. I still had my arm around her and she hadn't complained or shrugged me off. "I'm going to have to steal that line."

"You can steal whatever you want," I said. That made her blush.

"You're dressed down today," she said, pushing away from me and blushing even harder as she assessed my wardrobe. I was wearing cotton pants, a Dri-FIT shirt, and sneakers. My cleats and an extra shirt were in the backpack I had on.

"Ready for a War-k out," I said, winking.

She tore her gaze away from me quickly, but from the way her lips pursed I could tell she was fighting a smile. "I would love to see what a War-k out consists of."

"Really?" I asked, letting my eyes drift slowly down her thin yet curvy frame. "I'll give you a personal War-k out whenever you want."

The only ones I was interested in doing with her included her, my bed, and my dick, but I didn't want to say that aloud out of fear she'd slap me. She looked capable of doing something like that. She blushed even harder and looked away from me.

The three of us walked along, and Antoine walked a step behind, letting Camila and I walk side by side. When she waved at the guy in the corner store across the street, I waved with her, and Antoine shouted his greeting, which made the guy frown and look at Camila. She laughed.

"You know what the conversation at Pedro's will be to-morrow," she said, glancing at Antoine over her shoulder.

"Things I don't miss about living in the neighborhood: gossip," Antoine said.

We all laughed at that. Gossip was one of those universal things, that no matter whom you were or what you did, you could relate to. Everybody was gossiped about and few people liked it, but damn was it entertaining when you weren't the center of it. When we got to the bottom, I turned around to ask Antoine a question about the subway system, and by the time I turned around again Camila was handing me a card. I took it and looked at the blue and yellow Metro Card.

"Did you just buy this for me?"

"How else are you going to get on the train, Richie Rich?"

I tried really hard not to entertain her jab, but found myself smiling anyway. It was a small gesture, something that coming from anybody else I probably wouldn't have paid much attention to, but coming from her it was . . . progress. I decided not to be a prick and point out the fact that she paid for something and instead address her comment.

"I'm going to have to start calling you high blood pressure, or diabetes, or some other form of silent killer."

"Rocky isn't cutting it?" she asked, turning around. I followed, my eyes on her round ass. Fuck I wanted to grab it. She slid her card through the machine and I did the same.

"Your jabs are definitely worthy of Rocky," I assured her

as we walked on the platform toward the train.

At the sound of the screech, we turned toward the train and began to board when the doors opened. Once inside, we found no sitting room, so we were forced to stand by the door and hold on to the bars. Camila wasn't tall enough to reach the overheads, so she held on to the one beside her and I stood in front of her, my arms on either side of the bar above her, shielding her to keep from tumbling. She tilted her head to look at me and smiled.

"Welcome to public transportation, Mr. Silva."

"I've been on trains before," I said.

I'd ridden the Eurostar often when I was younger to go to Paris. This was nothing like the fucking Eurostar. This was all piss and sweat bundled into a small, enclosed, hot space. Jesus Christ. How did people do it? I looked over at Camila, who was looking at me.

"In Paris?" she asked.

"To Paris, yes." I smiled at the scowl she gave me. "Have you ever been?"

She seemed to stifle a laugh as she looked at me, her eyes twinkling. "I haven't had the pleasure. Do they look like this?"

I ignored her question and asked, "Would you like to go?"

She frowned. "To Paris?"

I nodded.

"I guess." She paused, a small frown forming over her top lip. "I've never really thought about it."

The train propelled me a little closer to her as it came to the first stop. I tightened my grip on the overhead bars. "You've never thought about going to Paris?"

"I guess not."

"Would you go?" I asked. "You're not one of those people who are deathly afraid of flying, are you?"

She looked right into my eyes. "I'm not deathly afraid of anything."

"Oh?" I raised an eyebrow and moved so the front of my body was almost touching hers and she had to tilt her head a little more. "You're afraid to go on a date with me."

"Oh God," she said, smiling and shaking her head as she looked away momentarily. "Really? You're going to use that right now?"

"Yes, really," I said, inching closer.

Her smile faltered a bit and her eyes widened, and from the way she held her breath, I could tell she was nervous as hell. For a millisecond I wondered if she'd slap me if I tried to kiss her, and chuckled at the thought. She'd probably punch me.

"Have you not figured out whether or not we're compatible yet?" I asked. "Isn't me getting on this train enough?"

She shook her head. "No, and definitely not."

I took and let out a deep breath. "Quiz me then. Let's see how well I do."

"That's ridiculous," she said. "I don't have to quiz you to know we're not compatible. Your statement about the train is more than enough proof that we're not."

I took a step back when we arrived at the next stop and decided to let it go. Evidently this was not an Elena situation I had on my hands. She'd been easy to pursue and conquer. In hindsight, she was probably conquered the moment she saw me step out of my red Bugatti.

"Talk to me about work," I said. Camila's mood picked up instantly.

"Right now I'm in charge of collecting funds for some

new parks we're building. We build them in low-income neighborhoods." She paused, tilting her face. "Actually, it's a lot like what Belmonte does, except instead of tearing things down and kicking people out, we build these parks and other extracurricular activity places that kids can go. It's about having a place they belong in."

I stared at her for a long moment, trying to figure out whether or not I wanted to tackle that Belmonte comment in the middle of a crowded, smelly train or let it be. I decided on the latter.

"What kind of parks?"

"Football fields, playgrounds, soccer parks . . . it really depends on the votes. The community gets to pick."

"So you're," I paused, frowning, "what's your title?"

She smiled. "I do a few things, but my current title is landscape architect."

"Sounds . . . formal? Is that what you went to school for?"

"I majored in psychology, which was how I ended up there in the first place. As a case worker. Most of us are kind of jacks-of-all-trades. When there was an opportunity with a higher salary and less work, I went back to school and the rest is history."

The tires squealed again and Camila was propelled toward me. She shot her arm out to my chest before she could fully hit me, and laughed nervously before she continued talking.

"Did you go to school?"

I shook my head. "I started football early and thankfully was good enough to skip over the whole college thing."

"You've been playing pro soccer a long time then."

"Very long time," I said, smiling. I wondered if she liked to torture me by calling it soccer right after I called it football.

"And your knees haven't gone to crap?" she asked, her eyes shooting toward my knees.

I chuckled. "My knees work quite well, thank you."

"Are you the best player on your team?" she asked lightly, then frowned. "Is that a rude question?"

I chuckled again. "It's not a rude question, and that's a tough question to answer, but I guess I am."

"Interesting. I don't think I've ever heard an athlete not boast about being the best one even when they're not."

I shrugged. "It's a team sport, and the team is as good as its worst player."

She gave me a bewildered look with a pout that made me want to bite her lips. I gripped the poles tighter. I kept talking in order to explain myself better.

"In basketball, for example, the team really depends on the best player. In American football, the team really depends on the quarterback. In real football, we depend on each other to pass the ball until we make the goal."

"Do you score a lot of goals?" she asked.

I sighed. How could I explain to her that even though technically I did, it wasn't the way it worked? I realized that I couldn't. It was something she had to see for herself.

"I have a game in a few weeks. You should come with me," I said.

"Where is it?"

"Manchester."

Camila gaped at me. "Manchester . . . in England?"

"Yes."

She smiled at me before glancing away. "Maybe some other time."

I hadn't said it as a joke, but I was almost relieved she took it as one. I needed to slow down with this one, and if she were anybody else I would have probably just walked away from the situation entirely. Between the chasing and the smell of bloody urine in the damn train, she had to know I was desperate to take anything she'd give me.

"So, you're spending your vacation away from playing soccer by going to Brooklyn and practicing with some kids?"

"I guess I am," I said. She studied me for a moment and I could tell she was dying to ask me something. "What?"

"Will there be cameras there to document this phenomenon?"

The spark in her eye told me two things: she was making fun of me and she was upset about the possibilities of the cameras. I wondered if she'd been testing my motives. I thought her test would consist of rappers' names and feuds, but evidently that wasn't where her interests lay. She was testing me. Trying to figure out what kind of person I was, and I was fucking losing. The media attention in Brooklyn would surely put the nail on the coffin.

"I have a question for you," I said.

"You still haven't answered mine."

I tilted my head and gripped the overhead bars a little tighter when the train came screeching to its next stop. "Are you wary of me because of my career or my involvement in Belmonte?"

She studied my face for a couple of beats. "Both. I have trust issues."

"So do I." I lowered my right hand from the bar above to rattle off the reasons I'd gathered thus far, starting with my thumb. "I have money. I invest in a company you have an immense hate for, and you have trust issues. Am I getting all of the reasons?"

"Pretty much."

"Let's start with the trust issues then," I said.

She gave me a nod. "My ex-boyfriend cheated on me and I've been trying not to let it affect me, but it's kind of impossible, so the whole possibility of going out with some rich, handsome soccer player who clearly has baggage and probably has groupies is a bit of a stretch for me."

Ah. I tried to fight back a smile, but failed. "What if I told you that this rich, handsome soccer player doesn't have groupies?"

"I'd say you were full of shit."

I chuckled. "Fair enough. What if I told you that I don't pay any attention to them?"

She searched my eyes with a serious expression on her face before shrugging. "Honestly? I'm not sure. Groupies or not, I still don't think we're compatible."

"My ex-fiancée cheated on me," I said, pausing for dramatic affect. "With one of my teammates."

Camila's mouth dropped. "No shit."

"Shit," I said, biting back a laugh.

Her eyes twinkled a bit before she began to laugh lightly and I joined, though the subject was no laughing matter. Every time I thought about Elena with Ricky, a quiet rage stabbed at me.

"Are they still together?"

I nodded in response.

"Is he still on the team?"

"Yeah. I've learned to move past it," I said, shrugging nonchalantly even though I was full of it. I was still trying to learn to move past it. I just hoped by the time the season started again I was a wise man when it came to that.

Camila's brows rose as if impressed. "Well, for what it's worth, I'm sorry that happened to you."

"I appreciate the sentiment, but if you really want to make me feel better, go out with me."

"I appreciate your tenacity," she said with a smile, "I do. But I have bigger things to worry about, like where I'll be living next month."

"Well, Belmonte is offering everybody in your building to transfer to one up the street temporarily, until everything else is settled and the new building is finished."

"Why would they do that?"

"It's the least they could do. We had a meeting about it yesterday and the board decided on it."

She looked at me for such a long time, I was sure she'd pry every bit of information out of me. "Was Javier part of that meeting?"

I sighed. I could feel her anger every time she said the name, and it made me wish I had no association with it at all. "It was a unanimous decision. I'm sure you'll be getting an email and a call about it soon."

"Okay. Thanks."

"So, now that your living situation is settled, let's talk about us."

She laughed. "I used to think it was a Dominican thing, the persistence and sweet talking, but I'm beginning to see it's just a man thing."

"Aren't you Dominican?" I asked, raising an eyebrow.

Her cheeks reddened. "Yeah, but I'm not going to sweet talk you, if that's what you're getting at."

"I won't object to sweet talking," I said, stepping a little closer to her. "And a date with me wouldn't be such a bad thing."

"Why not ask one of the other million women in this city? I'm sure you've met some that are more your type, or at least closer to your social status," she said, tilting her head to look into my eyes. I could practically feel her chest against mine and it made it difficult to concentrate on the words coming out of those beautiful lips.

"I have met a few of those, and they're not my type. My type is standing right in front of me in this smelly subway," I said. She laughed a bit, so I added, "If nothing else, at least you know I'm not a cheater," I said. "I'll never lie to you. I'll never purposely hurt you."

She didn't respond to that. We looked at each other for a long moment, too long for two people this attracted to one another to be standing this close to each other and not be doing something other than just looking. My heart rattled, my blood pumped louder in my veins, my breathing escalated. It was the same thing I felt every time the ball landed at my feet, as the anticipation of what could be began to make its way through me.

There was something about her, about her eyes, and the way she wrinkled her nose when she thought something was weird that intrigued me. There was something about her presence that made me feel I was where I was supposed to be. I'd only ever felt that way about football-related things. Never about a woman. And definitely never about a woman like this one.

Unlike every other time I met somebody, I didn't wonder what my mother would make of her, and how my father would insult her presence at the dinner table if he ever gave me a chance to share it with him again. I didn't care what my brother might have said about her and how many warnings about her background and what ulterior motives she might have. The only thing I saw was her. The only thing I cared about was what the next words out of her mouth would be.

And I really wanted them to be an agreement to going out with me. When the train stopped again, I barely noticed it, and would have missed our exit if it weren't for Camila placing her hands on my chest and trying to push me back slightly.

"This is our stop," she said, her voice a mere whisper.

I wondered if her heart was pumping in her ears, if her body felt as charged up as mine. I couldn't even make a joke out of things as we walked along the sidewalk or even as her steps began to slow in front of a brown brick building. Something about that moment had rendered me speechless.

Before she went inside, I said to her, "Call me. Don't even look at the time. Just call."

"You don't sleep?" she asked, her lips between a frown and a smile, as if she couldn't pick a side yet.

"Sleep is the cousin of death," I said, grinning when I was finally awarded with a real, melodic laughter from her.

"Two points for Warren," she said with a smile.

I chuckled and watched as she walked away, staring at her ass and the way it swayed slightly as she walked. It wasn't an exaggerated walk. I could tell from her quick steps that she wasn't necessarily thrilled that I was staring, and it was just one more thing that drew me to her.

Chapter
SEVEN

Camila

"A re you sure you'll be able to do this? You have a lot on your plate right now," Nancy asked for what felt like the millionth time since I signed on to help plan the charity auction.

"I can handle it."

I smiled to reassure her that I felt I could. And I did. I'd put together five networkers and auctions already for the other parks we'd built. I didn't see why this would be any different. In the company I worked for before I made the transition to Winsor, I'd helped design golf courses for retirement communities, and those were a lot more work than playgrounds and football fields. They definitely didn't leave me with the sense of fulfillment that this job did. I took out my sketchpad and opened it up to the page I wanted to show her.

"I was thinking," I started. Nancy put down the papers she'd been looking at and gave me her full attention, taking the pad I handed her. "This isn't finished, but I thought I'd give more options that didn't only include parks."

She looked at me over the thin frame of her glasses. "This is for the Y?"

"I'm not saying we should do this right now, but we've built three parks in that neighborhood, and I think in order to incorporate something that will be able to stand on its own long-term, we need a place like this, where they can go and read and use computers. We can scale it down and cut the costs a bit, but . . ."

"It's brilliant," Nancy said, looking down at the structure I'd drawn.

It really wasn't brilliant. I basically took components of the YMCA and changed a few things. "The orphanage is right next door to this lot, so I'm sure we can get their help with a few things," I added.

"How fast can we blow this up and print it?" she asked, pointing at my drawing. "We need to display it at the auction. Do you think you'd be able to talk more about it there?"

My heart skipped. I wiped my hands over my jeans. "In front of everybody?"

"There won't be that many people in attendance," she said.

"We have ninety RSVPs so far," I said, my voice a hoarse whisper. I cleared my throat quickly but didn't continue. Most people going to this event were either a CEO or private investor for a mega hedge fund company. There was absolutely no way I could stand in front of them and talk.

"I can have Adam present it, or Vanessa," she offered

with a kind smile.

I let out a relieved breath. "Yes! Either one, or both would be great."

Nancy laughed. "You never cease to amaze me, Camila."

I smiled though I knew she didn't necessarily mean it as a compliment, but she knew me well enough to understand I was not okay with public speaking. We spent the rest of the day going through the list, the contracts with the catering company, the entertainment, and gift bags people would receive. The auction items were already en route to the hotel and would be stored there until the weekend, so that was checked off the list. When I stepped out of the building, I found Trey, one of the kids I'd worked with in the past, standing outside with a basketball in his hand.

"Going home?" I asked him. He smiled when he saw me and nodded. "I'll walk with you."

We headed in the opposite direction of the train and neared the park I knew Warren was in. There were news trucks pulling out and cameras being put away. Trey commented about some celebrity that was playing soccer in there, and I listened to the way he described the park being packed and people standing around everywhere just to get a glimpse of this guy as if Jay Z himself would've shown up.

"Maybe he did," I said.

Trey scoffed. "Yeah right."

"Are things better at home?" I asked once we passed the park and I knew I wouldn't get a glimpse of Warren. Trey shrugged.

"I guess."

"Is your mom back?"

"Yeah. She's there. She got a new boyfriend."

I cringed. "That must be hard."

He shrugged. "Your pops still in jail?"

"Yup. He's supposed to get out in a couple of weeks," I said.

"Are you excited about it?"

We stopped walking when we reached the corner of the Whitman Projects, where Trey lived and we faced each other. He was only sixteen, but he was as tall as Warren, maybe even taller. As he waited for my answer, I felt like the tables had turned and suddenly he was the counselor and I was the one in need of somebody like him. If Warren had asked me this question, I would've had to think about it a lot. I would've tried to figure out how to go around the truth to make it sound more acceptable. Trey and I were cut from a similar cloth, though.

"I should be," I said, shrugging away the emotion that threatened to consume me.

Trey smiled his understanding and gave me a quick sideways hug before walking away. "You know you're my favorite, Miss Avila."

"You better remember that when you're playing in Madison Square Garden, Trey Andrews."

As I watched him cross the street and say hi to the friends that greeted him on the other side, I caught a glimpse of the crowd he most likely hung around when he left Winsor and the basketball courts and headed home each night. The picture wasn't one I liked, even though it was his reality and there was very little I could do about it. I turned my back with a heavy heart and headed back up the block, passing the park once more. This time, when I looked, I saw Warren bouncing the soccer ball with his knee as a small group of kids watched. A part of me wanted to run in there and experience that part of his life, but then I remembered his invitation to Manchester, and the fearful grip that had taken hold of me when he first asked returned, so I walked away.

Chapter
EIGHT

Warren

She hadn't called. I was sure she would. Maybe not yesterday, but today, I was sure she would. I'd never been turned down before. Ever. Well, maybe that one time I hit on a married woman (in my defense, I didn't know she was married). Aside from that, though . . . never. I tried to figure out where I went wrong. Was it something I said? She seemed relieved about Belmonte's building plan when I told her. Maybe she'd received the letter and didn't feel a need to call me. But why not call because she was interested in me? And she was interested. I could see it every time she looked at me. I could feel it anytime we were near. So why hadn't she called?

"Why does Dad call you War?" my nephew Cayden

asked beside me, jarring me from my thoughts. "Is it because your name is Warren? Do you like war?"

I looked down at him. His eyes were green and wide and full of wonder. I'd agreed to bring him to the movies for the premiere of a big blockbuster because I rarely got to see him. He'd been to a few of my football games with my brother, and whenever my mom came over to visit, we'd FaceTimed, but I hadn't actually held his hand in mine in over a year, and now that I was doing just that as we walked into the movie theatre, I realized how much I needed somebody to hold my hand right now. Even if I was too self-involved to admit that aloud, I was man enough to recognize it.

"It's a nickname, little man. I hate war," I said, smiling at the girl behind the ticket counter. Her jaw dropped and I knew instantly she recognized me. If not for her reaction, the bracelet she wore of my team colors would have been a dead giveaway.

"Are you—"

"Yes," I said, my voice hushed. "I can sign whatever you want, but I'm trying to be undercover while I'm here," I added with a wink.

The girl nodded, eyes as wide as her smile. She took the money I handed her and gave me the tickets and a few blank pages, which I signed and handed back quickly. Then, seeing how much meeting me meant to her, I offered to take a picture with her. As I walked away, I spoke to Cayden about the movie and our favorite superheroes. He was wearing an Iron Man shirt, and I wore a Captain America shirt, mainly because I liked the shield. Truth be told, unless it was on a cartoon I'd watched when I was a kid, I didn't know much about superheroes. Cayden, however, seemed to be an expert. If there were a job for an eight-year old superhero analyst, I'd hire him in a heartbeat. I was listening intently as we stood in the line of the concession stand when a familiar laugh caught my attention.

My eyes found Camila instantly. She was standing in the front of the line, talking to the guy handing her a bag of popcorn. I wondered if she knew him. He was obviously fond of her, from the way he was smiling, and the way they carried on what seemed like an endless conversation made me wonder how often she came here. On the counter in front of her was one bag of popcorn, one drink, and one box of peanut M&M's. Was she here by herself? Impossible. Right? It would be impossible.

Did anybody go to the movies by themselves? Did anybody that looked like *her* go to the movies by themselves? She was wearing a Yankees cap facing backward, and that alone should have been a red flag for me, especially since I was actually wearing my Mets cap. She fixed it a little, tucking her hair out of her face before leaning down slightly to pick up the three things she'd purchased. As she walked toward me, our eyes met. Hers widened immensely, as did mine, because even though I'd spotted her, actually seeing her all of her put my heart on overdrive. What the hell was it about this girl?

Her steps slowed as she reached me. "Did I tell you I would be here?"

Her voice was always low, always quiet, making her seem even more dainty than she already was. It should have steered me in another direction. All the women I'd dated were in-your-face kind of people, so sure of themselves that sidewalks parted at their approach. Camila was the opposite of everyone I'd ever known. It only made me want to get to know her more. Her quiet voice only made me want to find out how loud I could make her scream my name. I pushed the thought away.

"You most certainly did not, though I wish you would have," I said, tugging on Cayden's hand to bring her attention to the little man with me. "My nephew wanted to come watch the big movie."

"Oh." Her eyes flickered to him and she smiled.

"Are you here with somebody?" I asked. She bit the side of her pouty lip and glanced around as if she were looking for someone, but shook her head as her gaze met mine again. "Just me."

I smiled. Was she about to lie to me? I asked her as much, and she blushed fiercely and laughed it off, assuring me she was not, but it only made me think otherwise. I wasn't even going to ask her why she hadn't called. I wouldn't even think about asking her out again. I didn't think my ego could handle it if she said no a third time.

"What theatre are you in?" I asked.

"Ummm . . . " She switched the drink to her other hand and shrugged. Another blush crept over her face as she glanced up at me. "The ticket is in my back pocket."

My heart pounded harder. Was she inviting me to reach for it? Christ. Could I manage to touch this woman's ass without grabbing it? We looked at each other for a long moment, her face was no less red than it had been a minute ago, and I knew she was allowing me to reach into her pocket. I took and exhaled a long breath as if I was in the box preparing for a penalty kick. It might as well be just that. I took a step forward and gazed down at her as she craned her neck to meet my eyes. In that moment, with our eyes locked as I reached a hand around her slowly, I could feel the sparks of electricity between us, and I knew I wasn't imagining this thing between us.

There was no way I was, and when her eyes fell shut as I placed my chest flush against her, feeling her breasts press against me while I reached into the pocket of her jeans, I could practically feel her pulse zapping into mine. I took the ticket out and took a step back, putting a little distance between us. Even though I found the theatre number immediately, I looked at it as if my life depended on it as I tried to smother all thoughts of her naked against me. I needed to fuck this woman. The sooner the better. Somehow the feeling had gone from a simple selfish yearning to an absolute need.

I managed to swallow thickly and clear my throat before I said, "We're in the same theatre. We should sit together."

When I looked to her for a response, she simply nodded, mouth parted slightly, as if she was still recovering from whatever had just happened.

"You like Bucky?" Cayden asked suddenly, snapping us both out of our reverie.

"Who?" I asked, frowning. He pointed at Camila's white shirt. I hadn't even tried to interpret what it said, but now that I had, something I hadn't felt in ages threatened to take over my senses. Jealousy. "Bucky Barnes is your boyfriend?"

Her and Cayden shared a laugh and he let go of my hand and stood a little closer to her as if they had an inside joke going on that had instantly bonded them together.

"He's Captain America's best friend," Cayden said.

"The Winter Soldier," Camila added, as if that was supposed to give me some clarity. "Did you watch the last Captain America movie?"

I frowned. Had I? "I don't frequent the movies often. Things get a little . . . out of control over there."

"Right." She smirked. "Because you're soooo famous."

I smiled. She really had no idea. A part of me liked that

76

Camila was interested in me for me, and not for *War Zone*, relentless forward on the field, rumored heartbreaker off it. The sensitive side of me, the one I didn't even know still lurked under all my sorrows, wished she knew who the hell I was so it could incentivize her to hop into bed with me.

"Something like that," I said.

"Uncle Warren is kind of a big deal," Cayden said in my defense.

"Yeah, him and Jay Z."

I laughed. "You really have a thing for rappers. Maybe I should change my profession."

"Maybe I just have a thing for New Yorkers."

"I'm a New Yorker," I replied, raising a brow.

She scoffed. "Keep telling yourself that, pretty boy."

"Pretty boy?"

I couldn't help my smile as I reached the counter. The sound of the guy taking my order forced me to peel my eyes away from hers, which were filled with an amusement I loved seeing there. The guy, the same barely legal kid who'd been busy flirting with Camila earlier was glaring at me as he took my order. The only time he looked pleasant was when Camila smiled at him after I paid.

"Big fan of yours," I said.

"He and his brother live in Winsor," she explained, sounding distracted as she looked around.

"Were you supposed to meet somebody here?" I asked, feeling a frown on my face as I looked away and walked toward the theatre.

Surely she wasn't going on a blind date or something, right? Maybe she liked those online dating websites. I glanced over at her. She was so damn beautiful. Too beautiful, with her vibrant eyes, flawless olive skin, and dark hair.

"I thought maybe Quinn would come."

"Quinn, the guy from the band?" I asked. "Did you tell him to?"

"Sort of," she said as we waited for the ticket person to hand us back our stubs. "I told him I was coming. He usually comes with me, but then I left my phone at home."

"Hey, did you hear Spider-Man was going to be in this movie?" Cayden asked, interrupting our conversation.

"I did hear that," she whispered, crouching down to his ear so it was a secret between the two of them. "I read the comics."

Cayden's face lit up as he looked at her. "Cool! Dad said he would get it for me, but that was a long time ago. I think he forgot. He works a lot, so he forgets everything."

She looked at him for a long moment, and though I couldn't read her thoughts, a look of sadness clouded her features. We walked into the theatre and found empty seats. Cayden sat in the middle while Camila made room for me to pick my seat. I sat beside Cayden, and held the seat beside me down so that she could take it. There was no way I wasn't sitting beside her. The seats filled quickly, and when the lights dimmed giving warning that the previews were about to start, everybody hooted and catcalled. I chuckled.

I hadn't been to the movies in a very long time, but watching something in the States was definitely a different experience than England. But everything was different over there. In Barcelona I used to go watch movies while I visited with my mother's family, and they were equally as excited. In England people waited until you impressed them. It was a different approach and very similar to the way it felt when you were off the football field. As long as I was doing well, I was a god. When I wasn't doing as well, every bloke within a five-mile radius was going to let me know about it.

"I can't remember the last time I went to the movies," I whispered to Camila.

Her head jerked a little at the nearness of my voice. She turned her face and I could feel her breath on my face. Dim lights, movie I wasn't interested in watching, and a beautiful girl beside me could be a problem. I moved so that the side of my face brushed against her cheek as I brought my mouth closer to her ear.

"Last time I was in a theatre, my date wore a skirt for easy access."

I only heard her sharp intake in breath because my ear was so close to her mouth. God, how I wished she would say something naughty. I had a feeling she wouldn't, though. Camila was a tough one to crack.

"This isn't a date," she whispered.

"Come on, Rocky. Don't fight me on this."

I had the urge to move my hand and put it over hers, but didn't. I wanted her to make that move. I wanted her to make any move. I already told her what I wanted.

"We didn't even come together," she said.

"We can leave together."

She moved away, her cheek brushing mine as she did. I backed away and looked into her amused eyes.

"I thought we were having a moment," I said, keeping my voice light. The guy sitting in front of me turned around and shot me a glare. "The movie hasn't started," I said.

"Warren," Camila mumbled beside me, sinking into her seat.

"What?" I whispered, and was shhhhh'd by the guy in front of me.

I was going to kick his ass. I'd been involved in a few

fights back home, but they were over real things like the time my rival, Erik Vaden, trash-talked my awards. Or the time I'd accidentally hit on a new teammate's wife. Never in the history of my fights had I gotten into it with a damn comic book geek. But he wasn't letting me talk to Camila, and there was a first time for everything. Then, Cayden shh'd me as well, and I kept quiet. I hated the movies.

"Behave," Camila whispered.

I grinned. "That word isn't in my vocabulary."

She reared away slightly, enough so I could see her eyes searching mine. There was something about the way she looked at me that made my heart beat uneasy, as if it was warning me that this just might be the one to flip my world upside down. The thought was unsettling. Even as she shifted into her seat and faced forward, my eyes stayed on the side of her face. I'd been with a lot of women—beautiful, intelligent women like Camila—and none had captivated me the way Camila had. Why was that? As if hearing my thoughts, she glanced at me and smiled, then pointed at the screen as if to tell me to stop looking at her.

I smiled back and tore my eyes away from her and looked at the screen. When the movie started, some people cheered again, and I realized I was the one acting British while at the movies: reclining in my chair and waiting for the special effects and superheroes to impress me.

When did I become that guy? Throughout the movie, I alternated between glancing at Cayden and Camila, who looked equally as excited as everyone else in the theatre. And when the character written on her shirt came out on the screen, I frowned and tapped her arm trying to convey the question. She shot me a wide grin that took my breath away. Literally. As soon as she looked back at the screen, I wanted that smile back. That was when I knew I was in trouble. It wasn't every day that I felt my brain go haywire over a fucking smile.

After the movie, I watched as Camila and Cayden spoke animatedly about every single thing we'd just watched. Unlike other times I'd taken a date to a movie, I didn't feel the intense need to rush to the car and have her go down on me. Granted, I hadn't taken a date to the movies since I was a teenager. And Cayden did put a damper on those kinds of plans. As did Antoine, who was waiting outside. Still, watching Camila smile and laugh with my nephew tugged at something inside me. Maybe it was because she didn't act like she wanted to impress me. I gave her a once-over. Took in that shirt with another man's name on it (fictional or not, it bothered me), her tight jeans that squeezed those toned thighs and accentuated her ass, and her Converse. Her hair was up in a ponytail, and the blush on her cheeks was there from laughing hard at whatever Cayden was saying.

"Can we go get ice cream?" Cayden asked, widening his light green eyes in a way I wished I didn't have to say no to.

"No, buddy. Gran gave me strict orders to have you home early and it's pretty late already," I said, glancing at my watch.

"Please, Uncle War," he said before turning his pout on Camila. "You like ice cream, right, Peach?"

I balked at him. How the hell did I miss that part of the conversation? Was it when I was busy looking at her tits and trying to figure out whether or not she was wearing a bra, or when I was mentally bending her over my living room sofa and pounding into her?

"Now we're on nickname terms?" I asked, smiling at Camila, who was blushing furiously. Something about the sight of that did something to me. I chuckled. "It's cute."

"Maybe we can take a rain check on the ice cream. I have to be up early," she said, ignoring me and crouching down to meet Cayden's eyes.

She reached out and grabbed his hand in hers and he smiled. I'd always heard that animals and children had a sixth sense when it came to people, and that you could tell whether or not you were meeting a person with pure intentions from the way they reacted to newcomers. If there was any truth to that, Camila could probably sit at the same table as Mother Teresa. Because while I was aware that this was the first child I'd seen her in front of, Cayden was a hell-raiser when he wanted to be. My brother often told me about the way he made things difficult for his nannies. You'd never know it this instant, though.

"But Uncle Warren leaves soon and he never comes," he argued, sulking.

"I promise you I'm going to be coming home a lot more often," I said. His little head snapped up as he smiled at me.

"Really?"

"I promise," I said, crossing my heart with my fingers.

"So I have to wait for Uncle Warren to come back for you to have ice cream with me?" he asked Camila. She smiled.

"Maybe we can go for ice cream before he leaves. How's that?"

Cayden looked at me. Camila's gaze followed. And I just nodded. Anything to see this girl again.

"Why don't we take Camila home?" I suggested, not wanting our time together to end so quickly again.

"Uhh . . ."

"Yes, let's do that," Cayden said, smiling broadly.

I could see the moment she lost her battle at trying to come up with different excuses when her shoulders dipped and she nodded. I let out a breath. That wasn't so bad.

"You're good with kids," I commented as we walked back to the SUV.

"So are you," she said.

"You never called," I said, catching her completely off-guard. Her eyes widened before she looked away to hide her red face.

"I take it you're not used to that," she said when she looked back at me.

"No."

"Is it the thrill of the chase?" she asked.

"What?"

"Is that why you're so keen on getting me to go out with you?"

"No. Of course not," I said, frowning. "But what if it was?"

She shrugged. "You'd probably be in for some real disappointment."

I stopped walking when we reached the car and let Cayden in, asking him to buckle up. I turned around and looked at Camila, bringing a hand up to the side of her face slowly, so she could stop me from touching her if that's what she wanted. Instead, she gasped slightly and leaned into my touch. I could only compare that to how I felt when I ran out onto the pitch and heard thousands of fans cheering.

"If you're at the other end of the chase, it would be impossible for me to be disappointed."

I stepped forward, moving my hand along her jaw, and she swallowed, her breaths coming in shallow heaps from her parted lips as she gazed up at me. I could kiss her. I could kiss her right now, but what good would that be when I knew it would have to end quickly? I wanted hours with her. Sunrises and sunsets buried between her legs. I didn't need a kiss between us to confirm that. I didn't need a kiss at all to cement it, really. I wanted her. And I was determined to have her before I went back home.

"One date," I whispered.

She nodded slowly. "Fine, but we're doing New York my way."

"What does that mean?" I asked, ready to say yes to any fucking thing she suggested.

"I pick the place, time, and date. You just show up."

I grinned. "It's a date."

Chapter
NINE

Warren

"I can't say I'm surprised. You definitely have a type," Tom said over breakfast the following morning. I glanced up from my oatmeal, and he took it as a sign to continue. "Elena was penniless when you first met her. This one is probably worse off than she was."

"They're completely different women," I argued.

Tom shot me a look. "Maybe so, but don't all the women you meet want the same thing? Even when they deny it in the beginning?"

The feeling of doubt was one I'd grown accustomed to through the years, especially when I became a household name. This had been the same conversation our coaches, agents, and mates had every time one of us had a new woman in our lives. Was she a gold digger or not? It always became the basis of everybody we brought into the club. Did she want to be there for me or somebody else? I'd been fighting that battle for a good seven years, and I didn't want to start thinking about that again. Especially not here. Not now. Not with Camila.

"Camila doesn't even know about football. She doesn't understand who I am or how much money I make," I said.

"Because she lives here," Tom said with a deadpanned expression on his face. I nodded. "You think she doesn't have access to the Internet? Come on, War. Wake up."

I sighed and placed my folded napkin on the table. It's not like these things hadn't crossed my mind a million times. Of course I was paranoid. It's not like I didn't have reason to be. The last few women I'd dated had proven to be using me for something, and it was something I was sort of aware of while I was with them. Elena took it to another level, though.

"I'm only here for a few weeks. How much could possibly change in that amount of time?" I said, sipping on my glass of water.

"A lot," Tom said. "Especially with you already acting like this. I can count on one hand the amount of times you've gone this far out of your way for a woman. Actually, come to think of it, I only need two fingers. Buying cars for Elena and her brother was one thing, but an entire building? That's too far even for you. If you can't see it . . ."

I closed my eyes momentarily, trying to contain the rage I felt spreading through me. When I opened them again, I let out a breath and looked him dead in the eyes. "I know you don't understand it, and that's okay. I don't expect you to. You and I have had it all for too long. We've been so privileged, we don't even see the things we're taking away from others—"

"We're not taking anything away from them, goddammit. We're improving their fucking community."

"That's how we see it, but if somebody came and suddenly knocked down this lavish penthouse you live in—"

"I'd sue."

"Okay, you'd sue," I said. "These people don't even know when, why, or how to sue. Even if they did, do you think they'd have the money for attorney fees? That's why I did the thing with the building. There was no other reason."

Tom looked dubious for a beat before shaking his head. "Who are you?"

He was right, of course. I couldn't remember the last time I did something nice for a person, let alone a group of people. Sure, I signed autographs and posed for pictures, but that was my life. Actually going out of the way for people? . . . I let out a laugh.

"I have no idea, but for once in my life, I think I like who I'm becoming."

"You're definitely not going to be the next Javier Belmonte. I'll tell you that."

I grinned. "Thank God for that."

The moment I got up from the table, I called Camila. I'd considered the three-day rule for all of two seconds before I realized I didn't have time for that shit. I had less than three weeks to get this woman in my bed. On the phone, she made me promise her that I wouldn't push it. Keep your hands to yourself, Warren. It's a friendly date, she said.

I promised her I wouldn't try that, and I was going to do my best to abide by my words, but when she opened the door to her place, with tussled hair and wide caramel eyes, all thoughts of behaving went out the window. She was wearing the smallest pair of jean shorts I'd seen in a long time and a button-down Yankees jersey. Her feet were bare, toes the same shade of hot pink on her hands. The sight of that color on her did something to me, and on those fucking legs, which were lean and muscular and all I could do was picture them around my waist? Fuck.

"You look . . . incredible," I said, meeting her gaze again.

"You too," she said, pulling the door wider. "Come in. I have to put my shoes on."

"Fine by me. You made the plans."

I smiled as she closed the door and started to walk around. Her place was small. Minute. The size of my goddamn SUV. I wasn't even sure where to stand. She had a small kitchen, a bathroom I was positive I wouldn't fit inside of, and a bed on the floor. And it wasn't one of those IKEA types, either. It was just a mattress on the fucking floor. In front of it, on the wall, there was a television, and off to the side, a small futon with a desk in front of it. For the space being so small, she made good use of it. It reminded me of the flat I slept in when I went to boarding school. I guess my face must have shown my surprise, because Camila addressed it as soon as I looked at her again.

"It's not much, but it's all I need," she said, as if she owed me any kind of explanation.

"It's lovely. It suits you," I said, hoping my words betrayed my thoughts.

She shrugged and turned around, opening a door beside the bathroom. It was her closet. Jesus. Maybe Tom was right and I did have a type because the urge to lift her up and take her to buy a new flat was unbearable. I stood by the kitchen counter and watched as she sorted through her shoes.

"Am I dressed for the occasion?" I asked.

She'd told me to dress casual, so I'd worn jeans, black

tennis shoes, and a black T-shirt. She picked her head up and looked at me again. Her eyes trailed down my body quickly before she nodded and looked away, blushing. I held back an amused laugh. Never in my life had I felt so grateful for a woman's obvious attraction to me. Maybe she would crack soon, after all.

"We're going to a baseball game, and maybe a coffee shop," she added as she put on a pair of dark Converse.

"A baseball game? Do you think there are any good seats left?" I asked, pulling out my cellphone and opening up a ticket browser.

If there were none online, I could always ask Tom if his club seats were available. He barely used them anyway. Or I could call my assistant and have him make a call and try to get some tickets.

"What are you doing?" she asked. The confusion in her voice beckoned my attention. Sure enough, she was frowning.

"Looking for tickets."

Camila began to laugh. "Warren."

"What?"

"I already bought the tickets."

"What? What do you mean you bought the tickets?"

She shook her head, still smiling as she stood up to walk toward me. She grabbed a bag from the kitchen counter and threw it over her shoulder. Then, she stood in front of me and reached a hand up, using the tips of her fingers to push down lightly on the creases my frown created on my forehead.

"You asked me to show you New York, so I'm showing you New York."

I sighed, closing my eyes and relishing her touch. "That's not what I meant by you showing me New York. I want to pay for those tickets."

"That's too bad. They've already been paid," she said.

I opened my eyes when I no longer felt her fingers on me and watched as she picked up her keys and brushed past me. I followed her out and waited for her to lock the door.

"You're only obliging because I insisted. The least I could do is pay," I said as we walked down the flight of stairs. "You already paid for my train ride the other day."

She shrugged. "You can pay for the hot dog I'm going to eat at the game."

"And the coffee at the shop, and whatever else is consumed while you're with me."

She smiled as she looked over her shoulder, but didn't comment further. I wished I could record the moment for Tom just to show him she was different than Elena, who never offered to pay for anything while she was with me.

"I haven't been to a game since I was a kid," I commented as we walked outside.

"A kid like a toddler or a kid like a teenager?"

"I was probably around ten."

She tilted her head to look up at me. "Who'd you go with?"

"My dad and brother. I'm pretty sure neither one of them went back after that day either."

"Bad experience?"

"Not really. Just not their thing."

"Let me guess. Soccer is."

My lips twitched. "Football definitely is."

"Are they Giants or Jets fans?" she asked.

I sighed heavily. "Neither. I'm not talking about American football."

She smiled and looked up at me, her eyes twinkling, and I realized she'd been kidding. I shook my head, but couldn't fight my smile long enough. When I realized we were getting closer to the subway that headed to Queens, I looked around and spotted Antoine quickly. I explained to him what was going on and asked him to drive and meet us over there.

"I only got two tickets," she said when he left.

"That's fine. I would have been really upset if you spent another dollar," I said, smiling and reaching out to grab her forearm in reassurance.

She jumped at the contact. Was that against the rules? I decided it wasn't, and if it was I sure as hell didn't care. Camila moved to start walking again and I followed.

"Are all of your security guards oversees huge black guys?" she asked.

"Why would they have to be huge?"

She gave me a slow, intentional once-over.

"You know this is the second time I've caught you checking me out today. You better be careful. I may misinterpret it and think you find a handsome soccer player with money that invests in Belmonte properties attractive."

She tore her gaze from mine and looked across the street. "First of all, investing in Belmonte and being a Belmonte are two different things. Secondly, what are we going to do about Antoine? Does he need to sit with you?"

"I'm paying for our ride," I said when we reached the machine and she started to tap away on it.

"I already have a card," she said, smiling as she looked at the screen. "Loosen up, Warren. Let somebody treat you for a change. I'm assuming it's something that doesn't happen often."

She pulled out her card and slid it in before I could blink. It was a masterful movement and before I could stop her, she turned around with a smile on her face and held out a blue and yellow Metro card. My gaze held hers as I reached for it, my fingers brushing against hers as I slowly took it. I felt the walls of my throat close in that instant, and I knew that despite my promise not to come on to her, I had to have her.

"Thank you," I whispered. I cleared my throat and repeated my words.

Camila simply nodded, her lips slightly parted, her eyes still on mine as if she was under some kind of trance. A group of people came up behind us to use the machine and we moved. I followed her and mimicked her movement as she slid her card on the machine and pushed the bars, and when we got to the tarmac, I took a moment to look around. It was swarming with people in navy blue and royal blue shirts. Off to the right, a kid I recognized from the park the other day shot me a wave. I gave him a simple nod and Camila started to look around when she noticed. I couldn't help but smile. She really did watch me closely. She did a great job at pretending she didn't, though.

The train got there and we both turned toward it again. Out of fear of losing her, I grabbed the top of her arm as a wave of people got off, and kept holding on to her as we boarded. There were a few empty seats, and Camila wasted no time in taking one. I sat in the one beside her. It was a small space, much smaller than I'd anticipated. I was reminded of the last time we'd taken the train and how I had to stand with my hands over my head for forty minutes. This space was no better, and the smell of sweat and piss seemed even more prominent on this train than the last.

"We should've taken the car," I said under my breath. She smiled and looked at me.

"What's wrong, pretty boy? Afraid to get a little dirty?"

And just like that, with those softly spoken, yet fiery

words and the gleam in her eyes, my dick was hard. I shifted in my seat and threw my right arm around her, pulling her in close so I could whisper in her ear, "You have no idea how dirty I like to get."

I backed away, but left my arm over the back of her seat, and smiled at the large exhaled breath she let out. She sat up straight in her seat, her eyes snapping to mine once she seemed to gather her bearings.

"You are terrible at following rules."

"Rules are meant to be broken."

"You sound like every other privileged kid from the Upper East Side," she said, rolling her eyes.

"Do I look like one?" I asked, smiling when her eyes trailed down my chest, my arms, and made their way back to my face again.

"No, but anybody can put on a costume and pretend to be something they're not."

My eyes narrowed on hers. It was something I was tired of hearing, from less privileged teammates when I was younger, from less fortunate people in general. They always assessed my worth from my cars or my watches. It was never based on the things I said or the way I acted.

And I definitely did not act like a privileged kid from the Upper East Side. Normally, I let it roll off me. Just another thing people hated. Another thing I gave three shits about. Which was why I couldn't understand why Camila saying it bothered me.

"Is that what you think? That I pretend to be something I'm not?"

"I don't know. I don't think so, but I can't really figure you out." She scoffed. "Which is saying a lot coming from a person who psychoanalyzes people for a living."

We got off on the next stop and headed down the street, passing by the street shops along the way. It seemed like everybody on the block was selling some kind of paraphernalia. I couldn't remember the last time I was on the outside of a stadium like this. One *with* the crowd. I couldn't remember the last time I went to a game where I wasn't the one they were cheering or booing. It felt oddly exhilarating and freeing to walk with the large crowd toward the stadium. Camila looked over her shoulder to make sure I was still behind her. I reached for her hand and interlaced our fingers together. I felt her surprise in the way she stiffened and squeezed my fingers, but she didn't let go and she didn't stop walking, which I took as a good sign.

My phone vibrated in my pocket a few times, but I ignored it because I didn't want to pull my hand from hers. When we got to the front of the line, she dropped hers and rummaged through her purse to pull out two tickets. We walked in and I took a second to look around.

"This is the new stadium," she said.

"I know."

"I wasn't sure you did. You're looking at it like you're experiencing a part of history or something," she said. When I looked at her, she was smiling up at me.

"I kind of am." I tilted my head. "I've never taken a date to a baseball game before."

She was silent for a beat, her cheeks producing a hint of color as she tore her gaze from mine. When she looked at me again, she smiled. "There's a first time for everything, and technically, I brought you. Do you want a hot dog?"

I chuckled and let her lead the way. We got our hot dogs, beers, and peanuts and I waited for her outside the restroom. I pulled my phone out of my pocket and called Antoine back, who informed me that my assistant was able to get box seats for us.

"She bought these seats," I said in a low voice. "Do you think she'll be upset if I switch them?"

Antoine was silent for a moment. "If she was anybody else, I'd say she'd be thrilled, but I don't know about that one."

I chuckled. "Thanks. You go up to the box and I'll see what I can do."

When Camila came out of the restroom, I followed her to where our seats were. On our way up, I held back my laughter. Here I was, a man sought out for sponsorships by many reputable companies, some of which were displayed on the stadium walls, and this woman was leading me to the nosebleed section. We sat down and looked out into the field. The players appeared so far away that it made me wonder how people could see us playing from all the way up here. In baseball, you knew who was standing where. In football, we were all over the pitch.

"I take it you've never sat this high up," Camila said.

I shook my head. "I was just thinking about the people sitting up here and watching me when I'm down there."

"Doesn't it make you feel grateful?" Our gazes met when I looked over at her, and she continued, "To know that people sit all the way up here just to catch a glimpse of you playing and breathing the same air as them instead of watching from the comfort of their home?"

I'd never thought about that before. Of course I was grateful for everything I had, but I never stopped to consider people like Camila who used hard-earned and essential dollars to buy nosebleed tickets just so they could watch their favorite teams play. I'd never given it any thought at all. She hadn't torn her gaze away from mine and was looking at me so intently, that I was sure she'd find all the dark secrets I'd buried.

"Do you come to a lot of games?" I asked.

"Not really. Maybe one a year. They can be a little . . ." She shrugged. "I come when I can."

Was she about to say expensive? As shitty as these seats were, she'd spent her money on them, and I decided that if they were good enough for her, they'd have to be good enough for me too. We stood up for the national anthem and watched the first pitch, laughing at the way the guy missed the catcher by a mile.

"Do you think you can throw from the mound to home plate?"

"You bet your ass I can," I said. "And if I couldn't, I wouldn't be caught dead out there."

Camila laughed, that real, throaty laugh of hers and threw her head back. When we sat down again, it felt like we were a little closer than we'd been when we first got there.

"Do your parents live here?" I asked after chewing on a few peanuts.

"Upstate," she said.

Something about the way she said it made me want to know more. I sat up and put a hand over her knee so she'd look at me. When she did, she looked sad.

"Does it have to do with Belmonte?" I asked, and after seeing the mix of surprise and sadness in her eyes, I almost wish I hadn't asked at all.

"I hate them," she whispered.

"We don't have to talk about them if it makes you uncomfortable," I said.

I could tell she was debating it. I stroked the side of her thigh with my thumb as a sign of encouragement, and ignored the soft feel of her skin and the thought of running my hands up and down her silky body. She moved so that both her knees were facing me.

"Another time."

"Another time," I agreed, taking my hand from her knee and cupping her chin.

Despite the loud ambiance of the game, with the people cheering, and booing, and catcalling the people from the opposing team, in that moment, the only thing I saw was Camila. Camila and her beautiful almond-shaped eyes, and her pouty bottom lip. When she swallowed, my eyes followed the length of her thin neck. I resisted the urge to make a trail with my finger down to the first button of that shirt she wore. She cleared her throat and pulled away from me, but by then it didn't matter because I knew she wanted me just as badly as I wanted her.

We were quiet for a moment, watching the game, eating popcorn and drinking beer. The kissing camera came on and we watched as people did that. Then, marriage proposals started. Camila smiled through those.

"You think that's cute?" I asked.

Her eyes cut to mine. "Yes . . . and no."

"Yes and no?" I asked. I couldn't stop smiling. "How's that?"

"Yes, it's cute, but no, I would never want anybody to propose to me like that."

"Because it's impersonal?" I asked, tossing a kernel into my mouth.

"Yeah, plus embarrassing. The camera zooms in on you and you have to wait for the response." She shivered. "No, thank you."

I laughed. "I would assume if they ask in such a public

place, it's because they know the answer would be yes."

"You assume wrong," she said, eyes wide. "I've seen a no."

"No way." I shook my head with a chuckle. Her gaze dropped to my mouth. I kept smiling because I didn't want her to look away, but fuck it was hard not to lean in and kiss her right there.

She cleared her throat and looked away. "I'm serious. Last season against the Marlins. Someone got proposed to, and she said no."

The conversation went on a little longer, until we stopped talking about crazy proposals and started to laugh at the outrageous things people around us were saying. We talked to a few of them about the game and missing Jeter, who Camila was annoyingly obsessed with. It wasn't until we got out of our seats and headed to the bathroom at the top of the seventh that I noticed we never moved to the better seats.

"Do you want to stay?" she asked when we met in the middle of the hall.

"It's up to you." I shrugged nonchalantly, but I was hoping she'd opt on leaving.

"I think we can leave."

Her face was flushed from the beer, and the smile hadn't left her face since the fifth inning.

"Let's go. Do you want to take the car now? Or train?" I asked.

"We can take the car. The train is going to be insane right now," she said.

I relayed the message to Antoine, who told me where to meet him and we headed in that direction.

I looked over at Camila. "I don't want the night to end."

"I should get home," she said with a regretful smile.

"You should come home with me."

"I seem to recall the stipulation being that you wouldn't try to hit on me."

"And I don't seem to recall agreeing to that."

"I seem to recall you agreeing to exactly that condition." She smiled.

I wrapped an arm around her and pulled her into my side as we walked down to leave. We walked in silence, my arm still around hers, her body nuzzled against mine.

"You really want to go home?" I asked as she climbed into the back seat and I followed.

"No," she said, looking at me. "But I should."

I was caught between what I wanted and what I should do, and her sexy-as-fuck bare legs weren't helping, but in the end I told Antoine to drive to her house. We stayed in the car outside her building for a couple beats before she stepped out of the car.

"Thank you for coming tonight," she said as she looked for her keys in her purse.

"Thank you for taking me to the game."

"Thank you for the ride home."

We smiled at each other once more before she closed the door. I'd kept my mouth shut because I didn't know what to say to her, but the moment she turned around and started to unlock the door to the building, I bolted out of the car and jogged toward her. Camila turned around as I reached her.

"I'm sorry," I said, earning a confused look from her as I cupped the back of her neck and pulled her face to mine.

Camila gasped as my lips crashed down on hers, her hands flying to my chest, but not pushing away. She grabbed a fistful of my shirt and pulled me closer, as if any space left between us was too wide. Our tongues met in a crazed dance that had my cock hardening in an instant. I groaned loudly

99

when she pushed her pelvis flush against it. I broke the kiss and rested my forehead against hers, both of our breaths coming out as pants. The light bulb that was illuminating us suddenly sparked and caught our attention just as it burst and went out.

"See what we do?" I pointed at it. She laughed. "I know I said no coming on to you, but I had to kiss you."

"I'm glad you did," she whispered. I pulled away slightly.

"Does that mean you'll go out with me on a real date? One where I can hit on you and hold your hand and tell you how goddamn beautiful you look?"

She blushed and glanced away momentarily, but nodded when her gaze met mine.

"Tomorrow night?"

She laughed. "I don't know if I can tomorrow."

"Then Sunday."

"Sunday works," she said. "I'm going to see the apartments tomorrow morning and if all goes well, I should be moving in on Sunday. Not that it has any bearing on a Sunday night date. You've seen my place."

I cupped her face and leaned down to kiss her once more. "Let me know if you need help."

"I will."

I leaned down one last time and kissed her again, a slow, thorough kiss that unlike the first, was unrushed. When I backed away, her eyes were still closed, her lips still parted, and I wanted nothing more than to lead her through those doors, take her upstairs, and ravish her in that shoebox apartment of hers.

Instead, I walked away and went back to the car and went home, where I took a long cold shower and tried not to replay the way her lips felt against mine, because if that was making me lose sleep, I couldn't imagine what having my dick inside her would do to me.

Chapter
TEN

Camila

Warren: I can't stop thinking about you
Camila: That shouldn't happen again.
Warren: You know you want it to ;-)
Camila: Friends, remember?
Warren: Friends who kiss. There's nothing wrong with that.

I smiled so hard. I wish I wouldn't. I wish I didn't feel the pull I felt toward him, but I couldn't change the fact that I did. Despite what I originally thought of him, he proved that he was a good time. Before I could respond to Warren's text, I received a call from Quinn inviting me to a Jay Z concert in Brooklyn. Of course I said yes. When Quinn wasn't moonlighting as the singer of his band, he was setting up lighting for performers that "actually got paid for their art," as he said. He'd get me in backstage and I could watch the concert from a small area where the employees stood. I'd done it once before for an up and coming artist, so I knew I'd be watching it by myself mostly, but I didn't care. There was no way I was missing the concert. Another text message came in from Warren as I was filling out permit forms for the park Winsor was set to start building next.

Warren: I want to see you tonight.

My breath caught. My fingers froze on the screen momentarily before I started to type my reply.

Camila: Can't tonight. I have plans.

After a couple seconds of just staring at the three little dots waiting for his message to come through, I put the phone down.

Warren: What kind of plans?

Camila: The kind that include me going to the Jay Z concert in BK tonight.

Instead of text messaging me back, he called. I was startled by this for some reason. I was perfectly fine with volleying back and forth via text, but an actual phone call meant hearing his voice and picturing what he was wearing and how he looked when he was saying certain things. I took a deep breath and answered on the third ring.

"There's no way of asking this without sounding like an asshole," he said. His voice shot waves of warmth through me. "Who are you going with?"

I smiled. "A friend."

"What kind of friend?"

"The kind you kiss."

He breathed heavily into the phone line. "Here's the thing, Camila. I'm not opposed to playing games, if that's what you want to do. I like this thing we have going, the flirting, the getting to know each other, the kissing. I'm okay with that if that's what it's going to take for me to get you in my bed. Friends you kiss . . . I'm not okay with."

I set my papers aside and threw myself back onto my mattress, closing my eyes. Why did his words make my heart flip the way they did? Possession was something I usually didn't find attractive, but somehow Warren managed to make me want that from him.

"You're not okay with me kissing him or you're not okay with me hanging out with him because you think I'll kiss him?" I asked, smiling at the grunting sound he made.

"Neither. Both. I don't like it. I don't want to think about it."

"It's Jay Z. I already said yes and I'm not going to miss Jay Z just because you don't like the idea of me going with some guy you think I may or may not kiss. He's just a friend, Warren."

"I'll take you to the fucking concert."

"It's an exclusive concert. I think you have to be an American Express holder or employee, or something."

He stayed silent for a beat and I rolled my eyes thinking that he was about to tell me he had a Black Card or something. He didn't. He sighed into the line again.

"Fine. Go with your friend."

"I'll call you when I get home," I said with a small smile as I turned onto my stomach.

"Camila," he said before I could hang up.

"Yeah?"

"Please don't kiss him."

Butterflies swarmed my stomach at the sound of his plea. I smiled and promised him that I wouldn't.

I arrived early. A couple guys from his band were there as well, so we all walked around together hoping we'd spot Beyoncé. We didn't. When the crowd started pouring in and the lights began to dim and the DJ started to play, I slunk beside the rest of the band and the people who worked sound and lighting, and manned the stage. This was only the second time I'd actually stood on the stage to watch a show and my adrenaline was shooting through the roof. I couldn't stand still. I bounced from one foot to the other and swayed as the DJ played Run DMC and rapped along to Biggie. Quinn jogged over to us at one point and gave us a drink ticket, but I told him I was too nervous to move, let alone drink.

He frowned at me. "It's one drink. It's not like you're going to get drunk or anything."

"Yeah, but I might have to use the bathroom and I can't miss the show."

The guys laughed, shaking their heads, but didn't argue because they knew I was right. We speculated what special guests he might bring out. He always brought somebody out. I just hoped it wasn't P. Diddy or somebody stupid like that. When the concert finally started, my eyes were glued to the stage. I had so much adrenaline inside me I felt like I could pass out from it. I couldn't even imagine being the person the crowd was screaming for, singing along to, moving side to side for. I also watched Quinn moving from one side to the other making sure the lights were aligned with whatever plan they'd conjured leading up to this. I was watching him when Jay Z mentioned a special guest, and when I saw who it was, I gasped so loudly my breath caught in my throat.

I could feel Quinn's eyes on me without even turning

to look at him. I could only imagine him laughing at me for whatever I must have looked like when Nas walked out there and took his place beside Jay Z on the stage. I put a hand over my rapidly beating heart and mouthed *holy shit* as I looked over at Quinn. He smiled and gave me a thumbs up that I couldn't even return because my hands were shaking so much. The concert went on. They performed two songs together before Nas walked off stage and passed right in front of me. When our eyes met, he smiled a hello and I think I died right there.

I was busy staring at Nas as he walked away when Quinn nudged me. I jumped and looked at him.

"Isn't that your homeboy?" he asked, nodding at the stage.

My gaze followed his. My mouth dropped. I watched as Jay Z said hi to Warren like they were old pals. When they finished talking, Jay Z put the earpiece back in and ran on stage again to continue the show. Warren was wearing jeans and a blue button-down checkered shirt untucked, with the sleeves rolled up to show off his tattooed forearms. I tried not to picture those arms flexing above me and failed miserably. I also couldn't stop picturing him kissing me. His hands all over me. The way he looked at me and smiled at me. My heart fluttered. Still, what was he doing here? I told him I was coming and he never mentioned that he'd be here. Unless he came for me, but what the hell?

"Aren't you going to say hi to him?" Quinn asked, jarring me out of my thoughts.

Warren took his phone out and typed something. I felt mine vibrate in my purse. I took it out slowly, still watching as he looked at his screen, and saw his name on mine.

Warren: Having fun?

Camila: Yes.

Warren: With your friend?

Camila: Yes.

I watched as he scowled at the screen and found it difficult to contain my laughter.

Warren: What are you wearing?

I started to laugh, glancing up at him to see him staring at his screen. Forgetting that he was standing literally steps away from Jay Z, who was performing *Izzo*. He wanted to focus on what I was wearing.

Camila: A short romper. No bra. I'm cold.

He smiled as he typed.

Warren: Tell me where you are. I'll warm you up.

Camila: You already know where I am.

Warren: No. I mean where you are in the arena.

Camila: It's a big arena and it's packed. I doubt you'll find me.

Warren: Try me.

Camila: Are you here?

Warren: Yes

Camila: Where are your seats?

I watched as he lowered his phone and looked around. He looked at it again and typed.

Warren: Where are yours? I want to look for you.

Camila: What if I don't want to be found?

His brows pulled in slightly.

Warren: Too late.

My heart galloped. *Too late.* Such simple words, but damn. Finally, I put my phone away and walked up to him. He was still looking down at his screen and when I got close enough, I saw my name on his screen. I tapped his shoulder. He ignored me, staring at the screen. I tapped harder and heard him exhale heavily as if annoyed. His eyes snapped up to mine and widened. I smiled as he took a staggered step back.

"I'm not sure what should upset me more, the fact you're here and didn't tell me you were coming, the fact that you apparently know Jay Z and didn't tell me, or the fact that you seemed genuinely annoyed when I tapped your shoulder."

He wrapped an arm around me and pulled me into him, giving me no time to react before putting his lips on mine. He kissed me as if my lips contained the answers to questions he hadn't asked aloud—ravenous, hard, deeply. When he pulled away, his eyes drifted over my body, taking me in completely. They darkened as they met my gaze.

"No bra, huh?" he said, voice growing hoarse as he lowered his mouth to my ear.

I was surprised by the way his words made me feel, hot, needy, out of control. I swallowed, giving a small nod.

"Where's your friend?" he asked, tearing his eyes away from mine for the first time to sweep our surroundings.

"Working," I said. I smiled and explained myself, telling him that he works lighting and that was the reason I was backstage. "You know, if you keep showing up like this I'm going to think you're stalking me."

"Maybe I am." He grinned. "I haven't chased after a woman since I was seventeen, so you should take it as a compliment."

"A compliment," I said, unable to fight a laugh as I shook my head. "I'll keep that in mind."

Warren grabbed my arm and tugged me to walk away from where we were. I let him lead me behind the crew, behind large speakers, and into a narrow, poorly lit hallway. I could still hear the music from here, but it was much quieter and we no longer had to talk loudly into our ears. We stood facing each other without saying a word for a moment, just looking at each other.

"Are you upset I crashed your friend-date?" he asked, his eyes searching mine.

"Would it make a difference?"

"No." He sighed, running a hand through his hair. "Maybe. This is new territory for me, Camila."

"The stalking thing?" I asked, smiling at his flustered look.

"That and . . ." he shook his head, moving close to me again, pressing me flat against the wall behind me, "this."

His free hand traveled down my spine, stopping on my ass, which he grabbed a handful of this time. My lips parted as I gasped, watching the way his eyes darkened. Our lips met at the same time, our tongues crashing in each other's mouths in a wild escapade. I wrapped my arms around his neck, willing myself closer to him. My pelvis rocking against his very pronounced erection, my bare chest covered by only the thin layer of fabric brushing against the buttons of his hard muscled chest.

"You're killing me," he whispered against my lips, taking hold of both sides of my face. "You're fucking killing me and you don't even know it."

The fire inside spread through me, roaring through my veins with each touch, each drop of his lips on a different part of me, my shoulders, my neck, my collarbone. My stomach ached with the absolute need I felt for him.

"I don't want to want you this much," I whispered when our lips broke apart again.

His eyes searched mine, his gaze softening. "But you do."

"But I do."

"And you can't will the feeling away."

I shook my head, looking at him as if he was going to give me some kind of antidote for this. Whatever this was.

"Neither can I," he said, placing his forehead against mine. "Neither can I."

Chapter
ELEVEN

Camila

invited Warren to the cocktail party for Winsor. I hadn't planned on it. Normally I didn't take dates with me because it was a work event and I liked to focus on making sure I could navigate the crowd and keep an eye on everything. This event felt different, though. It wasn't my usual crowd. Nancy had invited her people and booked a hotel she fancied and asked me to do the rest as I normally did. I wasn't sure "the rest" would work in this setting though. I usually had cheap auctions in place, giving away things that middle-class workers would get excited about (an iPad, tickets to Hamilton, tickets to a Knicks game). This auction was all about art collections and items signed by famous athletes.

"Just relax," Vanessa said to me that morning when we

went to look at and sign the lease for my new apartment. "You always slay at these events."

"It's not the same."

"If what you're worried about is social status, I'll lend you a kickass dress and shoes, you'll do your hair and make-up, and boom. Nobody will know or care or even think about where you live or how much money you make." She paused, frowning. "Honestly, Peach, nobody cares about any of that anyway."

I closed my eyes and let out a breath. "I'm sure they don't, but it's easy for you to walk in there and mingle with them since you're kind of . . ."

"Part of them?" she asked, raising an eyebrow. I nodded. She laughed. "You think the people with old money welcome me with open arms because of my last name?"

I shrugged.

"They don't, but they're not bad people. It's like everything in life. You have to show people who you really are for them to see what makes you, you. You'll fit right in."

"Fine. Lend me the dress."

"And you'll have Warren," she said with a wink. "I can't wait to meet this unicorn."

He knocked on my door at nine thirty. He was definitely punctual. I placed a hand on the doorknob and took a deep breath to brace myself. I hadn't been able to do that the last time and seeing how good he looked nearly knocked me on my ass, so I needed to be prepared this time. I pulled the door open and swallowed. Next time. I'd do a better job preparing next time.

He was wearing a black suit that fit him so well, molding

THE PLAYER

over his broad shoulders and over his chest amazingly, I was sure it was tailored. I wanted to reach out, take off his jacket and tie and drag him to my bed. On that note, my eyes snapped back to his as I tried to regain my composure. Warren grinned as if he knew what I was thinking. As if he could hear my rapidly beating heart from where he stood in the hall and could read the illicit thoughts of him that were crossing through my head with each passing second.

"You look edible," he said, his gaze darkening as he gave me a slow once-over that made my heart feel like it was about to pound out of my chest.

"We should go," I whispered.

"We should," he said, lips turning into a slow smile as he took a step forward, reaching out to grip my waist as he looked down at me. "Or we can stay in."

My mouth opened. To talk. To gasp. To something that I couldn't manage to formulate with him standing this close giving me that look.

"I can feel your heart against my chest," he whispered, his eyelids suddenly looking heavier, his gaze heating. "You want this, Camila."

I swallowed, nodding as if in a daze. "I so want this."

"But we have to go." He cocked his head to the left as if doing that would make me change my mind about it.

"It's work," I managed.

"Let's go then."

We walked out and made our way downstairs. Warren was patient as he walked behind me, letting me take my time. I was so afraid of tripping in the sky-high heels that I stopped on each step. When we finally made it to the ground floor, I let out a long breath.

"That wasn't so bad."

Warren chuckled coming behind me and wrapping an arm around me to lead me out of the building. "It was painful to watch."

I smiled. The entire way to the event, he didn't stop joking and I couldn't stop smiling. When we pulled up to the luxury hotel, my unfounded fear and trepidation seemed to have disappeared. I felt at ease even as we got out of the car and Warren helped me make sure I wouldn't step on any cracks. Maybe it was his presence and the way he looked at me like I was the only thing in the world that mattered, but I didn't think about anything as we walked through the lobby. The feeling lasted long enough. As soon as we stepped in the room where the cocktail hour part of the event was taking place and I felt hundreds of eyes on us, I felt myself clam up.

Warren's hand moved from my hand to my lower back as we made our way to Nancy, who I introduced him to and let him speak to while I went to the back to make sure the caterer had given my message to the person handling the auction inside. When I got back, Nancy gave me a warm smile and hiked an eyebrow as she looked over at Warren. I tried not to react, but could feel my face heating up so I looked away.

"Don't let her work," she said to Warren as she started to walk away. "She needs to relax."

He picked up two champagne flutes as one of the caterers walked by and handed one to me with a raised eyebrow. "To relaxing."

I clinked my glass against his and held his gaze while I took a sip. In his eyes I found promises my mind was afraid to explore, but my body was so ready for. I looked away quickly when I felt my face heating once more. I took another sip and looked around for my sister. She was walking straight toward me, laughing at something some tall guy walking beside her and Adam was saying to them. Her eyes widened and her smile slipped off when she caught a glimpse of Warren. She looked at me and I gave her a knowing smile.

"That dress looks way better on you," Vanessa said as she hugged me.

"Thanks. I feel naked."

Warren chuckled, his eyes glinting as my gaze caught his. He splayed a hand on my lower back again and leaned in to say hi to my sister as I introduced them and Adam. When my eyes met the tall guy I wasn't sure what to say, so he introduced himself as Dominic.

"Oh. I finally get to meet the infamous Dominic," I said as we said hi to each other.

Adam and my sister spoke so highly about the guy that I was starting to think he was a freaking unicorn. He was definitely as good-looking as Vanessa had claimed, with longish dirty-blond hair and light brown eyes. He was tall, with the build of a swimmer, broad shoulders and a lean frame, much like Adam's. Not as good-looking as Warren though.

"I've heard a lot about you as well." His eyes lit up when he said it and I felt myself smile back. "And now that I've seen you I'm kicking myself for not listening to Adam when he wanted to set up that blind date."

"Oh God." My face heated. I felt Warren come even closer to me, if possible. He shook Dominic's hand and introduced himself.

"I definitely know who you are. I have your jersey in my closet," Dominic said, his voice catching. I could practically see the stars in his eyes without even looking at him. So apparently Warren was famous enough. I guess.

"I have one signed," Adam said proudly. "I was upset when I didn't see you on the roster for the Olympics this summer."

Warren chuckled, though it sounded tight and forced, unlike the other times I'd heard it. "Yeah, I was upset I couldn't make that work this summer. I had a bit of a family emergency, so I'll be in New York for the next couple of weeks."

"Oh. Well, we should get a picture of you here if you don't mind," Adam added in the end. "This is my parents' foundation and I know they'd love to have a picture of you on the website."

"I don't mind at all," Warren said. He looked at me. "As long as she's in it."

I felt my heart pump into my throat as if it had run out of places to visit. "What?"

"Aren't you responsible for putting this event together?"

Holy mother. Had I mentioned that to him? I felt myself blush and shook my head as I began to look around the room. "No, this is all Nancy."

"Really, Camila?" Adam asked in the voice he used when Vanessa went a little overboard with her online shopping. My eyes snapped to his. I tried to relay my *help me, I've gone overboard* look, but the plea either didn't carry or he didn't care. Adam turned to Warren. "She did most of this by herself, so she should definitely be in the picture."

He called over a photographer and Warren looked at me, eyes filled with amusement as he wrapped his arm around my waist and pulled me toward him, and dear God, I wanted to crawl into a hole and die right there. Because it felt so good, because it felt so right, and because it felt like everybody in the room seemed to turn and look at us at the same time as the camera began to snap. When we finished taking the pictures I looked around and realized that it wasn't the case. People were looking, but just in a conversational way,

not in the *who the hell is she and what is she doing here?* way
I was expecting.

Warren placed his hand on the small of my back again
and massaged the spot when we joined my sister, Adam and
Dominic again. I felt his touch everywhere. And when his
hand slid from my back to my waist ever so slowly, making
my flesh rise and my back straighten from the sensation, I
felt myself blush. My sister's eyes instantly found his hand on
my hip and came up to shoot me a questioning look. If only I
could get it off me without seeming like I didn't like it there.
I closed my eyes briefly and took a breath. He's your friend.
Your friend you enjoy kissing a lot. Your friend you can't stop
thinking about screwing. I really needed to stop thinking in
those terms.

I spoke to Vanessa while the guys spoke about soccer.

"Have you talked to Mom?" she asked suddenly. My
smile dropped instantly. Mood dampened.

"No. Why?"

"Johnny's coming back for good."

I bit my tongue. Hard. I really didn't need to voice the
many insults running through my head. Vanessa felt them,
too. As much as we loved him, we were both still bitter about
him leaving us when he did.

"Let me guess, Mom's going to take him back and let him
live with her again? She'll probably even do his laundry for
him," I said, unable to help myself.

My sister rolled her eyes even more exaggerated than
usual and pursed her red lips. I changed the subject out of
fear we'd both be too heated to carry on a conversation with
the sane crowd we were amongst and started talking about
my new apartment. She'd seen it, approved, and agreed to
help me move, which wouldn't be too difficult since I owed

all of three things. But in true Vanessa form, she also wanted to furnish the place for me, and that soon turned into an argument as well.

"I really don't need your help, Vee," I grumbled.

"Please," she said, giving me the pouty look she gave Adam whenever she wanted anything.

"I just got a raise. I can afford a new couch."

"And a bed frame? And decorative pillows? Those are expensive. Trust me, I know," she said, raising an eyebrow.

I resisted the urge to roll my eyes and sighed. "Not if you don't get them at Pottery Barn. Teresa has some pretty nice pillows at her store."

"Teresa?" Her eye widened at the mention of the consignment store owner by my building. "No, Camila. Absolutely not."

I laughed and plucked a glass of white wine from the next server that passed, sipping as I listened to her go on and on about what a terrible idea it was for me to buy pillows from Teresa. I looked around the room as she talked and almost spit out my wine when she lay down her last statement, "And she owns cats, which you're allergic to, so if you buy the pillows there you'll probably die in your sleep."

"And we definitely don't want you to die in your sleep," Warren said, jumping into the conversation. I smiled up at him, leaning in to his chest as he dropped a kiss on the top of my head.

Vanessa shot me a look and I stood up straighter. When the doors began to open, I excused myself to go to the bathroom. I needed to collect myself before I went in there and sat beside this man for the next hour. I saw Nancy on my walk over and she introduced me to a couple people. I was reapplying my lipstick when the door opened and my sister walked in. She strode toward me like a woman on a mission, her heels clicking against the tile in a quick tap, tap, tap, that sounded like Morse code.

"That is Warren Silva?" she asked, gaping at my reflection in the mirror.

"Yup."

"Jesus, Camila. I was expecting hot, but . . . Jesus." She paused, letting out a breath. "You guys cannot keep your hands off each other."

I frowned. "That's not true."

She shot my reflection a look. "It is so true, and it's not a bad thing. I'm just surprised. You look like you've been dating for a while."

"We're not dating. We're friends."

She shot me another look, rolling her eyes this time.

"We are just friends. We haven't . . . you know."

"Well, you better get to it." She laughed when my face turned bright red. "Just enjoy it, Peach. Have fun. Live a little for once. Isn't that what you said you were going to do?"

I nodded slowly. I had said that.

She walked toward a stall and I began walking to the door as she called out that we were at table ten. I smiled as I walked out, only to completely stop dead in my tracks when I spotted Warren talking on the phone a couple feet away from me. His eyes met mine, and when my feet began to move again, I walked over to him even though it was the opposite direction of where I needed to go.

"Listen, I'll call you back. We'll have to discuss this later, but the answer is yes, I absolutely want a meeting with them." He hung up and put it in the inside pocket of his jacket.

"You okay?" he asked.

His arm came around me, his thumb brushed against

my hip, sending a wave of sensation through my lower region. We were standing so close that I could make out every shade of green and every speck of light brown in his eyes. My lips parted slightly, ready to say yes, or no, or maybe, but unable to get any words out. His gaze dropped to my mouth momentarily and when he looked at me his eyes darkened a bit, his fingers tightened a bit. I felt like his hand was gripping my throat, and in my desperate search for air, I cleared my throat.

"I'm fine, but I can't think when you touch me like this."

His other hand came up and cupped my face. "Why, pretty girl?"

I closed my eyes momentarily, leaning into his large hand, his warm touch, relishing his delicious voice so close to me.

"Because," I whispered. *I want more and I shouldn't.*

"I tossed and turned all night again," he said. My eyes popped open to meet his. "I kept thinking about that kiss, and your lips, and your body against that wall."

"Please stop," I whispered. *Not here. I couldn't do this here.*

He inched closer, pulling my face closer to his as he did so. "Why?"

"Because," I whispered.

"Why?" he asked, matching my whisper as he kissed the edge of my mouth. I swallowed a gasp.

"We're from different worlds. You have to see that, especially in this setting."

"Fuck the world," he said, pulling away. My eyes snapped open. Warren chuckled. "Didn't a rapper say that?"

"Tupac. Yes."

"See?"

I smiled. "Just because you can quote famous rappers doesn't mean we should be more than friends."

"It doesn't mean we shouldn't."

We stared at each other, unblinking, until my heart began to pound in my ears. I had to speak up in order to distract myself from it.

"We already went out."

He grinned. "And I had one of the best times I've had in a long time."

"Even though one of those times was only a result of you stalking me?" I asked, smiling.

"I took you home, so yes."

His gaze dropped to my lips and it was clear he was going to kiss me. His face inched closer to mine, his hand splayed out on the small of my back, so warm and electric I nearly jumped at his touch. I let him kiss me chastely before pulling away.

"We should go inside."

His thumb brushed over my bottom lip as he let me go. "Come home with me tonight."

"I—"

"Don't fight me on this, Rocky." He smiled, tilting his head slightly, the sight of it making my heart plummet.

"Warren," I whispered.

"Please."

"Warren," I said again, this time a little louder, a plea.

He raised his hand and caressed my shoulder, where the strap of my dress covered.

"I'm physically aching for you, Camila," he whispered, there was a gruff edge to his voice and lust clouded his eyes as he gazed at me.

My skin tingled at the feel of his touch. The pounding of

my heart got louder.

Louder.

Louder.

Until I felt like it was too much. I closed my eyes for a beat, trying to steady everything I was feeling.

"At the very least, let's do something when this is over," he said, his words rushed. "It doesn't have to lead back to my house, but I don't want to end the night here. Let's do something else I can only experience here."

Somebody cleared their throat loudly beside us and we jumped away from each other, snapping our heads in that direction. It was Thomas Belmonte. Heat began to rise and cover my body, inside and out. I wasn't sure if the wave of anger was a result of his last name—and the bitterness that came with it—or the memory of us bickering at the meeting. Either way, all of my previous safe and wonderful feelings were completely dampened by his presence.

"May I have a word?" he asked, looking at Warren, not even glancing once in my direction.

"I'll see you inside," Warren said, giving my arm a little squeeze.

I nodded solemnly and walked away, leaving him to talk to his business partner.

The rest of the auction, I couldn't seem to shake my mood. Warren was no longer being playful or showing any kind of emotion, and I missed it. I missed the amusement in his eyes and the way my skin prickled every time he touched me. I glared at Thomas Belmonte's table a couple times when I caught him looking over at us, hoping he'd feel the burning hatred I felt toward him. I reasoned that people like him would always frown upon us. Vanessa's wide acceptance was because she and Adam met in college and again after that.

By the time their relationship was official, she'd already been around as a friend. When the auction was over, we stood and I looked at Warren to see what the plan was, but once again he excused himself because somebody from the Belmonte table was calling him over.

"Sorry. Business," he said with a groan. He kissed my forehead. "I'll meet you outside."

I sighed, feeling defeated, but nodded nonetheless. I couldn't expect to bring somebody like him to an event like this and have him all to myself all night. Still, I couldn't pretend that the instant mood switch didn't suck.

Chapter
TWELVE

Warren

I got an earful from Tom, warning me away from Camila.

"It's nothing serious, Tom," I muttered under my breath as I took a gulp of the scotch I'd acquired during the auction.

"I'm warning you as a friend," he said.

He brought up Elena, of course. As if it was my fault I fell in love with the wrong woman. But it happened. I couldn't change the past, and I didn't want to.

"I learned from my mistake," I said.

He scoffed, but didn't comment. I gulped down more of my drink, hoping the burn would get rid of the bitter taste in my mouth. I hadn't even slept with the girl and he was already warning me away from her. The not sleeping with her thing was already driving me halfway to the brink of insanity. When Tom opened his mouth again, it was to suggest I call Madison, the woman I fucked my first night in New York. I glared at him. Been there, done that. It wasn't that I didn't repeat, but I definitely didn't need to relive that one. Besides, my mind was already set on Camila. Every time I closed my eyes, the only thing I saw, felt, and heard was her.

After ending that conversation, he introduced me to the men he was with, and when I finished talking to them, I excused myself from the group and headed outside. I looked for Camila in the crowd, for her sister, her brother-in-law. I didn't spot any of them, so I went to the car. Maybe she was already there. Antoine opened the backseat of the SUV as soon as he spotted me and I was thankful for his attentiveness. She wasn't in there. I took my phone out to send her a text and Antoine cleared his throat. I lowered my phone and looked over at him.

"Are we waiting on Camila?" he asked.

"Yeah, she should be out soon. I think."

When she finally appeared, she was laughing at something her sister's husband was saying. I smiled at the sight. She looked carefree and happy standing with them. I watched as she took out her phone and looked at it, her head snapping up quickly and scanning the sidewalk, hopefully looking for me. She smiled the moment she spotted my car and put her phone away, leaning in to give her sister a hug and kiss, and doing the same for Adam. Right as she started to walk away, Dominic walked over and said something that made her stop and turn around. When she leaned up to give him a kiss on the cheek, he wrapped an arm around her waist and held her tightly against him, his hand fanned over the small of her bare back.

I'd never been a jealous man, not in the classic term of the word. Sure, when Elena told me she'd been seeing Ricky in private I got upset. Beyond upset. But once the dust settled I realized it wasn't about Elena or Ricky. It was a me thing. I couldn't believe she'd done that to *me*. I couldn't believe anybody would cheat on *me*. I couldn't think of a time that I'd ever felt envious of another man. But in that moment, while I was sitting in the car watching another man touch her, the sticky feeling began to build inside me. It wasn't his hands on her that bothered me. It was the realization that men like Dominic and Quinn from the band had months, years to prove they were worthy of her if they wanted to, and all I had left were two lousy weeks. The thought made me feel selfish, especially with the way those beautiful eyes of hers glittered in amusement as she walked toward my car.

Camila waved her phone around as she slid into the seat beside me. "I got tickets for something."

"Tickets? I thought we were . . ." I let the words hang because I didn't want to pressure her into going to my place, but I wanted to scream and yell and demand it. I'd never had this much trouble getting a woman in bed. I couldn't understand it. I sighed and shoved the thought aside. "I thought I told you not to buy things for me."

She grinned. "Oh, trust me, this was totally a gift for me."

She said hi to Antoine and told him to drive to the Brooklyn Navy Yard, which made his smile quickly turn into a rumbustious laughter that made me wary.

"I hope you're not going to make me do something crazy, Camila," I warned, leveling her with a stern look.

"What? Crazy? I would never. It's going to be so much fun. You're going to love it."

The way she smiled when she said it . . . I could picture

her giving me the very same smile as she lay in the center of my bed. Naked. My dick was getting hard at the thought of it, so I cleared my throat and attempted to rid my mind of the images. It was a difficult task with her sitting there in that tight-ass dress that gave me a view of her entire back. We talked about the auction and how it went. She asked questions about the people I was talking to, and I answered what I could. Soon the car stopped in front of what looked like a warehouse building and she climbed out.

"You going to be okay in those heels?" I asked, looking around the uneven pavement. "I don't know where you brought me, but I'm getting a sinking feeling in my gut."

"This is the third date I've taken you on where you've spent the beginning half of it questioning my judgment. Don't you remember how much fun you had at the game?"

"Third date?" I asked. "Is that how many we're up to? Do you have a three-date rule?"

She laughed. "No."

"That's odd. Women usually have weird rules they follow."

"I don't," she said, smiling up at me. "Are you done questioning my judgment? Can we go in now?"

I stuffed my hands into my pockets. Why couldn't I figure this girl out? I looked up and down the sidewalk once more. I was sure these streets hadn't seen such a well-dressed couple in a long time, if ever.

"I'm not questioning your judgment," I said as I followed her further into the yard. "I'm questioning your sanity."

And mine for wanting to be there so fucking bad.

Camila handed over her phone and the ticket person scanned the screen. She looked over to where Antoine was standing off to the left and called out, "I got one for you too,

Antoine."

He seemed surprised by this. I wasn't. Not because they
knew each other from high school, but because from the
short time I'd known Camila one thing I'd come to know
about her was that she always thought about others. I smiled
and wrapped an arm around her shoulder, pulling her close
as we began to walk. I kissed the top of her head and inhaled
the scent of her shampoo. It was dark out, so dark I could
only make out the lights of the buildings on the other side of
the Hudson.

"It's a late show tonight," she whispered.

I looked around and frowned when I read the signs.
Maybe I was right to question her sanity and my own for
trusting her so implicitly. "Pigeons? We're here to see pigeons
flying?"

She glanced up at me over her shoulder and shushed me.
Antoine laughed loudly beside us. I shot him a look and he
shrugged and shook his head as if to say *this bitch was crazy.*
I sighed in agreement. At the sound of a whistle, I turned my
attention to the boat in the middle of the Hudson, where six
guys were waving around sticks. I wondered what the fuck
kind of show this was. At the second whistle, I heard birds
flapping their wings and waited. And then, I saw the lights.

"You might want to close your mouth, New Yorker,"
Camila whispered. I shut my mouth quickly.

"What if they fly over here and shit on our heads?" I
asked quietly.

"They say that's good luck." She laughed. "Just make sure
you keep your mouth shut."

The pigeons laced the sky with ribbons of light, flying
in a synchronized form I had no idea they were capable of.
I looked over at Antoine and caught him snapping pictures,

a look of awe on his face. I had to admit, it was impressive. Soon, the pitch black, cloudless sky was consumed by strings of neon light.

"You've been here before?" I asked Camila.

She nodded her head slowly, keeping her eyes on the sky. I studied her profile, her small upturned nose and deliciously full lips. Her thin face and high cheekbones and those eyes that even from this angle seemed to shine as bright as her heart. I stepped behind her and wrapped my arms around her middle, pulling her to my chest.

"Thank you for bringing me," I said, tucking my head into the side of her neck. She shivered as I inhaled and exhaled a hint of the perfume she wore.

"You're welcome."

"Do you think a lot of people propose here?"

"Maybe. I guess it's less corny than at a ball game," she said, laughing.

I smiled. "Can we be more than friends now?"

Camila giggled and I felt my smile deepen. I'd never heard that sound before. She sounded like a young school girl when she did it.

"You have a one-track mind, sir."

I held her tighter, making her squeal while I squeezed her tighter and kissed her cheek. "Fine. I'll wait another date. But I am going to kiss you. And possibly grope you in that dress."

She turned around as I dropped my arms, tilting her face to look directly into my eyes as she wrapped her arms around my neck.

"That, I'm ready for," she said.

It was all I needed to wrap an arm around her back and pull her to me as I brought my lips down to hers. We kissed slowly by the Hudson, with thousands of pigeons making a beautiful light show above our heads and I couldn't think of any place I would've rather been in that moment.

Maybe in bed with *her*, but aside from that . . .

Chapter
THIRTEEN

Camila

If he kept at it, there was no way I would keep turning him down. Not with the way his arms felt when they were wrapped around me, the intoxicating way he smelled, the way he looked at me like nobody else was in the room, or the way he kissed me. Especially the way he kissed me, with skill and passion that only fueled thoughts of what being with him must feel like. And those thoughts were the reason I asked him to take me home after our pigeon date. I needed to mentally prepare myself before I had sex with this man. I couldn't just jump into it. I knew that as soon as I did, I'd be a goner and it would take me some time to get over never seeing him again if that's what ended up happening. Knowing he lived in another country kind of guaranteed that.

"Next thing you know, they'll have a job for sewer rats, too," he said as we headed to my place.

"Ew."

"What? Pigeons can get love but not rats? They're one and the same, you know." He chuckled when I fake gagged. "You sure I can't convince you to come home with me?" he asked, lowering his voice. He leaned in closer, his hand on my thigh. "I can help you get out of that dress."

My breath caught in my throat. "You shouldn't."

"Because friends don't do that," he said. I nodded. "But you want to. Admit it."

"I'm moving tomorrow," I said, changing the subject as I looked over at him when the car came to a full stop in front of my building.

"Tomorrow? That's fast."

"You've seen my place. I don't have much."

"You should come over tomorrow night then. We can celebrate."

"Wouldn't that require you to come to me since I'm the one moving into a new place?"

He tilted his head, pursing his lips as if deep in thought. "Will I fit in this new apartment of yours?"

I laughed. "You are so spoiled. Yes, you'll fit. It's bigger than where I'm at now."

"This car is bigger than where you are now."

I shook my head and opened the car door. "All right, Richie Rich. I'll take your invitation. Will there be food at this celebration party you're having in my honor?"

"Any kind you want."

"Chinese. I haven't eaten Chinese in a while."

"Chinese it is. Anything in particular?"

"Anything spicy." I stepped out of the car and stood

on the sidewalk, facing him as I held on to the door handle. Warren scooted closer to me and held my chin with his thumb and pointer, pulling my face toward him.

"Thank you for tonight."

He pressed his lips against mine, snuck his tongue into my mouth, and let me go on a breath. My only thought was that I would kiss him every second of every day if I could. The way his lips, soft and pillowy, felt pressed against mine, and his tongue eased into my mouth, gliding, stroking, consuming every inch of it was enough to drive me wild, but the way his eyes hooded each time he broke the kiss sealed the deal for me.

"See you tomorrow," I said, walking away and into my building.

"I'm looking forward to it."

As I pulled open the glass door to my apartment, I froze. Charlie was on the other side heading out.

"You just got home from the gala?" he asked, giving me a once-over.

"Yeah. You're just heading to the bar now?"

He nodded. "It's slow tonight."

"I'm moving tomorrow," I said when he brushed past me. "I have to wait until Monday. Are you on the fifth floor?"

"Eighth. There were no corner units left on the fifth."

"Let me know if you need anything," he said, starting to walk away again. He stopped suddenly and turned back around. "Hey, when did you say your dad gets out?"

"Supposedly next week," I said, adding a nonchalant shrug, though the occasion felt anything but.

Charlie knew this and didn't pester me about it. He turned back around and walked toward the bar with a wave and a see you later. The last thing I wanted to think about was my dad getting out of prison, my brother moving back from the Dominican Republic, and my mother's much anticipated party to celebrate both milestones. Every time I thought about it, I could feel the knots of anticipation building on my shoulders. As I walked into my apartment, my phone buzzed and I pushed the thoughts away.

Warren: I really wanted to peel that dress off you tonight.

My stomach clenched as I read it. I typed back a response as I slipped off my shoes and rotated my ankles.

Camila: I look forward to eating Chinese food tomorrow.

I set the phone down on the counter and smiled when I saw the three dots signaling his next response.

Warren: I'd much rather be eating other things . . . but I'm not sure if that's a stipulation in our friendship clause.

Holy mother. Did he really just . . . ? My stomach dipped. I tried to think of another response as I slipped the dress over my head, but couldn't because now all I kept picturing was his head between my legs. I groaned. I was playing with fire, and I knew without a doubt I'd get burned. Problem was, I couldn't find it in me to care. I hadn't felt this way about a man in a long time, if ever. He responded again before I could reply.

Warren: We can add it in if you'd like. I'm more than willing ;-)

I responded quickly.

Camila: You really love that winky face emoji. Do you even wink in real life?

Warren: LOL. That's what you want to focus on?

I stared at the screen. The future of our friendship slash relationship slash whatever the hell this was relied on these exchanges. It felt monumental and heavy and I wasn't sure I was qualified to deal with these things. Finally, I said to hell with it and responded.

Camila: I'm not sure I know you well enough to let your tongue go there.

I didn't see the little blue dots again, so I hopped in the shower quickly. When I got out, still damp from the hot water, I had two more text messages.

Warren: I think you know me better than most, but let's remedy that. What do you want to know?

And a second . . .

Warren: Why don't you think about it and ask me tomorrow when you come over? I'll send a car to your new building at seven.

When Vanessa and I went to look at the new apartment and I told her I hadn't Googled him, I thought she was going to spank me. How could you not Google him? He's actually on Google. How many people can you say that about? Of course I could think of one, but I didn't want to tarnish a conversation about Warren by bringing up Dad. Now that I knew Warren as much as I did, looking him up felt like cheating. He couldn't look me up, so why should I do it to him? Still, as I lay in bed thinking about him, I typed his name into the search engine on my phone and hit *Go*. What I found was page after page talking about the scandal with his ex-fiancée and a possible trade to some team in Barcelona.

The pictures I found of him were all the same: him smiling at the camera with a woman on his arm. In most of them he was pictured with the same woman, a busty blonde with big lips and hips to match. I zoomed in on her face. She had perfectly straight white teeth and a smile that would have been dazzling if it didn't look so forced. Her eyes were a sharp blue that didn't contain any humor in them. I looked at his smile, his face, his eyes. He also looked like he was forcing happiness. Maybe it had been taken when they were both tired of each other's shit; when she started cheating and he was suspecting. I looked at the other pictures of them together, but it was more of the same. Then the other pictures, the ones of him with different women: brunettes, redheads, you name it. Warren definitely didn't have a specific type. I wasn't sure if that should make me glad, mad, or just sad. The only thing all of those women seemed to have in common was the one thing I didn't have: social status. All of them were clickable names that took you to other websites where they also appeared. I didn't have that. I never would. If I ever showed up to an event with him, I'd be the first nobody. I didn't want to wonder. I didn't want the nagging question of *why me?* to infiltrate my thoughts, but it did nonetheless. On that note, I switched my phone off and forced myself to go to sleep.

Chapter
FOURTEEN

Camila

Vanessa and Adam showed up at my door first thing in the morning, both ready to get to work. It took us exactly an hour and a half to move everything to my new place. The three of us shared a laugh about it when we got back to my old place and saw how empty it was.

"Easiest move in the history of moves," Adam said.

"Right?" I laughed.

"Babe, we need to buy Camila some house-warming gifts," Vanessa said, tilting her head to look at him with a small smile on her face.

"Of course," he said, nodding at her. He looked over at me. "Just say yes. You know she'll show up every day and bully you into letting her do it eventually."

I shook my head and let out a long sigh. "Nothing too pricey."

Vanessa squealed and jumped up with a little clap. I couldn't help but laugh. Adam shook his head.

"Thank you. I'm so excited," she said before looking at him. "Let's get to work."

"Oh, I'm coming?" he asked, eyes wide. "I thought this was a sister-sister moment."

"No, I want to surprise her. Besides, Peach has a date tonight." She wagged her eyebrows when she said it. I blushed.

"I still can't believe you're dating Warren, *War Zone*, Silva," Adam said, shaking his head slowly.

"We're not dating," I argued with a frown. "And what the hell is *War Zone*?"

Adam balked. "You're kidding."

I looked at Vanessa, who had the same confused expression I wore, and back at Adam.

Adam fished out his phone and typed something in, then walked over to me. Vanessa followed. The three of us stood side by side looking at his phone screen as we waited on the YouTube video to start. When the ad finished playing, the soccer field came into view. A bunch of guys in red uniforms were playing guys in red-and-blue striped uniforms.

"I like those," I said, pointing at the red-and-blue striped uniforms.

"Wrong team. That's Barcelona," Adam said with a chuckle and pointed at the red uniforms. "You better start liking those."

"Red is a good color on me," I said.

My sister and Adam laughed as we watched the screen. The smile slipped off my face when I saw Warren kicking the ball down the field and dodging opponent after opponent. I grabbed Adam's arm and gasped, as if the game was on live television, when he got to a group of guys from the other team and braced myself for the ball to be taken from him. Suddenly, he stopped and placed his right foot on top of the ball.

"What is he doing?" I asked.

"Watch," Adam responded, jerking his arm from under me. "Dude, you're scratching."

"I can't see!" I waved my hands and lurched toward him to get his phone.

My sister laughed, plucking it from his hand and standing between us. "It's paused. He's still just standing there."

I bit my lip as she pressed play. I couldn't bear to watch. I couldn't. But I kept my eyes on the screen anyway and watched as he suddenly took off like a rocket between two guys. He was met on the other side by some teammates, who he kicked the ball to, but they kicked it right back to him and set him up for a goal, which he scored. The crowd roared. The commentators screamed their praises. My jaw dropped.

"And that, ladies and gentlemen, is why they call the area that surrounds him the *War Zone*," one of the commentators declared.

When the clip finished playing, Adam looked over at me and shrugged. "He's kind of a big deal."

"So I've heard," I said, thinking about Warren's nephew's words.

"And you took him to the damn pigeon show," he shot back with a chuckle as he took the phone from Vanessa and shoved it into his pocket. I rolled my eyes.

"I'll have you know that *War Zone* loved the pigeon show."

They left shortly and I walked back to my new place,

smiling as I walked in the door and was greeted with cold air conditioning. I set aside some clothes and showered, taking my time to shave and make sure I looked completely presentable. Just in case. My heart fluttered at the thought of that.

My phone buzzed as I was finishing applying mascara. I gave myself a quick once-over and nodded at my reflection. What I wore was simple: a short summer dress and sandals. The waves in my hair were cooperating without much primping, which was a rarity, so I felt pretty. I threw a gray cross-body bag over myself and headed downstairs to meet Antoine outside. We gave each other a smile and a quick hello before I slid in the backseat.

"You seem nervous," he commented as he drove.

I glanced up, meeting his eyes in the rearview. "Really?"

"You're quieter than usual. And that's quiet." He chuckled. I laughed.

"I guess I am a little nervous."

"It's a nice building," Antoine commented.

"Warren's?" I asked. I was sure nice was an understatement.

"No. I mean where you're living now."

"Oh. Yeah. It's very nice." I smiled. "Working air conditioning."

Antoine chuckled. "Always a plus."

"Definitely."

"I'm always wary about these dudes coming around and changing shit, but War's a good guy," he said.

"Yeah. Too bad he's not really involved in any decision making," I replied absentmindedly looking out the window, trying to keep my nerves at bay.

"He's involved enough to trade some of his shares for that building, though."

My head snapped to Antoine. "What do you mean?"

"The building you're at now."

"What about it?" I asked.

"Don't tell him I said nothing. I thought you knew and I really don't wanna get fired over this."

"I won't tell him."

Antoine shrugged. "I don't know the full details and can only go based on phone conversations I've heard, but from what I understand he sold Belmonte a lot of his shares so they'd give him that building. You guys lucked out. My mom still lives in the neighborhood and her rent skyrocketed this past fall."

We rode the rest of the way in silence, but I couldn't stop thinking about Warren owning my building. Should I be upset about it? I mean, it wasn't just me who moved from the other building to this one. It was all of us. It's not like he did it for me, and it's not like he did it for free, either. I shrugged it off as just another business venture on his part. Still, the feeling of gratitude lingered and stuck deep inside me. Antoine walked me into the building and cleared me past security in the front desk, then rode with me in the elevator, where he clicked on the penthouse button. When the elevator opened up, he signaled for me to get out and took a step back.

"I'll see you later."

"Thanks for the ride," I said and knocked on the mahogany door in front of me.

Warren opened after a few moments and stood on the other side wearing jeans, a black V-neck T-shirt—that fit him so well that I wanted nothing more than to rip it off him—and a black pair of Adidas sandals with no socks. At least he wore no socks with them. His eyes traveled down my body and back up quickly before pulling me into the apartment.

He wrapped an arm around me and pulled me against his hard chest. I closed my eyes just as his lips came crashing down on mine.

The kiss went from desperate to soft and sweet, but by the time we broke away from each other I was wired with need for more. His large hands moved from my back, up my waist and finally up to my face where he kept them as his eyes bore into mine.

"Those lips will be the death of me," he murmured, his voice low and raspy.

"There are worst ways to die though," I whispered.

He smiled as he placed one more chaste kiss on my lips and dropped his hands. I waited until my heart found its way back to normal speed before I cleared my throat and took a nice calming breath as I looked around.

"This is nice."

It looked very much like what I pictured: gray marble floors, chandeliers, nice tall vases with fresh flowers, dark wood kitchen cabinets with muted accents. The walls were warm, some white, some darker, and the couches were light tones that made me unsure of where to sit. There was a grand piano off to the left near a staircase that I assumed led to the rooftop.

"Thanks. It's my brother's," Warren said behind me.

His hand reached out and tugged at one of the straps of my dress, which crisscrossed on my back, and I felt my nipples pucker at the contact. I swallowed, trying to contain my nerves.

"You hungry?" he asked.

I nodded as I walked over to the floor-to-ceiling windows that overlooked Manhattan. "Starving."

We were quiet for a moment, my eyes skimming over

the buildings and lights. It didn't matter how many times I saw the scene in front of me, I was always in awe of my city. Warren came up behind me and wrapped an arm around me, his lips grazing over my shoulder softly. I shivered in his arms.

"It feels like you can see everything from up here," he said, his voice quiet.

"It does."

"Let's go eat. I want you to ask me all the questions your heart desires."

"Really?" I asked, smiling as I turned around in his arms.

"As long as that dress is on my floor by the end of the night," he said, chuckling when I slapped his arm playfully.

I followed him up the narrow circular stairs that led to the rooftop and gasped when everything came into view. There was a long table set up and lanterns lit up along the roof. As I neared the table, I noticed trays upon trays of food. There was enough to feed three families of four, and enough wine bottles to inebriate a sailor. Beside that table, there were pillows on the floor and a smaller table with two settings and tea light candles illuminating it. My eyes, wide and impressed, met his.

"You did this?"

He smiled. "Are you impressed?"

I nodded slowly, unable to take my eyes off his. He walked over and cupped the right side of my face with his large hand.

"Are you happy?"

The question shocked me. Had anybody ever asked me that? I thought about it and came up with a giant no. Not my parents, not my siblings, and especially not any guy I'd dated. I didn't even know they were words I longed for until he said them. *Are you happy?* When I looked at him again I nodded. "Very."

His lips met mine again, softly, tentatively. His hand moving from my face and threading into my hair as we deepened the kiss. I held his strong forearm and brought my other hand behind his neck, inching closer to him, seeking out his warmth. We tore apart slowly, breathing deeply and heavily, and kept our hands where they were as we looked at each other. I didn't want to pull away completely, and in his hand I felt the same reluctance. Finally, my stomach growled and left no room for question that I needed to eat. Warren chuckled. I blushed.

"Sorry."

"I invited you over for food and you're sorry you're hungry?" he asked, laughing as he dropped his hand and made his way toward the food.

We each grabbed plates and served ourselves.

"This is way too much," I said.

"Whatever we don't eat will be leftovers for tomorrow." He paused. "I'm sure Antoine will take some home."

I smiled, grateful he'd thought about somebody else's needs. We sat down on the pillows, our knees kissing as we ate and looked at the city lights. Cars honked, people laughed, some yelled, and Warren and I sipped on wine and ate the delicious food, stealing glances every so often.

"You never told me why you came here," I said, pausing to drink some wine. "You said you hadn't been here in ages and at the auction you said something about a family thing."

"You started out with a hard question." He chuckled as he leaned back against the front of the couch and looked over at me. "My dad is sick and I got tired of my mom and brother begging me to come see him."

"Is he dying?"

He nodded. "Bone marrow cancer."

"I'm sorry," I said, placing my hand over his between us. "When was the last time you saw him before this trip?"

"When I was sixteen and they took a family trip to Europe."

I gaped at him. Google said Warren was thirty-one. "When was the last time you came over here?"

He tilted his head, a small frown appearing on his face. I resisted the urge to iron out the lines it made on his forehead. "When I was . . . twenty or twenty-one when I got my first big shoe contract."

"Really?" I continued to gape. I couldn't imagine leaving New York that long ago and never looking back. "What about your brother and nephew?"

"They visit me pretty often. To be honest, this is the longest vacation I've taken in ten years . . ." he chuckled, "and that's saying a lot since it isn't exactly a vacation."

"Soccer really is your life," I said quietly.

"You have no idea."

I picked up my glass and leaned back, settling into his arm and tilting my face to look at him. "Tell me."

He took a deep breath and released it slowly before looking at me with a despondent look that made him look older, sadder. "I was fourteen when I left. My dad had just started a fast growing company that as suspected, became a huge success quickly. When I graduated high school he expected me to come back. I guess he thought the whole soccer thing was a phase. When I didn't come home and get involved in the family business, he wrote me off. Refused to see me, wouldn't take my calls . . ." He shrugged.

"Does it make you angry?" I asked.

"Not anymore."

"Does it make you sad?"

Warren gave me a lopsided grin. "Are we on the clock?"

I laughed. "Free consultation."

He pulled me closer, dropping a kiss on the top of my head and settling his chin there. "I guess I am."

I knew he was, but I wasn't expecting him to admit it. It used to take me weeks with some of the kids before they admitted to any kind of emotion. The ironic thing about his admission was that all this time I'd been saying we had nothing in common and what we did have was the one thing I wouldn't wish on anybody. But it was the key to making me open up more, which I seldom did, and that was a mistake I worked on trying to correct. We carried our stories so tight that we become suffocated with them, and more often than not, the person right beside us is suffering in the same silence we are. Of course that was easier said than done. It was easy for me to preach it to the teenagers at Winsor than it was for me to let it out, but I did anyway because I trusted Warren on some level.

"If it makes you feel any better, my dad got arrested ten years ago and took our visitation rights from me, my sister, and brother. Only my mom is allowed to go see him," I said, looking out to the dark office building beside us. An oddly comfortable silence fell over us.

"Maybe he was too ashamed to let you see him in there," he said against my hair.

"Maybe."

"Are you angry with him?"

"Yup."

"Do you think you'll forgive him?"

"Yes."

Warren reared back to look at me. His eyes searched mine. "Just like that? A sure yes?"

"Just like that," I said, smiling.

"Why?"

"That's what family does, isn't it? We put up with things from each other that we'd never take from anybody else. Even after being dragged through the mud and stomped on a few times somehow we still find it in us to forgive one another."

I knew that my eagerness to forgive him must sound crazy to an outsider, but my anger had been replaced by sadness long ago. Not that I didn't get angry every now and then, and I was sure another wave of that emotion would come my way when I did see him again. Right now all I felt was sadness for lost time; longing for the way he used to listen so intently as if nothing else mattered when I spoke. Sometimes, when I was feeling extra sad, I'd wrap my arms around myself and pretend they were his arms giving me a hug. Dad always gave the best hugs. I exhaled at the memory of them.

Warren shook his head. "I'm not sure I could."

"Have you forgiven your ex-fiancée for cheating on you?"

"No." He pursed his lips. "She can go fuck herself."

I laughed. "You should work on that."

"You forgave your douchebag ex-boyfriend?"

"Yeah."

"Why?"

"The way I see it, when it comes to forgiveness, we only have two choices. We could stay here moping and thinking about how much better a person we are while they keep living their lives, or we can prove that we're the better person by letting go." I shrugged. "Life is short. We're only here to chase moments. I'd rather make those moments worthwhile."

"So you choose to let go?"

"I choose to keep living."

"Hmm."

"Hmm." I bumped my shoulder against his. "You should try it."

"To chase moments?" he asked, a whisper.

I smiled. "To chase moments."

We were quiet for a long time, my head on his shoulder, before he spoke again.

"When does he get out? Your dad."

"Next week."

I felt him stiffen beside me. "That's soon. Are you going to go see him?"

"My mom's throwing a huge party for the occasion. My brother is moving back from DR and everything. Imagine that," I said, rolling my eyes into the dimly lit space.

"I take it you're not a fan of his?"

"My brother? I love him, but he's an asshole. Back to the family forgiveness circle of healing," I said, shooting him a smile. He chuckled. "How's it going with your dad?"

He grinned. "Ah . . . it's going. He's no longer refusing my visits to the hospital, but he ignores me the entire time I'm there."

"So what do you do while you're sitting there?"

"Think about you." He said it with a twinkle in his eyes that made me bump my shoulder against him again.

"I'm serious."

"So am I. It's all I do these days," he said, bringing his right hand up to the left side of my face. My heart roared in my chest, my veins, my ears.

"I like this," I said, my voice quiet.

"Being in my arms like this?" he asked, his voice hoarse,

eyes darkening when I nodded. "Tell me."

He shifted a bit, so that the tips of our noses were almost touching. My eyes searched his, my breathing escalating at the possibilities of all the things that could happen between us.

"I like . . . being with you."

His eyes softened for a moment, so quickly if I blinked I would've missed it, and then his face was coming closer. I closed my eyes just as his lips touched mine. It was a soft graze at first, so soft and delicate it took my breath away. When I took my next breath, it was his tongue I felt against mine as his hand stroked the side of my arm. His mouth felt like everything I envisioned heaven and hell must feel like: warm and welcoming, hot and seductive. The way he used his hands to skim down my body set me on a path to ecstasy and I was still clothed. I couldn't imagine. Didn't know if I wanted to imagine doing more, but I knew I didn't want to stop it from happening. With one hand he slowly pulled down the strap of my dress and began to touch me. I arched my back, desperate for more than just the soft, tentative touch he provided.

"We don't have to—"

"I want to."

"We can stop whenever—"

I pulled away from him so I could look into his eyes. "I don't ever want you to stop."

That seemed to be enough for him. He pulled my dress over my head and let his gaze slowly travel down the length of me.

"Bloody perfect," he said, his voice low and grating, his eyes dark and hooded, and the only thing I could do was picture this man putting his mouth in other places, his hands in other places. The thought alone made me clench my thighs together.

I brought my mouth back to his and met him in a desperate kiss, much rougher than the one before, much needier, and tugged the hem of his shirt, bringing it over his head. My eyes widened as I took him in. It didn't even occur to me to stop because we were exposed outside on a rooftop. It was dark, and the lounge area was beneath a small retractable roof that seemed to shield us from wandering eyes, if there were any this high up. Furthermore, neither one of us cared. We kissed as we undressed, each one taking off an article of clothing from the other until our lips were swollen and we were completely bare to one another.

I couldn't stop looking at him. He was a work of art, from the tattoos to the ridges on his perfect figure. He was perfect, with thick thighs and cut arms, but what called my attention most was what was between his legs. He was thick and hard. I couldn't imagine any sane woman passing any of this up. With his left hand, he began to stroke himself, and I felt my own breath quicken, my heart beat frantically as if I was the one experiencing his touch.

"Camila," he said, voice gruff, hand still moving. I met his eyes. "I hope you believe that I'm not just saying this because you're standing naked in front of me. I can't remember the last time I wanted anybody the way I want you. If ever."

And just like that, he dropped his hand and I dropped all pretenses and lunged toward him. He caught me, wrapping my legs around him and crashing his lips against mine. Our tongues clashed in a wild devour, our hands clawed against one another, his on my ass, mine on his muscular back. He carried me with ease, and set me down on the sofa, his hand reaching in between my legs as he did. His fingers thrummed against me softly, methodically, and I arched my back as the familiar sensation of an orgasm began to spread through me. I gasped, wondering how the hell that could happen so fast, and gasped again, louder, when it began to completely consume me. Warren kissed the side of my mouth and dragged his lips to the base of my throat as his fingers continued to work. I threw my head back and reached for him, stroking the way he'd been doing, and he let out a loud groan.

"Fuck, Camila."

I pulled him closer, still stroking, and stopped suddenly. He followed suit and looked at me.

"Too much?"

I shook my head, and licked my lips, my face burning. I'd never been so forward, but I figured if there was a time to be forward this was it. "Do you have condom?"

Warren grinned, dipping a finger inside me, then two, and moving them in a motion that made me writhe beneath him. I began to stroke him again, faster, harder, and he groaned. Our eyes locked in that moment, our expressions unmasked, our need exposed. He pulled out slowly, folding his fingers against my inner wall as he did so and stroked my clit again. I began to pant, still looking at him. His expression alone could have made me come undone. It was craze and wonder as he brought me to the brink again. I was still panting, writhing, when he slid on a condom and parted my legs a little wider. He settled between me, placing his forehead against mine, and with our gazes still locked, he tugged my hand and placed it over his heart, where I could feel it beating wildly, unrestrained.

"This is how I feel when I'm near you."

There was a raw honesty in his eyes that held me hostage as he pushed himself inside me. There was no room for doubt.

Chapter
FIFTEEN

Camila

I barely got any sleep at all, not that I was complaining. I'd never been with anybody with a sex drive as voracious as Warren's. We'd gone from the rooftop, to the living room couch, to the shower, and finally ended up in bed. Even after we were both sated, we stayed awake, talking about our past sexual history. I was expecting him to have crazy stories, but when the threesomes came up, I began to feel panicky. Suddenly all I could do was wonder if I was good enough. It subsided when he wrapped an arm and leg around me and kissed my bare shoulder. I experienced a sense of comfort as I lay there, blanketed the warmth he provided.

The ache between my legs and the soreness of my muscles were the first things I felt when I woke up. I peeled my eyes open slowly, expecting to find Warren beside me, but the bed was empty. I sat up and looked around, letting my eyes adjust to the overbearing sunlight coming in. I stretched my arms over my head as I pulled myself out of bed and headed to the bathroom. Switching on the light, I caught a glimpse of what was on the counter and froze. Last night, I mentioned I couldn't stay over because I didn't even have a toothbrush with me, and there, on top of a folded fluffy white towel, sat a pink toothbrush.

I smiled as I picked it up and took it out of the packaging. After showering and slipping on the dress I wore the night before, I exited the room quietly in search for Warren. His voice, loud and stern, was coming from somewhere in the house, so I followed it down the hall, passing closed doors I didn't dare open. When I reached him, I stood outside the door, not wanting to interrupt and waited for him to finish.

"I asked you twice to stop meddling," he said. His temper surprised me, but I edged closer nonetheless. "You know what? Fuck right off. I'm here for two weeks and suddenly you think you need to reclaim your title as big brother? You can keep the whole fucking company for all I care. I don't need it. I want no part in it if it's going to bring me this grief." He paused. "Yeah. I don't care."

He was silent for a long moment, and I finally decided to move and step into the threshold of the door. It was an impressive office with a clear view of Central Park on the other side of the street. Warren was shirtless behind the mahogany desk, with his clenched fists on it and his head down. The pose pronounced his shoulder blades and the muscles on his arms. I felt myself blush at the memory of being beneath him last night while those strong arms held him above me. It took me a second to find my voice.

"Hey."

His head snapped up first and he straightened up quickly. My gaze made its way from the waistband of his shorts slowly over his rock-hard abs covered in ink, and all the way up to his neck, his jaw, his lips, and finally those hypnotizing eyes of his. They held an angry, fiery look that anchored me where I was standing and made my skin prickle.

I watched him walk around the desk, taking long strides to get to me, a different muscle flexing with every move. When he reached me, he cupped my face and leaned down to kiss me, hard and thorough, his tongue sweeping into my mouth with no preamble, so crazed, I had to hold on to his forearms to keep up. He broke the kiss and pinned me with his stare.

"Don't leave."

"I have to be at work in a couple of hours."

"Fair enough." He gave me a nod, still looking upset. "I'll take you home and make sure you get to work on time."

"If you come with me, I won't make it to work on time," I said, smiling to lighten his mood.

His expression morphed slowly from anger, to confusion, and finally, amusement. "That makes me want to go more."

"It'll give you something to look forward to." I reached up on the balls of my feet and kissed his lips chastely. When I came back down, he was looking at me like I was some kind of puzzle to solve.

"Come home with me."

I smiled. "I'm already here."

"No. I mean home. To Manchester. I have to fly back for practice and I want you to come."

"Manchester?" I asked, fully aware of the squeak in my

voice.

He'd asked me this once before, but unlike the last time, he was completely serious this time. Warren chuckled, amusement glinting in his eyes as he pulled me into a hug, wrapping one of his long arms around me.

"Yes."

"What makes you think I even have a passport?" I asked against his chest. He pulled away and looked down at me.

"Do you?"

My passport was renewed last year when I'd planned to visit my grandmother in DR. Stranded looking after one of the kids from Winsor here in New York, I'm still saddened my plans fell through. Vanessa and Adam went on the trip and came back with pictures, a handmade scarf from my grandmother, a package of Soy Turey crackers, and so many stories that only made the ache in my heart worsen.

"Yes," I said slowly. "But I can't just take off."

"Please, Camila," he said, pulling me and kissing me sweetly. "Say yes?"

I sighed. "I Googled you last night before I came over."

"What?" He dropped his arms instantly.

"I didn't click on any of the articles," I said, looking down at my hands momentarily.

"They were mostly about you and your ex. But I did click the pictures and . . . I'm not sure I can keep up with Manchester Warren."

"Manchester Warren?" he asked, raising an eyebrow. "Is that some kind of action figure I'm not getting paid for?"

I rolled my eyes and looked away again, thinking of the pictures of him with a different woman in each shot . . . I wasn't sure I could deal with being the girl in the next three shots until he brought me back and discarded me. Warren pinched my chin and tilted my face to look at him. His eyes were soft and sincere when he spoke again.

"It's just practice games. I have a couple of things I need to do while I'm there, but I'll make sure you don't feel out of place." He paused and sighed. "You showed me New York. Let me show you my home. Please."

We gazed at each other for a long, quiet moment. I could feel how much he wanted me to agree to it, and so I did.

"If they let me take days off," I said, adding another *if* just before he wrapped his arms around me and lifted me off the ground.

Chapter
SIXTEEN

Warren

"**W**hy haven't you brought her around?" my mom asked after I told her where I was spending all my free time.

"Because I know how welcome the three of you make the women I date feel."

She raised an eyebrow. "So, you're dating?"

I opened up the newspaper in front of me and flipped through it in vain.

"Is she a New Yorker?" Mom asked.

I glanced at her over the paper. "Yes."

"Where does she live?"

"Washington Heights."

"Really?" She raised her eyebrow again as she picked up

her tea and took a sip. "What does she do for a living?"

"She has a regular nine-to-five job and is just waiting for somebody with a hefty bank account who only thinks with his dick to knock her up and marry her," my brother said as he walked into the room.

I glared at him. He glared right back.

"Is this another Elena?" my mom asked, looking at my brother as if he knew something about the women in my life. She looked at me quickly. "Warren, you can't deal with another Elena."

"She's not another Elena. She works with the Winsor Foundation and has three degrees from credible universities. Three," I repeated, looking at my brother. "How many do you have?"

He scoffed and shook his head. "All that means is she has triple the student loans to pay back, and I know what Winsor pays their employees isn't much so she can probably barely make ends meet."

I stood up from the table and grabbed my suit jacket. The tips of my ears were already starting to burn and I knew if I stayed another minute we'd end up arguing again. "I have to go. Have fun knocking down all the women I've ever dated. Your wife is lucky to have you."

"She is," he called out as I walked away.

I scoffed. "I'm sure she's at the spa right now telling all her friends what an asshole you are as she charges up your AMEX."

It was a low blow. I knew that. I had absolutely nothing against my sister-in-law, but she was the only thing I could use against him. I wouldn't dare use Cayden, and I really loved my brother when he wasn't talking about my love life. That always led to arguments and which caused us both to revert back to our petulant teenage selves. I was sure Camila would call us spoiled brats for the way we acted. *Over-privileged kids from the Upper East Side,* she'd say with an eye-roll. The thought of her made me smile as I reached for the door handle, my mood instantly boosted. And then my brother scoffed and pointed out to my mom that this girl lived in another country.

"He wasn't a saint when it came to Elena. Stop trying to put all of the blame on her," I heard my mom say in Spanish.

I walked out the door before I could hear his response. That fucking relationship was going to haunt me for all eternity. Her cheating, my lying, my cheating, her lying. The relationship was toxic and doomed from the start. It was nothing like what Camila and I had. But then, what did *we* have? A guilty urge that bloomed into an unlikely friendship and continued to blossom into this. Whatever this was. The only thing I knew was that it would come to an end and for once in my life, I was dreading the moment it did.

Chapter
SEVENTEEN

Camila

"I wanted to ask for days off," I said to Nancy after we went over some case studies.

"Oh?" She took her off her reading glasses and looked at me. "For your dad?"

"No. For me."

Her eyebrows shot up. She smiled. "Well, that's great news."

"Thanks," I said, smiling.

"How many days will you need? Last time I checked you had ten saved up. They roll over, you know."

"I know," I paused, "but four should be enough."

"I'm taking my vacation days," I told Vanessa over lunch. Her brows rose as she stabbed at her salad.

"For Dad?"

I sighed. "No, not for dad. For me."

"You?" she asked, clearly surprised. "To fix up the apartment?"

"No . . . Warren wants to take me home for a few days."

"Home as in . . . Barcelona?" she asked, frowning.

"He lives in Manchester."

She eyed me for a second. "You're serious."

"As a heart attack."

Vanessa dropped the fork, eyes wide, as if she just now believed me. "No shit."

"Shit," I said, unable to contain my amused smile.

"Things are moving . . . fast, huh?"

I sighed. "We're friends."

"Friends who have sex and take each other on expensive vacations?"

I tore my gaze away and looked out the window. That's what I didn't like about the whole thing. The money factor. I was okay with paying for stupid baseball tickets and the subway because I wasn't the one with something close to a million dollars in the bank. I'd be lucky to have seven hundred dollars after paying my bills. And even that was on a really good month. I told Vanessa how it made me uncomfortable and she laughed.

"Look, I'm saying it as a compliment. Just have fun. If he has the money and wants to spend it on you, let him."

Easy for her to say.

A manila envelope in front of my door was what greeted me when I arrived home. After picking it up, I went inside, tearing it open as I set my keys down on the little table by the door and walking to the kitchen. There was a note, typed on a sheet of computer paper in *Times New Roman* font. I knew it because I'd used the stupid font all through college.

He's not who you think he is.

My heart launched into my throat as I read the words over and shook the envelope to release the enclosed USB drive. I clutched it in my hand and walked over to my laptop, turning it on as I examined the USB. It was just plain, no name brand, no company logo. Who the hell would send this to me? Who cared enough to warn me about somebody? Not that I knew who the somebody was. It could be my dad, my late grandfather . . . Once connected to the computer, I clicked on the first file.

Then froze.

It was Warren. Warren with a curvy and busty blonde. I squinted, zooming in on the picture and recognized her as his ex-fiancée. I kept scrolling until I reached an image of him making out with another woman. The sight of it left a bad taste in my mouth. I didn't want to see him kissing another woman. Once I got over that, I noticed the timestamp and clicked on the previous picture. Only one had a time and date, and it didn't take a rocket scientist to see just by Warren's slightly thinner frame that they had been taken when he was younger. The only photos that looked more recent, with his same hairstyle and frame were the ones with his ex-fiancée.

I sat back in my futon and kept clicking. Finally, I reached a photo of him and not one, but two women—a blonde and a brunette with their hands between his legs. The three of them were topless, but the two women were wearing skirts and he was wearing dress pants, his face tilted toward one of them as he kissed her and cupped one of her breasts. I ejected the USB drive out of the computer, my heart pounding.

I wasn't an idiot. I knew he wasn't a saint. I had a television and watched reality shows about their wives and their cheating scandals. And I'd been around long enough to hear crazy stories about athletes and some he'd told me himself the other night. I just didn't understand why anybody would go out of their way to send this to *me*. I wasn't even his girlfriend. I got up and took a long shower, hoping it would clear my mind. All it did was confuse and enrage me. I'd gone from *why would they send this to me as if I would care?* to *he's so disgusting; I can't believe he'd do that* in the matter of thirty-five minutes.

It wasn't what he was doing in the photos. It was just that in my mind, the Warren I knew wasn't like that. The Warren I knew didn't flaunt women or cars or talk about flashy things. The Warren I knew was a bit snotty, but not snotty enough to complain about sitting in the nosebleed section at the Yankees game. The Warren I knew took his nephew to the movies on a Thursday to watch a superhero movie the night it opened. He just wasn't who I saw in those photos, and it made me question everything. Did I even *know* the real Warren? Did they?

As I thought about it, my stomach began to growl. I went to the kitchen, opened the fridge and found the only two things I didn't feel like eating right now: eggs and cheese. I picked up the phone and dialed the Puerto Rican diner across the street and ordered the only comfort food I could manage to get quickly. Then, I called Warren, who answered the phone on the second ring, his voice scratchy and deep.

"I miss you."

The words caused butterflies to ignite deep in my core. I pushed them back, trapped them and put them in a box. I had no room for those feelings right now.

"I got a package in the mail."

"Oh?" he asked. I could practically see the lines of his frown and the way his full lips pursed.

"A USB drive with pictures of you and some girls. I mean, TMI pictures."

He was quiet for a beat. "I'm coming over."

"No." I paused, eyes wide. It was the loudest word I'd ever said outside of the bedroom. "I just got out of the shower. Let me just . . . give me a few minutes. I just couldn't not call you."

"You sound upset," he paused. "At me or what you saw?"

"Both."

There was a knock on my door that had me spinning around quickly, my towel coming undone. I cursed under my breath as I adjusted it over my boobs and opened the door. I asked Warren to hold on as I talked to the teenager delivering my food and signed the paper.

"I'm so sorry," I said to the kid, whose eyes were wide as saucers. He didn't respond before I closed the door and set the bag on the counter.

"Did you just open the door wrapped in a towel?" Warren asked.

I clutched the towel harder. "I told you, I just got out of the shower."

"I'm coming over. Now."

"I don't want you to."

That brought on another bout of silence. When he spoke again, his voice was a low and tentative. "You don't want to see me?"

"Not right now."

"So you are mad at me," he said. "You realize that whatever it is you saw was taken before I met you, right? I haven't so much as looked at another woman since I met you,

Camila. Not once. I swear that on my life."

His words brought a warm feeling with them, one that spread through me and stuck. I had no reason not to believe him. I had no reason to be upset at him, except that I was and I realized I was upset because I trusted him.

"I believe you," I whispered. "I do. And I promise you I'm not mad at you. Just . . . give me some time to digest. Maybe if I sort out my apartment I'll sort out my head."

"Okay."

"Okay."

"Camila?" The way he said my name sent a slight shiver down my spine.

I closed my eyes and swallowed back the memories of him saying it in my ear, rasping it as he bit my earlobe and fucked me.

"Yeah?"

"Please don't take too long."

After I ate my dinner I felt more at ease with everything. I put the USB drive and paper back in the envelope so I could give it to Warren and then threw myself into the task of putting everything away. Clothes, shoes, pots and pans. I was setting aside the laundry I needed to do when Vanessa called me to remind me that my furniture was due to arrive tomorrow afternoon, so I set aside time in my calendar to be home early.

I tossed and turned the entire night, thinking about my dad and brother, about my grandfather, about Javier Belmonte, and how he'd probably never pay for putting my family in ruins but how oddly enough he was what brought Warren into my life. I realized that amongst everything else, Warren Silva was not really a problem at all. And the fact that even saying his name made my heart thunder the way it did proved it—and also scared the hell out of me. He'd be leaving soon. So soon. And what would happen then? We'd become pen pals, writing each other emails and catching up via Skype when time allowed? Maybe I should just take a page from my own long book of advice and just enjoy it.

Chapter
EIGHTEEN

Camila

Adam and my sister got me a new bed, dresser, small dining room set, and a sofa set. Vanessa came by around three-thirty when the movers were finishing up and I was chasing behind them making sure they didn't scratch any surfaces of what they were delivering. She came with two different movers and lugged a huge television into my living room.

"It's a hand-me-down. I hope you don't mind," she said.

I gaped at her, at the TV, and back at her. "You guys are completely insane."

I hadn't realized how small my old TV was until I saw this one. I looked around in awe. I'd never owned this much furniture. Not my own. Not brand new from Restoration

Hardware of all places. After staring at the dark wood low bedframe and the beautiful sleek gray couches and the size of the flat-screen television, it sank in and I began to cry. Really cry. I couldn't believe my apartment looked like a real home and not some space deemed for a homeless person to squat in for a couple nights. A real home, warm and cozy, filled with all the things one needed to host a legitimate dinner party. My sister threw an arm around me and pulled me tightly into her.

"You deserve it, Peach. You so deserve it," she said into my hair as she held me.

"I can't believe you guys did this for me," I said and cried some more on her shoulder. I hugged and kissed her cheeks a few times before I was able to collect myself.

"I have to get home. We have a cocktail party tonight, but I fully expect a dinner invitation next week after the whole thing with Dad is done," she said.

"Thursday," I called out.

She smiled brilliantly over her shoulder. "Thursday it is. Enjoy your new bed. Maybe call lover boy to come help break it in."

My face heated at the thought of that. I hadn't even called him back yet. Judging from the radio silence on his end, he probably thought I didn't want to hear from him at all. I cleaned the new furniture, the floor, the counter tops, and headed to the basement to do my laundry. My new bed was now covered in clean sheets. I headed back down to get the second batch out of the dryer and marveled at how much easier it was to use the elevator. As I stood there, waiting for it so that I could go back upstairs, I jutted out my hip to settle the basket of clothes. And then, as if on cue, the un-mistakable sound of the elevator, air conditioning, and light switches came to a halt and went out all at once. My mouth dropped as I stared at the metal doors.

"You have got to be kidding me."

I let out a heavy sigh and turned toward the stairwell to head upstairs. Two flights of stairs later, I decided to stop by the front desk and ask what happened and when I could expect the power to come back on. I did have a new television to watch, after all. As I neared the front desk, I heard a persistent knocking on the glass door and glanced up, nearly dropping my basket at the sight of Warren standing on the other side. I froze for a second before walking over and opening the door.

"Your name isn't on the list yet," he said, tearing his gaze away from the list of names on the buzzer and looking at me from my sandal-wearing-feet, ever so slowly up my bare legs, taking in the tiny cotton shorts and off the shoulder shirt I had on until he finally reached my face.

"Oh."

It was all I could manage to say, and when he flashed me one of his wide smiles and my heart beats doubled in speed, I backed away slightly.

"Need help?" he asked, eyeing the basket in my hands.

"I . . . I'm fine. You can come up though, if you'd like."

"I'd like," he said.

He put his hands on my basket and I tried to resist, but he tilted his head and gave me a look that made me want to just give him everything, so I relented and let him take it from my hands. I pivoted, my wide eyes on the staircase as I tried to calm down. Warren Silva was coming up to my apartment, and even though he'd been to my old one, nobody had seen this one, this newly furnished one, my new home. I tried in vain to remember what panties I was wearing, but couldn't recall. My heart rattled with each step he took behind me. I hoped the squeaks of the floorboard were loud enough to mask my heavy breathing.

"Some of these need to be replaced," he commented.

I nodded but kept my eyes in front of me. It was bad enough that he was walking right behind me, no doubt looking at the tips of my ass that peeked out of my shorts. I tugged them down a little and he chuckled behind me.

"Please don't. I'm enjoying the view."

My face flushed and I was glad he couldn't see it.

When we finally made it to my floor, I practically pranced toward my apartment, and halfway there, the power switched back on.

"They're doing something to the power right outside the building," Warren said behind me. "I guess they must be done."

I stayed quiet, but opened the door and held it for him. I watched his face as he took the place in. His eyes bounced everywhere, from the kitchen to the television, couches.

"When did you get this?" he asked, meeting my eyes.

I smiled. "My sister and Adam bought it for me. They delivered it earlier today."

His eyes swept over the place once more before he looked at me and smiled, a heart-stopping smile that made my heart skip a beat.

"Where should I put this?"

"I'll take it," I said, but he refused to hand it over. I smiled. "You just want to see my room."

His lips twitched. "I thought you'd never ask."

"I didn't ask." I smiled. "Give me a second, though. I need to make sure it's not embarrassing."

"I want to see it just the way it is," he said, pinning me

with a gaze that warmed my skin. "The messy and out of control, and definitely the embarrassing."

He made me feel like he was talking about much more than just a messy bedroom. I pushed the door open and moved to push the decorative pillows back so he could set down the basket on the bed. He did and walked straight to my vanity mirror where I had put a picture of Vanessa and me, and one of Johnny, Vanessa, Mom, Dad and me. I watched as he carefully examined the one of my family. The only pictures I had with my dad were when I was a kid or a teenager and that one in particular, of us hanging out in Boca Chica was my favorite. It was one of the only memories I allowed myself to keep from that life, and only because we were happy then.

"You were even beautiful as a teenager," he said, his voice a low murmur.

I focused on my pillows, placing them on the bed strategically, small, big, small, as if I ever cared to do it on a regular basis. My hands stopped moving as Warren walked over to me, his scent enveloping me from behind as he placed his hands on my upper arms and leaned down to place a kiss on my bare shoulder.

"We need to talk," he said, but his tone unraveled me and I couldn't find it in me to talk about anything.

I turned around and tilted my head to look at him. I was sure he was going to kiss me, push me back on this bed and have his way with me. I wanted it. I wanted him so much.

"I can't think when you're this close to me," I whispered.

"That makes two of us," he said.

He dropped his face to mine until our lips melded together in a slow, soft, earth-shattering kiss. I held on to his biceps, my fingers gripping the grooves of his tight muscles.

The feel of his arms, the memory of the way he flexed each time he moved when he gripped me—my ass, my waist— made my heart work overdrive, my core tighten with need. I moaned into his mouth, deepening the kiss.

"You're not expecting any company right now, are you?" he asked, breaking the kiss.

I shook my head and grabbed a fistful of his shirt, urging him to take it off. He did quickly, pulling it over his head and tossing it to the side. My eyes made their way down his chest. I reached out a hand to touch him. No man-made sculpture would ever do his body justice.

"You're killing me here, Rocky," he said, his voice a low groan.

My eyes snapped back to his. "Undress me."

He didn't reach out right away and rip my shirt off (like I would have if he'd said the words to me). No, Warren took his time. His eyes searched mine as his hands gripped the hem of my shirt, his fingers tucking beneath it to caress my abdomen softly, slowly, as his eyes anchored me in place. I was beginning to feel suffocated with longing, with a need so powerful it buzzed through my veins. I closed my eyes and focused on breathing, on getting my heart to a more suitable beat, one that wouldn't make me feel like it was going to leap out from my throat. I'd never in my life wanted anybody this badly. I never thought it possible.

His hands moved then, slowly up my shirt, skimming my waist and cupping my breasts.

"I knew you weren't wearing a bra under this," he whispered.

"Please, Warren."

"Please what, pretty girl?" he said, bringing his mouth to the side of my neck. "Tell me what you want."

My heart leaped again. "You. Please."

I opened my eyes and met his gaze, and suddenly he began to move into action. He peeled my shirt off quickly, tossing it toward his, and tugged down my shorts and panties together and tossing them aside, his eyes blazing when they met mine again.

"You're a work of art," he said. I was breathing too hard to answer him, to tell him that *he* was the work of art.

He shook his head, stepping close to me again and grabbing me by the nape of my neck as he lowered his head to kiss me again. Our tongues clashed until I was dizzy. My hands flew to his belt, unbuckling it quickly.

"Take these off. Please," I said, my voice a grating tone I'd never heard before.

"I want to make you feel good," he said, kissing his way down my body and kneeling before me.

He made his way up my legs, kissing my calves and sucking on the insides of my thighs, his stubble brushing against me with each movement. I'd managed to stifle a moan at the feel of that, but when his tongue began to draw slow strokes over my clit, I shut my eyes and moaned out his name. My hands gripped on to the sheets beneath me as he parted my legs and stroked faster, my body flooding in hyperawareness with the feel of it. Of the tips of his fingers biting into my thighs as he pulled me farther apart and the way his mouth moved over me like a starved man. I felt myself convulse before I could lie back on my bed, my legs shaking relentlessly as jolts of ecstasy traveled through me.

"Please. Just . . . please," I pleaded, a loud chant as he continued pushing his tongue inside me in a fast pace before pulling it out and running it over my clit. Over and over. Repeatedly. Slowly, but effectively not letting the tension stop building inside. "I need to feel you inside me."

I was laying on my back, breathing heavily, my eyes closed when I heard the unmistakable sound of a condom wrapper. My eyes popped open. I'd missed the show. I'd seen it the other day, but still. I'd missed him taking his jeans and briefs off. The condom was in his right hand as he stroked himself with the other. I leaned up on my elbows to take in the size of him. There was no part of Warren that wasn't massive. The sight of him pleasuring himself as he looked at me was making me feel like I was going to come apart again. I sat up and got on my knees, placing my hand over his and pumping the way he was. He groaned loudly.

"Oh fuck, Camila."

I adjusted myself and leaned forward, my tongue darting out to lick the tip of his cock as my hand continued to move over him.

"Oh shit," he moaned, and when I put my mouth completely on him, he let out a long, deep groan that traveled all the way to my toes.

Soon, his hands were on my hair, pulling and making sure it didn't interrupt my pace, and his moans got deeper, my name dripping out of his mouth every time I did something he liked. I reached down with my free hand and found the ache in between my legs.

"You're touching yourself," he said, his voice a rasp. "Fuck. I'm going to come from the sight of you. From the feel of your mouth around me."

I moaned as my clit pulsed beneath my fingers.

"Camila," he said, voice low, breath heavy. "You need to stop. You need to fucking stop. I want to fuck you. I need to be inside you right now."

He pulled my hair so hard I had no choice but to move

with him. His chest was heavy with his breaths as he looked down at me, his eyes half-mast, lust-filled, crazed.

"You'll be the death of me, pretty girl," he said, grabbing my arms to position me so I was on all fours facing the window. He rammed into me with a force I'd never experienced, and I screamed, a full-out unexpected shriek.

"I want you to be loud. It's all I ever think about," he said, pounding into me, one hand gripping my waist, the other circling around my hair and pulling it tightly so I was arched. "How loud I can make this quiet little girl scream out my name," he said, pounding harder, if possible. I yelped, and he roared out his next words, "I knew you'd be loud. Fuck. You feel so good."

He let go of my hair and leaned forward, his rock-hard chest on my back as he quieted his movement and found my clit again. I felt like I was going to die from over-stimulation. It was too much. Too much. The pressure building, and building, my toes tingling, and when he pinched my clit and let go to hold my sides so he could ram into me hard. So fucking hard. I could feel him everywhere inside me, and my orgasm spread over me.

I screamed his name loudly, unabashed, and he groaned out mine one last time before emptying himself inside me. Even that was prominent, the feel of him dripping into the condom while he was inside me. I felt everything. I was glad I wasn't looking at him in that moment, because I feared he'd read right through me and see that this was no longer a friends-with-benefits fuck. I was afraid he'd see just how much I felt.

Chapter
NINETEEN

Warren

I hadn't planned on barging in the way I did, but once I saw her I couldn't stop myself. And I was glad for it. I was sitting at her new dining room table with a glass of whatever it was she'd served me. The last time I had real lemonade was when I was living with my grandparents in Barcelona. I took a small sip, cringing at the tart taste. I looked into the cup with a frown.

"What am I drinking?"

She laughed from the bedroom. She'd stayed in there folding clothes while I came to the dining room and took over her computer to look at the photos in the USB she'd been telling me about.

"It's called *Morir Soñando.* Do you like it?"

I felt my frown deepen. "To die dreaming?"

"Yes. Do you like it or not?" she asked, standing in the doorway of her room.

She placed a hand on her hip and raised an eyebrow, awaiting my response. I tried to keep my face neutral as I took another sip. Truth be told, it was delicious, whatever it was.

"I can tell you like it, you know," she said, her eyebrow still holding a challenge.

"Oh yeah? How's that?"

"Your get a distinct look in your eyes. It's like they widen a bit in wonder, and your bottom lip curves slightly."

I pushed my chair back to stand, not taking my eyes off her. As I walked over, she dropped her hand from her hip and swallowed visibly as her gaze made its way up my body. It left a scalding trail on every inch it wandered and I felt my heart pound louder. When I reached her, she tilted her head to meet my eyes just as I brought my hand up to cup the side of her face. Our bodies seemed to be in sync, yielding to every touch. Her breathing picked up as we looked at each other, my thumb caressing the soft skin of her now-colored cheek.

"Is that the look on my face right now?" I asked. Her eyes widened slightly. If I didn't know any better, I would've thought she was panicking. I whispered, "Tell me."

"I . . . I don't know," she stammered, tearing her gaze away from mine.

"Yes, you do."

She nodded slowly, her eyes sliding slowly back to meet mine. I lowered my face to kiss her. I couldn't be this close to her and not kiss her, not hold her, not touch her. And even though it was a bittersweet feeling, even though I knew I wasn't worthy of her, I kissed her again, and again, and again, until we needed to break apart.

"I don't deserve you," I said, a murmur against her lips. "But I can't let you go."

I dropped my hand and walked back to the table, taking a seat again and going back to the task at hand. I finally opened the first file of images and cringed, looking up at her again. She was still rooted to the same spot I'd left her in.

"You looked at these?"

She shrugged. I looked back at the screen and kept scrolling before skipping the second and third to open the fourth folder. It was a grainy image of me at a nightclub, the photo probably wouldn't have processed had it not been for the purple lights shining right at me at that very moment. My hair was different—shorter. My frame was thinner. I must have been twenty at most, but there was no mistaking it was me. There was also no mistaking what the blonde in the black dress was doing as she kneeled before me. There was a table blocking her from view, but my hand gripping the top of her head and my head thrown back . . . there was no mistaking that. My heart sank into the pit of my stomach. What the fuck had I been thinking? I shook my head. Even as the rage began to teeter inside me, waiting for an excuse to unleash at whoever sent this to Camila.

"Did you look at all of them?" I asked, swallowing as I waited for her response. I couldn't even look at her.

"Like four or five. I stopped when I got to what looked like was about to become a threesome."

Her soft voice beckoned my attention. When I finally looked at her, she was chipping at her nail polish with a disinterested look on her face, and that broke my heart more than an angry or upset look would have. I closed my eyes momentarily to gather my thoughts.

"Are you okay with what you saw?" I asked.

"Why wouldn't I be?" she asked, looking at me again. I stared at her, unable to think of anything good to say. "I'm not here to judge you, Warren. If that's how you live your life, then . . ." She shrugged again.

I groaned and stood up again, this time taking long, fast strides until I reached her and wrapping my arms around her to pull her closer. "That's not me anymore. That's stupid, young, bad-judgment, hot-head, twenty-something-year-old Warren."

She pulled back and looked up at me. "What's thirty-one-year-old Warren like?"

"Calm, cool, collected, classy, and very good in bed."

"And modest. You forgot modest," Camila said, shaking her head with a laugh.

I grinned. "Extremely modest."

While Camila put her clothes away, I packed up the USB and the letter with the full intention of going to my brother's house and confronting him about it. I just hoped by then I'd calm down and wasn't overcome with the urge to beat his face in. The last thing my mother needed was more heartache, especially because of me. I snuck out of Camila's bed around midnight, kissing her forehead lightly and smiling as the gentle snores she swore she didn't make. It would be easy to stay. It would be easy to tell myself that I was doing the right thing by wrapping my arms around her and holding her close to me all night. It was what I wanted to do, and that was exactly why I needed to leave.

Chapter
TWENTY

Warren

By the time I got to my brother's office, anger was all I felt. I tossed the manila envelope on his desk and crossed my arms. He tilted his head with a frown.

"You should leave and come back when you've calmed down and you find your manners," he said.

"Sure. Right after you find your balls."

He let out a chuckle and leaned forward in his seat to open the envelope. The USB slid out of it as did the paper. He read it with a confused look on his face.

"What am I supposed to do with this?" he asked, picking it up and sliding it into his computer drive.

I paced the length of his office as he clicked on the mouse.

"What the hell is this, War?" he asked. I could hear the

clear confusion in his voice, and I stopped pacing to meet his gaze.

When we were kids we'd play the staring game more than anything else. He'd always cave first, falling into a fit of laughter before we even got to half a minute. When he lied about something, I was always the first to call his bluff. We may not be kids anymore, but we were still brothers. Through good and bad, like Camila said. No matter how long we were apart, we were brothers. Family. A year ago, I wouldn't have forgiven him if he did this to me, but as I stood there, looking into the same green eyes I had, thinking about our childhood and Camila's words, I felt like if he explained himself and apologized to her, I just might.

"Did you do this?"

"Do what?"

"Send this to Camila."

He rolled his eyes and scoffed. "Of course this is about that girl."

"Did you?" I asked, louder, getting closer to his desk, bracing myself on the opposite side of him.

"Why the . . ." He let out a harsh breath and shook his head, pinching the bridge of his nose. "Warren, do you really . . ." He paused again, shaking his head as if he was trying to make room in there for something so crazy it might not fit.

"Answer the question!"

"I don't know what concerns me more, that you think I have time to play these stupid games or the fact you're this worked up about it. This is you, War. This is you. Maybe it's better she sees it now and not after you buy her a goddamn apartment." His lips twitched. "Maybe I should use another example."

I sat down in one of the chairs in front of him and

sighed. I wasn't in the mood for volleying insults right now, no matter how stupid they were. I had to figure out who the fuck would send this to Camila. Nobody else knew about her.

"Who would do this?"

"Maybe Sergio."

Sergio, my agent. I shook my head. No way. I hadn't even told Sergio about her. I told my brother as much and he shrugged.

"Whoever did it has access to you. It's someone you're with often." He looked back at the screen. "How many threesomes have you had?"

"Enough."

"Christ. I should've blown off my last name and moved to Spain."

Despite myself, I laughed, though it fell flat the moment my gaze caught on the Manila envelope on top of his desk again. My brother noticed.

"Does this girl really mean that much to you or are you just scared these pictures will get out and tarnish your reputation?"

My lips curled into a tight smile. "You mean confirm my reputation."

He chuckled, amusement glimmering in his eyes. "So this is about the girl?"

"She's not like Elena," I said, hoping the finality in my voice traveled through to him.

"If you say so."

"She's not. She's . . . good. Real."

"Because she doesn't have fake tits and lip injections?"

I rolled my eyes. Most of the women I'd dated had fake tits. That didn't make them any less smart or beautiful. "Melanie has fake tits."

His smile widened. "I paid good money for those."

"You're such a dick."

He let out a heavy sigh and rubbed his face. "Look, War, you know I love you and despite all the stupid shit you've done, I try to stand by you, but after what happened with Elena—"

"It's not like she emptied out my bank account and left me scraping for money. I do make a good living, you know?"

He shot me a look. "You acted like a lost little rich boy after she fucked you over and we were the ones who had to deal with the questions and fucking CNN calling us on a daily basis to get exclusive interviews about Warren Silva and his grim future in soccer."

I bent my head and looked at the floor. It wasn't something I'd been proud of. Getting those calls from my mom in hysterics, and worse, my grandparents telling me they didn't raise me to be the kind of young man who treated women with such disrespect after I called Elena a whore in a local newspaper after a night out of heavy drinking. The biggest blow was when my father finally did give his exclusive interview and called me a "no-good bastard" whom he "always knew would turn out to be a let down." Those words would forever be etched in my brain. I looked at my brother again, meeting his gaze one last time before I got up to walk away.

"Camila is the best thing that's happened to me in a really long time, and I'm not going to let anything mess this up."

"Warren," my brother called out. When I looked over my shoulder, he was looking at me with a solemn expression. "I hope you realize that you don't need any help fucking this up, and even if you don't, you live in different countries."

He wasn't wrong, but I was going to do everything in my

power to enjoy the time I had with her and that meant not letting anybody else come between us.

Chapter
TWENTY-ONE

Camila

'd been at Penn Station for two hours waiting for the train to be fixed. With each passing minute, the sinking feeling I wasn't going to make it to my mom's house multiplied. My phone buzzed in the back pocket of my jeans and I sighed as I reached for it.

"Is this Camila?" a little voice asked.

I frowned, looking at the screen, which had Warren's name written across it. "Yes. Who's this?"

"Cayden."

I smiled. "Hi buddy. How are you?"

"Good. Can you come over today? I have ice cream."

"I would love to, but I can't. I'm at the train station and the train is broken. I'm waiting for a superhero to come fix it."

"Which one?"

I shook my head, still smiling and looked up and down the platform. "I'm not sure."

"Maybe Thor will go."

"Ha. If Thor shows up I'll never leave."

"Why not?"

There was clear confusion in his voice and I decided not to respond to that. Explaining the whole crush on Thor thing didn't seem like the right thing to do when talking to a kid.

"Where's your uncle?"

"He's here. He came to visit me at home. You should come next time," he said before whispering his next words, "He says you're prettier than Wonder Woman."

I smiled.

"I said you're the most beautiful woman in the world, Cayden. Get it right if you're going to relay messages for me," Warren said into the line.

"Hey," I whispered.

"I miss you," he whispered back.

"I miss you too."

Why the hell were these butterflies so persistent and why did he insist on saying things that put them there to begin with?

"Did you make it to your mom's house?"

I sighed heavily, leaning against the cold wall behind me. "No, and from the looks of it I may have to wait until tomorrow. They've been fixing this train for two hours."

"Where are you?"

"I just . . ." I shook my head, realizing he had no idea what station I was in. "At Penn Station."

"I'm coming to get you."

"What? No. If they cancel again I'll just go home and try

back again tomorrow."

"Stay there. I'm coming right now."

"Warren."

"Camila, stay there. I'm already on my way."

I begrudgingly agreed and went outside to wait for him. When the SUV arrived, I walked toward it swiftly. Warren got out of the driver's side and rounded the car to open the door for me.

"What the . . . ?" I frowned, squinting to look inside the cab. "You're driving?"

"Antoine had the night off."

I climbed in the car and waited for him to do the same. As I buckled my seatbelt, I glanced over at him. "You know how to drive?"

He shot me a look. "Obviously."

"Hey, I don't know how to drive. I'm just asking."

"You don't know how to drive?"

"No. Why would I need to know how to drive? I take the train everywhere."

My phone vibrated in my hands as he was pulling out of the space, and I answered it when I saw my sister's name.

"Are you coming?" she asked.

I explained to her the entire situation, which she explained to my mom who was in the same room as her, and when she responded there had already been a collective vote on, "Bring Warren."

"Vanessa," I hissed, and lowered my voice into a whisper, "you told her about him?"

"Didn't you just hear me repeating every word you said? Bring him and stop being an idiot."

"I'll see." I hung up the phone and glanced over at him. "Why are you smiling?"

"You want to keep me a secret," he said, still smiling as he looked over at me.

"I . . . It's not . . ." I sighed. "You don't know how my mom is. She's crazy."

"I like crazy."

"This isn't the kind of crazy you like."

"How do you know what kind of crazy I like?"

I shrugged. "She's judgmental. She'll take one look at you and decide you're in a gang."

He chuckled. "Because of my tattoos?"

"And the whole super-ripped body and pierced-nipples thing, yeah." I turned bright red when I said the last part, thinking about the way they felt beneath my fingers.

"I don't mind being judged," he said. "Trust me, I have thick skin. I want to go. I want to take you."

"Did you hear me when I told you how far of a drive it was?"

"Three hours."

"Don't you have things to do? This is a weekend thing."

"Camila," he said, beckoning my eyes when he stopped at the next red light. "Stop stalling. There's nowhere I'd rather be than with you."

Chapter
TWENTY-TWO

Warren

"**I**s your dad already there?" I asked.

We'd stopped by the apartment to get my clothes and while I was there I made some calls and sent some emails to my agent and publicist to let them know I'd be unreachable for the next two days. I never said that, but I knew it was the only way they'd respect my time away.

"He gets home tomorrow morning," she responded.

I nodded, wondering if I should keep probing the subject. She'd been through enough for one night but I was curious and we had a long drive ahead of us. And I was going to meet the guy.

"You said your mom is judgmental, so I'm assuming your dad is the opposite?"

She was quiet for so long I thought she wasn't going to answer my question. I glanced over quickly, and caught her as she readjusted herself in the seat, folding one of her legs under the other. She rested her chin on her knee and smiled. I looked back at the road and waited for her to talk.

"I don't know. I don't know enough about him anymore." She paused. "He didn't used to be, though. He was smart, and kind, and a genius. And I'm not just saying that. He really was. He moved here from DR when we were small, studied for a degree, accepted a great job at a bank and just succeeded in everything he ever did. At least that's what it seemed like."

She lifted her head and looked out the window. I let go of the gearstick I'd been holding on to out of habit and reached over to squeeze her knee. Her face whipped to me.

"How'd he end up in jail?" I asked.

"Javier Belmonte offered him a job he couldn't refuse. Bonuses, health care, an apartment upgrade, private schools for his kids. Back then we were living in a small two-bedroom in Queens. I don't know who was happier about the promotion, my dad or my brother, who was seventeen and had been sharing a room with Vanessa and me for years."

I smiled. "I'm sure they were both equally as happy."

"We moved to this huge apartment on the Upper East Side and suddenly went from sharing a room in that tiny apartment to having a closet the size of my parents' bedroom all to myself. It was fun while it lasted." She paused, smiling. "Anyway, one day that was our life. Next, I'm waiting for my mom to pick me up in my dad's office, and the next police officers are reading him his rights over a Ponzi-type scheme."

My eyes widened. I kept my eyes on the road. Javier had only done two months in jail, from what I recall. I'd gotten the cliff notes version of the story from Tom a while back, and remembered there were other colleagues involved, but never thought to ask what happened to their families. I glanced at her.

"Why do you think your dad did so much more time than Javier?"

"My brother says it's because of Javier's powerhouse lawyers."

"What do you say?"

Our eyes met briefly. "I think he pinned it all on my dad."

Chapter
TWENTY-THREE

Camila

I was glad we got it all out in the open on the way to my mom's and were able to talk about lighter things afterward, but when we reached the woodsy area around her house and Warren started squinting in the dark to see if he could find the house, the light feelings were overshadowed with nervousness.

"It's that one," I said, pointing at the last house on the block.

"It's nice," he commented as he drove between the trees alongside the driveway and parked in front of the two-car garage.

My mom's house was nice. It was one of the things she'd accepted from Javier when my dad was arrested and Javier was set free. The other was a monthly check to cover expenses. It still came in every month, even after she told him she'd found a job and no longer needed it, and while I was put off by the idea of using the money the court had been sending me until my eighteenth birthday, my mom welcomed it. I saw it as blood money, she saw it as a right. Warren took both of our bags in his hands when we got out. I looked over at him to examine him again. He was still wearing jeans and a black T-shirt, showing off his toned arms and tattoos, which I loved to see, but my mom would definitely have words with me about.

"You don't seem nervous," I said.

"Should I be?" he asked, raising his brows as I rang the doorbell.

I shifted from one foot to the other. "Remember, if my mom gives you dirty looks, it's only because she doesn't understand some things. Specifically tattoos. So if she stares just . . ."

His eyes twinkled in amusement. "Should I hide them?"

"Very funny."

"Is that why you're so nervous? Because of my tattoos?"

"I guess." I pushed the doorbell again. "Why aren't you nervous?"

"Parents always love when women bring me home with them."

"They do?" I asked, looking over at him.

Jealousy unfurled deep inside me but I pushed it down. He wasn't mine and whatever he did before me was not my business. I'd seen enough of his past to know he had quite a string of women's houses to visit if he wanted. Warren turned his body to face mine and looked at me for a long, silent moment before a smile bloomed on his otherwise serious face.

"I don't think I've met one parent who liked me, but if it makes you feel any better, I hope yours do."

I reached a hand up to brush his perpetual five-o'clock-shadow just as the door opened. I instantly dropped my hand and whipped my head in that direction. My mom was studying Warren, and from the way her eyes cut to mine fast and wide, I was given no time to figure out whether or not she approved before she threw her arms around me and pulled me into a tight hug.

"You're finally here," she said as she let me go and kissed both my cheeks. "We were so worried you wouldn't make it."

"I'm only here thanks to Warren." I turned to him. "Warren, this is my mom, Rosa."

In a completely uncharacteristic move, she threw her arms around him and kissed his cheek as well. "Thank you for picking Camila up and bringing her to me. I hope you stay the weekend."

He smiled as they moved away from each other. "No need to thank me. There's nothing I'd rather be doing. Thank you for inviting me."

She frowned. "Where are you from?"

"New York." He chuckled when she put a fist on her hip and her frown deepened. "I live in England now and the accent seems to have stuck, though according to them I sound like a Yankee, and according to everybody here, I sound like a Brit."

Mom laughed. "You definitely don't sound like a us."

I wanted to point out that she didn't either, but didn't bother. Vanessa and Adam joined us in the kitchen shortly after we arrived, and by the end of the night, after Mom insisted we had bread and hot cocoa, she and Warren were speaking to each other in Spanish and having conversations as if they'd known each other their entire lives while my sister and I shot shocked glances at each other. I excused myself from the table and started cleaning up with Vanessa's help, Adam excused himself because he was exhausted, and my mom looked over at Warren.

"Come. I'll show you to your room so you can settle Camila's and your things in there," Mom said in Spanish.

Vanessa dropped the spoons she was washing, causing a loud clatter and I stopped walking dead in my tracks, just barely keeping hold of the mugs in my hand. We all looked in my sister's direction. She just stood there, water running onto her hands, with her mouth agape. It was most likely the same expression I held on my face.

"Vanessa! Watch what you're doing before you break something and get hurt," Mom chastised before walking away with Warren, who shot us an amused look over his shoulder.

"I'm in shock," my sister whispered.

"So am I." I set the mugs down shakily. "Like, really shocked."

"Maybe this is a test. Maybe she's expecting Warren to decline that offer and say he'll stay elsewhere since you guys aren't married."

"Probably."

"Remember when she did that to Adam in Punta Cana?"

We rarely took family trips, and it was even more rare for us to visit DR and go to a resort. We normally bounced between family members' houses and never worried about rooms or food, which were plentiful. When Vanessa and Adam first got engaged, we decided to celebrate by going to DR and instead of staying with family the entire time, we stayed in one of the hotels our friends so often bragged about. We'd booked four rooms: one for me, one for my mom and grandmother, one for my brother, and one for Vanessa and Adam, or so we thought. Until my mom laughed and looked at us like we'd all lost our minds.

"No. One room is for you and your sister to share. Adam can stay with Johnny," Mom specified after getting quite a laugh at the situation. Of course the remainder of the trip was spent with Adam and I sneaking out in the middle of the night and swapping rooms so my sister could sleep with her fiancé. Even though it was annoying, it was better than the alternative, which would have included me sharing a room with the two of them.

I scoffed. "How can I forget?"

"You have no idea how easy you have it. Johnny and I paved the way for this moment," she said, shaking her head. "I can't believe she's letting you guys sleep in the same room under her roof."

I didn't know what she wanted me to do. Thank her for being the first daughter and guinea pig? I didn't say anything at all and continued to pick up the table instead. Mom joined us when we were finishing up.

"I like him," she said.

Vanessa rolled her eyes. "But not Adam?"

"I love Adam."

"Is it because Adam doesn't speak Spanish?" my sister asked, still annoyed.

Mom shook her head, smiling. "I already told you. I love Adam. Stop acting like a spoiled brat and get over the Punta Cana thing. These are different times."

"That was like four years ago, Mom."

"Bueno, Vanessa. No se que decirte," Mom replied.

"You don't know what to say because there's nothing to say."

"Can't you just be happy for your sister?"

"I am happy for my sister," Vanessa said, raising her voice. "My being happy for her and being upset that you clearly don't accept my husband are not mutually exclusive. I can be both, you know?"

"I have bigger things to worry about right now, Vanessa. Por favor. Your brother gets in tomorrow morning and he needs a room to sleep in. I don't have enough room for him, your uncle, your aunt, and your sister's boyfriend so they have to share a room. Grow up and get over it." Mom started to walk away, shaking her head. "And Adam knows I love him like a son, so don't give me that shit."

We both stayed quiet as she walked away. My sister had stopped wiping the mug in her hand in the middle of my mom's rant, and I just stood there, eyes wide as I watched her walk away, her big hips swaying exaggeratedly in the black dress she wore. When my sister and I began developing our curves, my aunts would have elaborate conversations about which one of us would end up with the body type of my mom's side of the family: thin waist, thick hips. Or my dad's side of the family: long and lanky. We were a mix of both. Vanessa was taller than I was, and I had a little more room in my hips than she had, but not much. Though we both had decent-sized boobs and butts, neither one of us had quite developed the vivacious Gonzalez hips. When mom disappeared into the back of the house, we both sighed and faced each other.

"I'm going to bed," I said. "Are you going to wake up early for breakfast with Johnny?"

She shrugged. "Are you?"

"I don't know. I guess we should, right?"

"I guess."

By the time I made it to my room, Warren had completely made himself at home. He was lying down, shirtless, under the plush white covers with his phone in his hand. He put it down and glanced up at me, a slow smile spreading over his lips.

"I was going to unpack for you, but wasn't sure you wanted me snooping through your underwear."

I looked over at the bags we brought. "You unpacked?"

"Your mom made it very clear I should make myself at home and unpack. She even opened up the empty drawers and offered to help."

My eyes widened. "She didn't."

"She did," Warren said, looking completely amused. Sinful, welcoming, and amused.

"Vanessa was having a fit because we're sharing a room."

He frowned. "What does it matter to her?"

"Long story, but my parents are old school and not okay with this kind of stuff."

"You're in your mid-twenties," he said, as if I needed a reminder.

"Like I said, old school."

Warren sighed, running a hand through his hair. "I get it. My grandmother is the same way. When I lived with her I wasn't allowed to have girls in my room."

"I can imagine that put a damper in a lot of teenage playboy Warren's plans."

He chuckled. "Not really. I snuck them in when she went to bed."

"Of course you did," I said, smiling and shaking my head.

I put away my things and took my pajamas into the ensuite bathroom with me. I stepped into the shower with the full intention of washing away the day's worry, but as soon as I closed my eyes under the spray, I started to cry thinking about seeing my dad tomorrow. By the time I got out of the shower, instead of looking sexy for Warren, I looked like a hot mess, with puffy red eyes. At least my lips look soft. I sighed as I looked at my reflection while I brushed my teeth and shut the lights after picking up after myself. I tried to hide my face by turning off the lamp on my side of the bed and not looking directly at Warren, but I could feel his eyes on the side of my face and knew I was doing a shit job at it.

"Come here," he said.

The scratchy tone in his voice made him impossible to ignore. I climbed into bed, taking my time to pull the covers up to cover me as I scooted in beside me. His arm went around my shoulder and he pulled me into his side, pressing his lips to the top of my head before pulling back to look at me. A small frown formed on his face as his eyes searched mine for a beat before he pulled me into his side again.

"I've got you, baby."

His voice was so soft, so caring, so unlike every other time it was near my ear that I nearly cried again. Instead, I pressed the side of my cheek onto his chest and breathed him in, relishing the way he smelled and how it felt like nothing could touch me as long as I was inside the protection of his strong arms. The thought of him leaving soon came crashing through me, and I had to blink away tears at that too. We were quiet for a long moment as we lay there.

"Your mom said no funny business," he whispered, his breath tickling my ear. "So try not to rub up against me tonight."

I smiled. "You're not the only one who used to sneak people into their bedroom, you know?"

He reared away to get a good look at my face and raised

an eyebrow, lips twitching. "Is that right?"

I nodded.

"Well, in that case, try to keep your voice down," he said, dipping his hand into the front of my boy shorts as he crashed his lips to mine.

Chapter
TWENTY-FOUR

Camila

Johnny rang the doorbell at nine o'clock in the morning and from then on, the day seemed to move fast. Vanessa and I cleaned up the house while the guys set up tables and chairs for the party. Warren and Adam went on ice and beer runs; Johnny set up the music equipment that Adam said looked a decade old and prompted Warren and him to go to Best Buy and buy new speakers and music playing equipment. Vanessa shook her head as they brought the boxes in. I gaped at Warren while he laughed.

"I can't believe you bought this. My mom is going to kill you, just so you know," I said. He grinned and winked as he opened one of the boxes.

"Yeah, she may even kick you out of the room and make

you sleep elsewhere," Vanessa added.

Warren's smile instantly fell. His eyes snapped to mine, waiting for me to dispute her words. I shrugged, trying to fight a smile. "I told you, my mom's crazy. You never know."

Adam chuckled as he set up one of the speakers. "Don't listen to them, man."

"Listen to them about what?" my brother asked as he joined us in the patio.

He frowned as he looked at Warren. They hadn't met because when he arrived, Warren had gone out for a run, and when he came back to take a shower, my brother had gone out to fill up Mom's car with gas. Now they were standing, facing each other like they were ready for a duel. My brother would inevitably lose, if push literally came to shove, but would one-hundred percent win if it was a battle between who could give better insults. I wasn't sure I wanted to introduce them.

"What the—" my brother started. "Are you Warren Silva?"

Warren's eyes bounced to me and back at my brother. Mine bounced to my sister and back at my brother. How the hell did he know who he was? Warren wiped his hand over his jeans and put it out to shake Johnny's.

"Pleased to meet you," he said.

Johnny's jaw dropped as he shook his hand. "What the hell are you doing in my house?"

"Mom's house," Vanessa mumbled.

I tried and failed to contain a smirk. Johnny glared at her momentarily before looking at Warren again.

"I'm here with your sister," Warren explained.

Johnny, if possible, frowned even more. "Which one?"

I rolled my eyes. "Me, dumbass."

"You?" he nearly shouted before looking back at Warren and lowering his voice to a near whisper, "You're kidding."

Warren seemed confused by his reaction. I wasn't. Vanessa, who under any other circumstance would have egged Johnny on and turned him into even more of a jerk until they both managed to make me cry, rolled her eyes and came to my defense instead.

"Why's that so hard to believe? You move to DR for three years and you think you know us so well?" she said, crossing her arms.

Johnny chuckled. "What happened? You move back to the hood and dropped the fake princess vibe you had going in that pretty little brownstone of yours?"

"You're seriously going to start this on the day Papi gets home?" I asked, glaring at my brother.

That sobered him up. He took a deep breath and let it out slowly. "Sorry. I just wasn't expecting this and I definitely wasn't expecting him to come with you."

"What is that supposed to mean?" Warren asked.

His voice was calm, cool, and collected, his words spoken nonchalantly, but he looked murderous. Johnny must have been paying more attention to the way his eyes were shooting daggers at him and his jaw was clenching, or maybe the way his knuckles seemed to have gone white as he gripped the bubble wrap in his hand. He moved back with his hands held up in defense.

"I didn't mean anything bad by it. I just wouldn't expect a broke girl living in Harlem who's paying a million student loans meeting a guy like you." My brother looked over at me. "Do you even know what soccer is?"

I put my middle finger up to him, not bothering to respond with words. Sometimes silence was the best answer.

And a middle finger. That helped.

"She knows me," Warren said, looking right at me. "And that's worth much more than her knowing me for the sport."

Johnny seemed satisfied with that response. He nodded and smiled as he scratched his goatee. "How long has this been going on?"

"Not long," I said.

"Long enough," Warren said at the exact same time.

Our eyes met. My heart dipped at the expression in his eyes, as if *long enough* meant more. He gave me that flirty, lopsided smile of his that he knew damn well drove women everywhere, including myself, wild, and I felt my face heat.

"Mom's letting them share a room," Vanessa said.

Oh mother. I closed my eyes with a sigh.

"She what?" Johnny yelled.

When I looked over at him again, he was studying Warren closer, as if he was no longer some prized soccer player he knew about, but some random guy we let into our house. My brother had never accepted any guy we brought home with ease. It was always an interrogation, a background check provided by his cop buddies, a long talk with Mom as to why it was a terrible idea to let us date the guys. Mom always listened politely and then laughed it off with us over wine. He's just trying to look out for you, she'd say. It's what your father would have done, she'd add. It always annoyed both my sister and me. We didn't want him doing what our father would've done. We wanted our father back.

"Stay out of it," I said.

"Not gonna happen, bruh," Johnny said, looking at me and then at Warren. "But I'll let it be for now."

For now took an hour, tops. I heard him talking to Warren and Adam while I was filling the coolers outside.

Mom had gone to pick up Dad. She said she wanted to go by herself so they could catch up on the ride home, though I couldn't imagine how much catching up they'd need given she'd been the only one allowed to visit him all those years. Warren and Adam went out to give us privacy when Dad arrived. I wasn't sure how Vanessa felt about it, but I was glad for it. The three of us paced the living room, the kitchen, the dining room, and finally, stood by the window peering out. When Mom's old black Mercedes pulled into the driveway, my left hand found Vanessa's and Johnny's closed over my right. We walked like that, hand in hand, toward the door and stood there, our grips tighter as the door opened. I thought Johnny would break my bones for sure, but it was fleeting, because when Dad walked in the three of us took a collective breath and the force of it made me feel like I was going to pass out.

He looked old. And shorter than I remembered him. I was expecting him to be skinny, in shape even, but his belly was round and pressed to the plaid short sleeve button-down he was wearing. His hair had more white than brown and his skin was more pale than I remembered it. His eyes were honey, the same color as mine, but the warmth had left them, the light had been drained from them. I also expected to feel something when I saw him again. Anger, pain, happiness . . . something. I'd felt more in the years, the weeks, the days, the hours leading up to the moment than I did right now. I did feel something unexpected as I looked around the room, at my brother, my sister, my mother, my father . . . I felt peace.

I wasn't sure who moved first, maybe Johnny, but we ended up in a group hug. When we managed to pull ourselves together one by one, again in birth order, we went back for individual hugs. Mom took pictures on her phone from the corner.

"You've grown up so much. Mom shows me pictures, but . . . it's not the same," Dad said, his voice hoarse as he looked at me.

"It could've been the same. You could've let us visit," I managed to say through my tears.

Then he started to cry. Really cry. He pulled me into him and I let him because the onslaught of tears that came and my heavy breathing as I tried to hold them back to no avail made it impossible to stop. I took a deep breath and even though he didn't carry the scent of his cologne, he smelled like cigarettes. My dad always smelled like cigarettes. And that was enough to make me smile. I backed away and wiped my eyes as he held both my shoulders with his hands, his face still wet from previously shed tears.

"I'm sorry," he said.

It was all he needed to say, and I couldn't find mine to say anything at all. Thankfully, Mom brought back food and gave us something to do while we killed time before people started to arrive for the party. I heard the door open again while we were clearing the table, and Adam walked in. My sister jumped up quickly and introduced him to Dad and they hugged as if they'd known each other forever. Dad had never been a man of many words, or many hugs, so this version of him was foreign. Then, Warren walked in. He stayed back, waiting for Adam to have his moment. He looked unsure of what to do, so Mom introduced them. They looked at each other for a long time. I held my breath. He was going to say something about his tattoos. He was going to insult him and tell him to get out. I was prepared to leave if he did that.

Instead, Dad did the most unexpected thing. He started to cry again, quietly, wiping the tears as they escaped his eyes so they didn't even reach his face. He shook Warren's hand and looked at me as if he couldn't believe I had a boyfriend. I didn't bother to tell him that Warren was not my boyfriend. Not that Mom had introduced him that way. She'd said he was my friend—Mom had called my boyfriends my *special friends* until I was twenty and begged her to stop.

Around eight, the music began to play, and people started to arrive. Warren and I hadn't had a moment to ourselves since that morning and with each passing hour I was regretting I'd left the comfort of his arms so early. My brother brought out a roasted pig, with the help of a few cousins, and my aunts contributed with rice and other sides. Everybody was joyous, drinking, eating, and dancing. The women in my family seemed more interested in talking to Warren than they were in finding out how my dad had held up. All of them. I hated every single moment of it, but Warren was smiling at them every time I looked over, so I had no choice but to let it be. When I looked again, he was talking to my dad, and that was a conversation I didn't want to intrude in.

Instead, I danced. With my cousins. With old family friends. With friends my brother grew up with who knew Dad and had come to show support. One in particular, Tony, was a little tipsy and wouldn't let me sit down. When the music changed from merengue to bachata, I paused on the dance floor. Tony didn't skip a beat. He gave me a salacious smile that I'd seen work on my cousin Lari five New Year's Eve parties back, and pulled me tighter, until my chest met his and our pelvises were in sync. When he started to move and I had no choice but to move with him, but before Romeo Santos even got to sing the hook, Warren was at my side.

"I think my girlfriend has been too generous with her time," he said, not bothering to ask if he could cut in on our dance before he pulled me away and stood in front of me, mimicking the same stance Tony and I had a second ago. I smiled up at him.

"You don't know how to dance this, do you?"

His eyes sparkled as he chuckled. "No, but I wasn't going to stand by and watch you dance it with another man."

"You had no issue with the million other songs I danced while you talked," I said.

I started to lead the dance, trying to test out whether or not he could pick it up without me actually having to count the one, two, three, bounce steps.

"You weren't standing this close to anybody when you were dancing those," he said, his voice in my ear as he moved in sync with me. "This is a bedroom dance."

"It is," I said, surprised I could even find my voice with my heart pounding that hard against his chest. "You know, when my mom was growing up she couldn't even dance this at parties. It was reserved for engaged and married couples only."

"Yeah?" He pulled back to look at my face. He lost his step and stopped moving. I nodded seriously. He leaned in again and began to move. "I like that rule. They shouldn't have changed it."

I laughed, squeezing the arm I had behind his back and hugging him a little closer. "We wouldn't be dancing if that was the rule."

He reared back again to meet my gaze. "I would have to propose."

My breath left me in an instant. My smile dropped. My heart stopped.

I blinked.

And blinked.

Finally, not because I wanted to, but because my brother brought out the guira and began to play it along with the music and told us to keep dancing, I swallowed and moved again. I was grateful my chin was against his shoulder and my eyes were on the instrument my brother was rattling. Why would he say that to me? Why would he say that to me and look at me with such a serious expression? He's not supposed to make me fall in love with him. He's not even my type. He doesn't even belong in this world. But as we stood there in the middle of a makeshift dance floor, surrounded by people who'd watched me grow up, helped change my diaper, some whom I'd changed, I couldn't help but feel like this was exactly where we belonged. Together.

That was until he stepped on my foot. I stopped moving and looked up at him. He flinched.

"Just one question before I teach you how to dance this correctly, what do you dance in Spain? Flamenco?"

Warren smiled. "I can do paso doble."

"Okay." I laughed. "No idea what that is. This is easy. It's three steps repeated over and over, the important part is remembering when to do a little hop and to move your hips. Always move your hips."

"I don't have a problem moving my hips." He winked.

I blushed. "You need to stop flirting with me in front of my family."

"I really want to kiss you."

"Warren."

"And fuck you," he said, bringing his face closer, until his lips were beside my ear and his voice was more of a purred growl. "I really, really want to fuck you, pretty girl."

Oh mother. My knees began to shake. "Please dance."

"Can you feel how badly I want you?" he pulled me

closer to him. I could definitely feel it. I closed my eyes and moved. One step, two steps, three steps.

"Bring your foot up a little here," I whispered, swallowing.

"I want to take you upstairs right now, pull up that tight little red dress you're wearing, and bend you over the bed."

One step back, two steps back, three steps back. "Remember to do a little hop here."

"And slam into you," he said while doing the little hop I told him to do. "Balls deep."

I felt my heart plummet into my stomach. My breath picked up. I stopped moving, no longer being able to put up the charade. He was affecting me too much. My body. My mind. My heart. I couldn't take it. He gave me a knowing smile that I had the sudden urge to slap away. Instead, I squeezed the hand I was holding. Warren chuckled.

"Good thing I don't need my hands for my career."

"No, but you need your knees," I said, narrowing my eyes. "You've been warned."

That made him laugh harder. We spent the rest of the night like that, with family, laughing, talking, eating, and I threw caution to the wind. I let myself be happy, be in the moment. Dad motioned for me a few times, danced with me once, cried again when he danced with Vanessa at the regret that he hadn't been there to dance at her wedding and promised to make amends for everything he'd missed. It felt right. The night felt right. Everything clicked in place for our family. Sure, it would take time for all of us to get used to the dynamic again, but we'd do it. Having Warren there to hold my hand and kiss my cheek every so often helped, and despite knowing that he was leaving soon, I let my guard down completely and relished every moment.

Chapter
TWENTY-FIVE

Warren

The morning I left for Manchester, I had knots in my stomach. I wasn't sure why. I'd never been a nervous flyer before. Maybe it was because Camila had stayed behind, though she promised she'd get on the plane and meet me there Thursday. Maybe it was because my father's health was going from bad to worse and I didn't know how to feel about it. On one hand, I hadn't had a relationship with him for over ten years; on the other, seeing the way Camila welcomed her dad with open arms made me reconsider my own situation. Maybe I needed to try harder.

Thankfully, I slept during the flight. When I landed, I switched on my phone expecting to see a message from Camila—I'd given her the number before I left—but all I had were emails and social media notifications that I didn't feel like scrolling through. As I walked down the hall that led to the private lounges, I spotted my agent Sergio waiting for me with a tight smile on his face as he spoke on the phone. I put my phone away as I reached him and gave him a quick hug as he continued to talk on the phone. Sergio had become more than just an agent to me. *He* was family. We'd spent Christmases together in his family home. I was the godfather of one of his children. His wife treated me like her own son, and everything they'd ever done for me was in my best interest, so I didn't question him when he got off the phone and told me that the club in Barcelona was interested in paying me and my club to loan me for five years.

"What do you think?" he asked as he drove me to his house, where I'd left one of my cars.

I sighed, leaning back in my seat. What did I think? Even before they'd acquired the great footballers they had, Barcelona had been where I wanted to play. That was before Chelsea acquired me and Manchester after that. Each time, I'd hoped for Barcelona. I had a non-trade clause in my contract, which meant I had the option to take or turn down any offer made, but every summer when the transfer window opened up between July first and August thirty-first, I held my breath waiting for the moment Barcelona might make an offer. That was before Stephen came over to our team, though. We'd finally built something that felt more like family and were playing like it.

"I thought this would be good news," Sergio said as we pulled into his driveway. "You've been waiting for this. It's great money."

"Not everything is about the money."

Sergio glanced over, blue eyes wide. "What? I'm sure I've

misheard you. Did you just say that not everything is about the money?"

I got out of the car and walked over to the back of his Ferrari as he popped the trunk. He was still staring at me as I took my carry-on bag out and placed it on the ground.

"What?"

"Aren't you going to come inside and say hello to Miriam? I think we have some food leftover from earlier."

I smiled and followed him in knowing damn well that wasn't why he wanted me to stick around, but unable to resist a home-cooked meal. Sergio didn't like to leave conversations unfinished. He preferred his clients slept over if they needed to as long as he received a conclusive answer as to what they were going to do. Miriam was in the kitchen putting dishes away when we walked in.

"There you are," she said, coming around the counter to kiss her husband before giving me a tight hug. "I missed having you around here. How was the US? How many broken-hearted women did you leave behind this time?"

I chuckled and ignored the question. "Where's Penelope?"

"You just missed her," Miriam said. "I'm sure she'll be sad to know her favorite uncle came by while she was out."

"I think she's seeing one of the guys," Sergio grumbled. "I just don't know which one. He better hope it's over before I find out."

My eyes widened. "You're kidding."

He shook his head; Miriam shrugged. Sergio and Miriam housed guys that attended one of the local boarding schools and couldn't afford to go home during the summer. I hadn't met any this summer, but they were usually a good group. Some of them had already started playing professional football. Penelope had never shown interest in them in the past, though, so I didn't think Sergio could be right about that. They were older than her, not by much, but old enough to know better than to be with the daughter of the man who put a roof over their heads and fed them.

"I'm so glad I don't have a daughter to worry about."

"At this rate you'll never have any kids to worry about," Miriam said, rolling her eyes.

I sat down in one of the chairs and waited as she served me some casserole she heated up. As I ate, I checked my phone again. Still nothing.

"You waiting for a call?"

I looked up at Sergio.

"No, why?"

"You haven't stopped looking at your phone since your plane landed."

"I'm always looking at my phone."

"How's your dad?" Miriam asked as Sergio gave me a suspicious look.

I went on to give them an account of how my time in New York went. How my dad ignored me every time I went to visit him in the hospital. How Belmonte had kicked people out of an apartment building and I helped relocate them for the time being, and how I hoped that never happened with any of the buildings I invested in here. I tried to leave Camila for last. I didn't even want to tell them about her because I didn't want them to think she was just another conquest. When Elena came along, she was dubbed the woman who tamed the lion. I didn't object. She had tamed me in a lot of ways, though it was short-lived.

"You didn't get into any trouble that I should know about," Sergio said, rather than asked.

"I'm sure you would've heard about it by now."

214

"Just checking."

"No women staking claims yet?" Miriam asked with a hopeful smile.

My heart tapped faster. I checked my phone again. Nothing. When I looked up, they were both looking at me with the same questioning expression on their faces and their arms crossed. I smiled, unable to hide it.

"She lives in New York."

"Ah. We have a confession," Miriam said with a laugh.

"She's not . . . she's not just another woman," I said. They exchanged a glance. "She's coming to visit in a couple of days."

Sergio sighed and closed his eyes briefly. "This isn't the best timing."

I looked at him for a long moment. I hadn't thought about it before, but now I wondered . . . "You wouldn't happen to know anything about a USB filled with pictures that was sent to her, would you?"

Sergio frowned. "What kind of pictures? Threatening ones?"

I exhaled and rubbed my hands over my face. I thought by now I would have figured out who sent her the damn photos. It could have been anybody, but the fact that somebody knew where she lived. They'd left them in her new building. Not her apartment, but her building, and the envelope had her name on it.

"Never mind," I muttered.

"You have a big decision to make, War. And with Elena and Ricky still around . . ."

Normally, the thought of that gripped my heart. There was a burning feeling that came with the notion that I would have to see my old coach and my ex-fiancée walking together in public, kissing, but today I felt nothing. Instead, I shrugged.

"They deserve each other."

Sergio's brows rose. "First you don't care about money and now this? What did they do to you in New York?"

Miriam laughed. "He said he didn't care about money?"

I thrummed my fingers on the kitchen counter. "Is that so hard to believe?"

"Coming from a guy who owns three cars that cost more than my house, yes."

I rolled my eyes. "I've had those for a long time."

"You switch them out any chance you get," Miriam said, but there was no judgment in her eyes.

"You took out your frustrations on the pitch every time you scored a goal because you felt you weren't getting paid the amount of money you deserved," Sergio said, raising an eyebrow.

"I was young and stupid."

"That was last season."

I rested my forehead on the palm of my hand. "You're giving me a headache."

"Tell me honestly, Warren, how much money will it take for you to stay and how much would you leave for?" Sergio asked, beckoning my attention with his serious tone. "I need to know."

At the mention of money, Miriam walked out of the kitchen and left us alone. Normally I had an answer for that question. It was an easy, no-brainer question. I knew what my mates were paid in a year. I knew who to compare myself with more or less. But I couldn't concentrate. I was too busy wondering what it would take for Camila to move over here for good, and knowing I would never get the answer I wanted if I asked her that question tore me to pieces.

"I don't know, Serg. That is my most honest answer. Give me a few of days to decide."

"You're expected on the pitch in two days for practice."

"And I'll be there."

"And your New York girl?"

My eyes flashed to his. "Don't call her that."

"Until proven otherwise, that's what she is," he said.

I hated that she was being placed in a category with all the other notches I'd collected in different cities. I didn't bother to explain myself. I knew Camila wasn't just another notch, that she wasn't my New York Girl. The term was something that had never bothered me in the past. I fucked around with women in different cities and after I left, they were vocal about it. I never gave it much thought, but thinking about the media turning Camila into one of my city girls was different, because she was different. I hadn't gotten her into bed and left. I'd worked for her and even after getting what I originally wanted I kept going back for more.

She wasn't my New York Girl.

She was my game changer.

And after spending the weekend with her family and seeing how hard she tried to embrace her father after he'd been gone for so long, after the pain she'd been through in his absence, I knew it for a fact. She wasn't the kind of woman you fucked and left. She was the kind of woman that made you want to stay and confront life's chaos with. I just hoped that when she got here she was able to embrace my life as well as I embraced hers.

Chapter
TWENTY-SIX

Camila

England! How the hell did I end up here? It was all I could think about when I got to the airport and cleared security. Then again when I boarded the plane and sat down inside of a private cubicle in first class. I was in heaven. I was sure of it. The last time I'd flown was in the last row of an overcrowded airline that had been delayed seven hours. And now I was sitting here, in this comfortable chair that I had no idea how to recline or move. I watched the people in the row beside me for a little while, trying to figure out if I could mimic their movement. After two hours of fidgeting, I swallowed back my embarrassment and asked the flight attendant for help.

I hadn't seen Warren in a few days, and it felt like an eternity. I wasn't sure how or when I'd become so accustomed to him, but I missed him. I slept most of my flight, which was good because when I landed in Manchester it was only eleven o'clock in the morning, which was six o'clock my time. I went straight into the bathroom to freshen up after I deplaned. My heart was vibrating wildly as I finished and took one last look at myself in the mirror. My cheeks were flushed, my eyes were bright, my hair was cooperating with no frizz in the soft waves that went down to my shoulders. Warren had warned me that it would be in the fifties most of the time, so I was wearing a white long-sleeved cotton shirt and green jacket on top.

Walking to the front of the airport, I passed by a few men with signs, but did a double take when I saw my name written on one of them. The man noticed and waved it a little until I nodded my confirmation. I walked over to the guy, who was wearing a jacket over a nice button-down shirt and jeans. He was tall and looked maybe about fifty, with dark red hair and matching light beard. His eyes were the bluest of blues, and his smile was . . . non-existent. He looked almost bothered by my presence, but after everything Warren had told me about Elena and how she used him, I figured the people in his life would be cautious about a newcomer and decided not to let it get to me.

"Hi," I said as I stood in front of him.

He lowered the sign, blue eyes inspecting my face for a long moment. Finally, he offered to shake my hand. "I'm Sergio, Warren's agent."

"Camila." I blushed, glancing away momentarily. "Obviously."

"I've heard good things about you," he said.

I stared at him for a long moment. "You don't sound anything like what I was expecting."

"Ah." He smiled. "I'm a Spaniard living on English territory."

Well, that explained it. The chatter around us was definitely more of what I was expecting. My head turned to and fro as I watched friends and family members greet one another. It was soothing to hear everybody speaking the language I spoke at home, but odd to hear it in such a different accent. I'd been expecting it, but actually experiencing it was a different story.

I looked at Sergio. "Is Warren in the car?"

"He had to go to practice so he asked me to come get you. Or demanded it, more like it." He grumbled the last part.

I hadn't come under the false pretense that we'd spend every waking moment together, but a small part of me was a little disappointed he wasn't there to greet me. We reached a red Ferrari and he popped the trunk. I gaped at the car for a moment as he put my bag in the front of the car. The front of the car . . . what? I blinked rapidly.

"Are all trunks in the front of cars here or just this specific one?"

Sergio chuckled. "Just some cars. This model being one."

He reached over and opened the door for me and I lowered into the seat, putting on my seatbelt as he closed the door and went around the car.

"This is . . . low," I commented as he sat down. My eyes bounced on every detail of the car. My brother would die if he saw it.

"They say this style is similar to the Maserati, though I beg to differ."

"Oh," I said.

I had no idea what a Maserati was or looked like. He must have realized and disapproved of this, because he shook his head with a single laugh and began to drive. I looked out the window, taking in the scenery, the greenery, the people walking and talking, the cars that went by. We stopped at a red light and my eyes widened when I caught a glimpse of the billboard we were approaching. I ducked in my seat and narrowed my eyes.

"It's him," Sergio provided.

Warren was on the billboard wearing a sharp dark suit and holding a soccer ball in his hand. He was looking into the camera with one of his seductive smiles and wearing one of those ginormous watches he wore sometimes. I only knew the brand because everybody on earth knew the brand.

"I didn't know he modeled," I commented.

I knew he had sponsorships, but I had no idea he actually stood in front of the camera and modeled. Sergio didn't say anything about this. Instead, he made a sharp right turn, and drove onto the highway, which had small lanes. There was another billboard with his face on it. This one had five guys wearing red shirts and white shorts. It simply said, "We're back. We're ready." And beneath the television ad, the words, "We're United".

"I didn't expect it to be this cold right now," I said to Sergio. "It's hot in New York."

"We have switched winters," he said.

"That's what Warren said."

He looked over at me. "I bet your friends are excited you're dating Warren Silva."

"Not really."

"They don't like how much time he's taking you away from them?"

"No, they just don't know who Warren Silva is," I said, waving a hand outside as if all his billboards were lined up in front of me. They weren't but they might as well have been. I caught a glimpse of two more.

Sergio scratched his beard. "You don't watch football?"

"No. I like baseball. Sometimes I'll watch a Giants game," I said. Upon seeing his confusion, I added, "American football."

"So when you met him you didn't know who he was?"

I shook my head. "Not a clue."

"And you didn't have a good impression of him?"

I smiled, shaking my head.

"And then he took you on a fancy date and you got over it," he said, chuckling as he turned into another street.

"Not exactly," I said, but didn't feel the need to expand on that.

I thought about all of our odd dates and his time in the "smelly" New York City subway and smiled. I'd been hesitant to take this trip after seeing the way Warren seemingly lived his life here, and I had been right to hesitate. He was a completely different person over here. That was clear from the way his agent spoke about him and looked at me like I didn't belong in this life. I pushed the thought out of my head. I knew Warren and I was here to see him.

My eyes widened as the stadium came into view. It was as big as MetLife. Sergio tried to make another joke, but I ignored him. My entire body was buzzing with the realization that I was going to see Warren soon. It wasn't like I hadn't seen him in a long time, but it felt that way. After driving back from my parents' house last weekend, Warren had stayed in my apartment every night. He'd go to practice, I'd go to work, and then we fell into a routine where I'd come home, make dinner for the two of us and we'd sit down and eat together. On Tuesday he *made me dinner*, which consisted of him crossing the street and getting takeout from the Puerto Rican restaurant. I smiled at the memory.

Sergio and I stepped out of the car and I waited by the trunk to get my bag, but he shook his head.

"This is Warren's car. You can leave it."

Interesting. I remembered Warren say something about him not letting people drive his cars. I said as much to Sergio, who shrugged and smiled.

"He wanted a favor, so I took the car."

He said it in such a good-natured, funny way, like a kid who took their parents' car out to get milk, so I had to laugh. He walked me over to security and got me a visitor's badge. We walked past three more security stops, and finally into a large room with two televisions, some kids' games and books off to the side, and a clear view of the field. There were three women sitting in there. All of them had giant designer handbags on the floor beside their feet and were dressed nicely, like they were going out to dinner and not sitting in a soccer stadium. Maybe they were going out to dinner after this, who knew? The three of them turned their heads to me and began sizing me up quietly. No greeting, no questions, just eyes going up and down my body so fast, I felt like I was being violated. I cleared my throat and put my best smile on my face.

"Hi," I said.

The three of them blinked a few times, green eyes, brown eyes, blue eyes, and turned their heads away from me and continued to talk amongst themselves as if I wasn't standing there. I clamped my mouth shut. I always thought people in Europe were nice. Why did I think that? I could have sworn I heard somewhere that they were more polite than Americans. Definitely more polite than New Yorkers . . . apparently whoever said that was full of it.

"You can wait here," Sergio said. "She's waiting for Warren."

My head whipped around to where he was and I widened my eyes in complete horror. He couldn't be serious. He couldn't just leave me with these vipers. He wouldn't.

"You'll be fine. They take time to get used to newcomers," he whispered, smiling as he shut the door behind him.

I stood there, gaping at the door well after it closed. I couldn't very well turn around and face those women again. They started talking amongst themselves about their nails and their hair, and I finally turned around and sat down in a chair behind them. Taking out my phone, I sent my sister an email to tell her I'd arrived and the predicament I was already in before slipping it back in the pocket of my jacket. I looked around again. The room was pretty simple with two televisions on either side, and a terrific view of the soccer field. I looked at the three women again. They were probably all older than me, but not by much. They didn't look mean, except I already knew they were.

They didn't stand up or make any movement when men in red long-sleeved shirts and black sweats with red lines on the sides started to run onto the field. I stood and held my breath. I couldn't help it. It was the first time I would be seeing Warren out there. I wanted to leave the room. I wanted to run onto the sideline and watch him up close. I wanted to . . .

"Where are you from?" a female voice asked.

She sounded sweet, so I turned my attention to her. It was one of the blondes with pretty green eyes.

"New York."

She smiled. "I love it there. Is it your first time in Manchester?"

"Yes," I said.

"How do you like it so far?" she asked.

Her two friends rolled their eyes and whispered things to each other as if they were displeased at their friend for talking to me. I was grateful for her questions, even if I wasn't completely sure she was genuinely interested or was about to flip the switch and start acting bitchy.

"I came here straight from the airport."

She raised her eyebrows. "Oh. You must be exhausted."

I shrugged and offered her a smile before looking back out at the field. I didn't want to make small talk with somebody I couldn't figure out.

"Another one of Warren's toys," one of the other girls said with a sigh.

"Well, we all know Elena is bound to appear back in his life. They never stay away from each other for too long."

"She made her choice," the blonde said, looking at me. "Don't listen to her. Once you cheat with another teammate, you're pretty much done. The rest of the team is pretty adamant about not having her around."

I smiled gratefully at her, but shook my head to let her know she didn't have to stand up for me. I didn't owe them an explanation. They were obviously mean girls who had decided I wasn't worthy of being in their circle and that was fine. They started talking amongst themselves again, harsh whispers, about me I was sure. I tried not to listen, knowing that all it would do was upset me more, but I was human, and I caved and listened anyway.

"She's pretty."

"She's only here for a moment, so I hope she enjoys her time."

"Do you think Elena knows?"

"Stop talking about Elena. She screwed up."

"I'm not saying I like Elena but how many women will we have to meet, get to know, end up liking for nothing? He always fucks up with them."

I bit down on my lip and leaned on the counter in front of them to get a clear view of the field, or the pitch, as apparently it was called according to the signs. I felt like I was back in high school. In private school the girls didn't accept me because I wasn't rich enough. In public school they didn't accept me because I was too rich. Too rich meant my Converse weren't stomped on repeatedly, which they then took upon themselves to do. That little initiation led me to the hospital to treat a broken foot and my mom didn't let me live it down since we'd just lost our health care benefits. Maybe that's what this was—an initiation thing for them. I wasn't about that life, though. After my Converse ordeal, I stayed away from anything that required one. I hadn't even thought about joining a sorority in college because I didn't care to be a part of any movement that felt like I needed to be tested in order to join. You either wanted me or you didn't. There was no in-between. The door opened up and I turned around to see Sergio standing there. He waved me over and I left without bothering to turn to the women in the room.

"Did you make new friends?" he asked.

I ignored the question. "Are you taking me to better seats? I can't see anything from that angle."

"Warren asked me to move you so that you would be closer to the field, but the girlfriends and wives prefer to stay in the warmth of their suites."

I looked over at him. "I'm from New York. I can deal with the weather."

"Were they being rude?" he asked, shaking his head.

"Rude is all I've dealt with since I landed here."

"We're a tight-knit family. It's hard for us to let outsiders in, especially when it comes to Warren." He glanced over at me. "We'll get used to you . . . if you stick around."

I tore my gaze away from his. It seemed like everybody was trying to get a rise out of me. Either that or they had little faith in Warren, though I was sure it wasn't that. I sighed and was grateful when we took one more turn and ended up outside, walking toward the field. There were a few chairs set up on the sideline that he ushered me to.

"You can watch from here."

I thanked him as he walked away, and looked around in complete astonishment. There were guys running to and fro on the field, talking, laughing as they did. They were all dressed in the same team gear. I knew Warren was in there somewhere, but instead of looking for him, I looked around the stadium in awe. The seats were red with the team letters drawn in big white letters. I breathed in deeply, relishing the way it felt to be here; the way the players must have felt to hear their name being cheered by loud, rumbustious fans. I'd never been to a soccer game before, but if it was anything like American football, I was sure this place got wild.

After a moment, I sat down in one of the chairs and looked up at the field. I saw a couple of guys glance over at me and say something to each other that ensued laughter, and I tightened my coat and wrapped my arms around my middle. I'd only been here for a few hours and I was already regretting it. I felt like I was trapped in a fish bowl and everybody was poking at the glass, trying to figure out what kind of specimen I was. I tried not to avert my eyes from where they were standing, to show courage, to show I didn't care they were talking about me right in front of me, but that was short-lived. I glanced away and looked around, hoping to find Warren, but I couldn't see him out there. I sighed and leaned back in the uncomfortable folding chair and waited.

Finally, from the corner of my eye I spotted a couple guys coming out into the field. My heart swelled at the sight of Warren. He was wearing the same tracksuit everybody else had on, his hair bounced in the wind as he sprinted across the field, a huge smile on his face as he made his way to the rest of his teammates. Without a word (or not one that I could hear), they all stood in a circle and began to stretch to the right, and then the left. It seemed like a wordless chant, the way they swayed side to side with their arms around each other as they squat, jumped, shifted, and repeated.

When they broke formation, Warren glanced up and looked around the field quickly before his gaze found me. He was far, but I knew he'd seen me from the way his lips spread into a slow, wide grin. I shifted in my seat, unable to hide my excitement, and suddenly everything that had happened previously began to fade away. After that, he kept watching me, glancing over every so often in between drills. The rest of the guys seemed to realize what I was doing there and started to say things every so often that I couldn't hear but made him laugh as he looked over at me. The other men standing around, the ones that weren't wearing the tracksuits, started leading the drills and once that started Warren stopped looking.

My eyes never left him. Not when Sergio came back and offered me something to drink. Not when I heard female voices behind me that I thought might be the women I'd been sitting with before. And most definitely not when Warren began to strip his jacket off and toss it aside. Then, all I could do was stare at his athletic form in the tight Under Armour shirt. The moment practice was over, he looked at me and called me over. I nearly jumped out of my chair, but as I made my way over I wasn't sure if I should jog or just walk swiftly. I walked at a normal pace.

The last thing I needed was to fall on my face in front of all these people. Warren didn't let me think about it much. He sprinted over to me with ease, as if he hadn't just done the most intense workout I'd ever seen in my life. He stopped in front of me for a second before wrapping his arms around me and squeezing me to his sweaty chest. I licked my lips and tasted the salt from his shirt. His chest was still heaving heavy breaths from his workout when he loosened his grip to get a better look at me.

"You're here." The sides of his eyes crinkled.

"I'm here," I said, smiling.

He grabbed my face with both hands and pressed his lips to mine, and everything around us seemed to fade away. I was a long way away from Manhattan, but I was there with him.

Chapter
TWENTY-SEVEN

Camila

Being outside of New York with Warren was definitely different. He drove his own car here, and even though he didn't have security detail, he seemed to have people around him at all times. His agent, his assistant, teammates, employees, just people everywhere all. the. time. I waited for him to shower and dress after practice and we headed to a restaurant with his "mates" as he called them. In the car, he held my hand and smiled.

"Are you sure you're up for it? I can cancel," he said, but I could see he didn't want to cancel, so I smiled and reassured him it was fine.

I wondered if the mean girls were going. If they were, it was going to be a long meal. But, I had to eat anyway and I really wanted to see Warren in his element. He'd been with me to so many places he would've never normally stepped foot in. It was the least I could do.

"Do you like what you've seen so far?" he asked as he shifted gears.

I kept my hand beneath his, which meant we were both switching gears together. That also meant I feared any minor movement I made would send the car into overdrive or something so I kept my hand as limp as possible.

"I haven't seen much aside from billboards, hot soccer players, and hot soccer players on billboards."

He grinned, keeping his eyes on the road. "Was I naked in any of them?"

"Who said anything about you?" I asked, looking out the window to hide my smile.

"You said hot soccer players."

"So you assume I'm talking about you?" I asked, laughing as I looked over at him.

His gaze cut to mine. "I don't have to assume, baby. I know."

I rolled my eyes.

"Have you seen the one of me in my underwear?"

"What? No!"

He glanced over at me, eyes crinkling with amusement. "I'm not sure if you're saying it that way because you missed that one or because you're jealous other women see me in my underwear."

I took the hand that was beneath his and put it on my lap as I looked out the window again, watching the cars going the opposite direction fly by us. I didn't really love the idea of other women ogling him in underwear, but it's not like they got to see the whole package, though based on the pictures I'd seen, many of them had.

"Camila?" he said, his voice tentative.

"I guess it doesn't really bother me." I looked over at him with a shrug. "I mean, I could pose in lingerie for some photographer and have my photos posted for other men to see and it couldn't really bother you, so . . ."

He scowled deeply. "Of course that would bother me."

"Yeah?" I tilted my head. "Why?"

"Because you're mine."

I looked at him for a long moment, studying the side of his face and the way his lips were set in a fine line. His frown was still clear from this angle, his jaw set as his teeth ground together.

"So what you're saying is that you're not mine," I said finally.

His eyes cut to mine. "I never said that."

"Sounds like it to me."

"Camila." He blinked and looked back at the road. "I never said that."

But he hadn't said otherwise, either. I stayed quiet. I didn't want to fight. I was tired and hungry and the last thing I wanted to do on one of my three days with Warren was argue over stupid pictures and his feelings for me, but it was all I could think about the days leading up to coming. I was growing attached. Way more attached than I expected to. Way more attached than I should have allowed being that we were not only from different worlds, but lived in different parts of it too. My heart hurt just thinking about our goodbye. Because goodbye was inevitable. It always was.

"I missed you," he said, pulling me out of my thoughts.

"I missed you too," I whispered.

"I mean, I really, really fucking missed you."

His voice was a thick whisper. Those big green eyes of his that filled with raw honesty and desire, made my heart skip a beat. He was saying he missed me, but it felt like he was saying much more. He tore his gaze away and remained focused on the road for the rest of the car ride. We talked about his car, and then his house, which I was looking forward to seeing later. He seemed more nervous than I was at my being there. When we reached a nice neighborhood with pretty storefronts and restaurants, he pulled up in front of one of them. I spotted the valet's eyes widen as we stopped in front of him, and he jogged quickly to my side, opening my door and offering me a hand to help me out of the low car before going to Warren's side and opening his.

I made my way over to Warren and stood beside him as the valet spoke to him. Warren smiled and listened intently as the guy went on and on about last season and how excellent he was on the field. Finally, when another car pulled up behind Warren's, the valet snapped out of it and excused himself. Warren grabbed my hand and led me away, toward the restaurant beside us. I smiled as I looked up at him.

"I guess you are kind of like a big deal."

He grinned as he opened the door for me. "Ah. Have I finally managed to impress you?"

"Not quite," I said, pursing my lips. "But close."

He chuckled as we walked up to the hostess. She was also in complete awe to be in his presence, and when one of the waitresses came up to us and saw him, she might as well have been the heart-eyes emoji. As cute as it was to see people this affected by him, I had to fight the urge to roll my eyes. No wonder he expected women to want to drop everything to go out with him. We were escorted to a private room in the back of the restaurant where there were three couples waiting. I only recognized one of the women from earlier. I looked away from her quickly and followed Warren as he made introductions. Stephen (and his wife Ally), Felix (and his wife Ana), and Juan (and his wife Evelyn—the bitch). I said a polite hello to each one and sat down beside Warren, directly across from Felix and Ana.

The other two wives, unlike Evelyn, had warm smiles on their faces as they looked at me and made me feel good about being there. The men seemed friendly. They didn't ask me anything right away, instead choosing to talk about the practice they'd had and how grueling the schedule for the season looked. One of them asked Warren about rumors of a trade, which spiked my interest. He tucked his arm under the table and slid his hand over mine on my lap, holding it as he spoke.

"Nothing is a sure bet," he said in response.

"But it's true that you're thinking about it?" Felix asked.

The expression on all of their faces fell when Warren shrugged. I moved my hand and threaded my fingers through his, relishing the warmth of his large hand against mine. That alone made me feel safe. I squeezed his hand and he glanced at me for a beat, his mouth tipping into a hint of a smile.

"How could I not?" he said, looking around the table. They all nodded in agreement. "But you'll be the first to know my decision."

The waiters took our drink and food order as they continued to talk. The women joined in, chatting about the grueling schedule and their kids, and I listened intently as they spoke. While we were eating, one of them, Ally, asked me how I liked Manchester, and I told her the same thing I'd told everybody else who'd asked me—I just got here, but I liked it so far.

"Have you ever been to London? We like to think this is

better than London," she said, smiling.

"I've never been. I'll have to plan a trip there next," I responded, smiling over my glass of wine.

"You'll have to go to Barcelona first," she said with a wink. "If Warren takes the contract, we'll all have to go knock on his door and stay in his castle."

"Well, if there's a castle, I guess I'll have to go," I said.

The group laughed and I joined in, meeting Warren's smiling face when he wrapped an arm around me.

"His family really owns a castle," Felix added. "I've seen it."

"Not my castle," Warren said, his expression suddenly serious.

"Family castle, same difference," Felix said.

"Not the same difference." Warren shot a look at Felix that made him clamp his lips shut and acquire a serious look on his face. "How did Cristiano react to you coming over here?"

Felix chuckled. "Probably just as bad as I'll take it if you leave after I came all this way to play with you."

"Ah, there's the pressure," Warren said with a laugh as he dropped his arm from where it was around me and picked up his glass of wine.

They explained to me that they'd gone to school together in Barcelona and hated each other their first year until they were forced to room together and finally hit it off. Juan also met them back then, but he was in a rival school.

"So, Camila, how'd he manage to rope you into coming?" Juan asked after telling a funny story about Felix back in high school.

"I'm still wondering that myself," Warren said before I could answer. He put his hand on mine over the table. "It took me days of chasing for her to even agree to go out with me as friends."

The group laughed, even Evelyn (the bitch) found that amusing. Amusing enough to actually smile at me.

"For once the flashy cars didn't work?" Felix joked.

"Have you ever been to New York?" Warren asked him.

"Once, when I was about ten."

"That was a long time ago," I said. "It's changed a lot."

Warren snickered. "Did you ride the subway?"

"I believe I did," Stephen said with a frown. "Because at the time I was convinced the Ninja Turtles lived down there."

"Yeah, well, it smells like they do," Warren said, grinning at me when I nudged him.

"Wait. You took public transport?" Ally asked, her eyes widening.

"I've been known to take trains once in a while," Warren said with an easy smile.

The entire group outright laughed. I still had a smile on my face from before, but didn't understand the humor in it until Evelyn spoke up.

"So you're saying you took the subway?"

"Yes, I took the subway," Warren insisted and threaded his fingers through mine on the table. "I wasn't going to let some germs keep me away from this woman."

Evelyn raised her eyebrows. "Weren't people all over you?"

I tried so hard not to roll my eyes, but from the look and laugh Felix gave, I failed.

"What?" he asked.

"We're not big on soccer over there. At least not where I live."

Warren raised a finger to argue. "Actually, a lot of people

in your neighborhood recognized me while I was walking."

"Who?"

"I don't know their names, but I stopped for autographs a few times," he said. I shot him a disbelieving look, and he chuckled, looking back at his friends. "You see what I have to deal with?"

Felix laughed. "Somebody who keeps him on his toes. I've waited seventeen years for this moment."

"Are you really such a snob that people don't believe you'd take public transportation?" I asked with a frown.

They laughed hard at that.

"I'm not a snob. I just like nice things," he said, smiling at me.

His lips looked so damn good when he smiled like that. I wanted nothing more than to lean over and kiss him right then, but held back because I really wanted answers. He wasn't a snob. He'd sat in the damn nosebleeds in the Yankees stadium and hadn't complained once. I took him to see a pigeon show, and while he did have a lot of comments about that, he didn't act like he was too good for it either.

"He likes extravagant things," Felix added, snapping me out of my thoughts.

"Luxurious," Stephen provided.

"Very high-maintenance," Ally said with a smile.

"And he likes his women the same way," Evelyn added, eyeing me up and down, "which is why this is surprising."

I tried not to give her the satisfaction of reacting, but felt my resting bitch face sitting in place nonetheless. Her husband nudged her and shot her a serious look and she got serious for a moment.

"I didn't mean anything by it," she corrected. "I think it's good."

I shrugged. "I don't care either way. I'm not into flashy things or fancy cars and know absolutely nothing about soccer. Warren knows this and he seems to be okay with it."

He wrapped his arm around me again, pulling me into his side. I inhaled the scent of his fresh body wash and cologne and tilted my face up with a smile as he looked down at me. "I'm more than okay with it."

Our lips met then. It was a soft, chaste kiss, but it was long and made a feeling of warmth spread through me nonetheless. The table was quiet when we pulled apart, and we continued to look at each other. I sensed a promise of wicked pleasure that would come later, and felt heat flood my cheeks. The rest of the meal was uneventful, and eventually, when they eased up on the questions and started to tell me about their pasts together, I felt comfortable.

Even stepping out of the private room we dined in was an ordeal. The waiters went to the front of the restaurant and informed the valet to get the cars and we said our goodbyes and waited as we were called, as if we were in school. It was odd, but once Warren and I walked out and I saw the crowd of cameras that had gathered outside of the restaurant, I understood the reason for it.

Warren's protective arm came around me and he pulled me to him once more as we walked toward the car.

"Keep your head down," he said, low so only I could hear.

I didn't question him and did as I was told. I could sense that his head was also down as we walked. When we climbed in the car, the cameras gathered around it, taking photos, filming, people with cellphones out snapping shots of him, of me, of us. I could hear their questions persist as we drove away. "Is it true you may trade to Barcelona?"

"What's going to happen this season?"

"Is it true you missed practice today?"

"Who's the lucky girl?"

"Holy Moses," I said, placing a hand over my rapidly beating heart. "What in the world was that?"

"That," Warren's gaze cut to mine as he shifted gears, "was the media."

"Is it always like this? It can't always be like this."

"Pretty much."

I gaped at him. "You're joking."

He didn't respond, just shook his head with a tight expression on his face as he continued to look forward. I figured he didn't want to talk about that, so I changed the subject.

"Why does everybody keep asking about Barcelona?"

"They want to make a trade for me."

"Oh." I paused, thinking about baseball players. "Do you get a say or do you go with them if they trade for you?"

"In this instance, I get a say."

"But you don't want to go to Barcelona?"

"It's not that. Barcelona was where I dreamed of playing ever since I was a boy." He sighed and I watched him and waited for him to continue. "I feel like I'm finally on a great team. I've played for good teams before, but this is finally feeling like a family on the field. I'm not sure I'm willing to trade that."

"Your grandparents live in Barcelona, though, right?"

He smiled at the mention of them. "My grandmother is dying to meet you."

"You told her about me?" I asked, smiling.

"I tell everybody about you." He reached for my hand and brought it up to his lips. "How could I not?"

"Stop making me blush," I whispered.

He chuckled as he lowered my hand, setting it on his

lap. "I'm going to do everything I can to make you blush all weekend."

I felt his words deep in my core. I knew damn well he'd make good on that promise. I looked outside to hide my smile . . . and blush.

Chapter
TWENTY-EIGHT

Camila

I'd been in Manchester for twenty-four hours and only had Warren to myself when we got back from dinner last night. In the morning he woke up before me and left me a note saying he was off to a meeting and would be back soon. I would have worried about food had it not been for the huge spread of things delivered for me around lunch time. It was thoughtful, and beautiful, but sitting at the long dining room table, where the food had been set up by the caterers made me feel a pang of loneliness.

When he finally came home, he was on the phone for an hour before he was able to have a normal conversation with me and it wasn't long before he got another call that whisked him away again. It seemed like the man couldn't get a minute to himself. I was sitting in his movie theatre room, snuggled up with a blanket when I heard him get off the phone and call out to me. I was flipping through the almanac of movie titles when he came into the room and plopped down in the plush chair beside me.

"You look tired," I said, looking over at him.

"I am. So tired and I have a meeting to go to in an hour," he said, closing his eyes and rocking the chair to and fro.

My shoulders slumped. I turned my attention back to the screen in front of us. It wasn't like I could expect him to change his life for my measly visit, but I had expected a little more attention. When I looked over at him again, he had fallen asleep. He looked so gorgeous with his plump lips slightly parted and the peaceful look on his face, that I couldn't bring myself to stay upset for long. I let him sleep a few more minutes before I shook him to wake up.

"If you're going to make it to the meeting in time, you have to go get ready," I said.

He nodded sleepily and stood up, stretching as he did so. He turned back around and leaned over me, placing both hands on either side of my chair as he looked into my eyes.

"I'll be back at nine thirty. Be ready by then. I'm taking you out," he said, pressing his lips against mine.

"What should I wear?"

"Whatever you want. It'll be chilly tonight, so jeans will be fine."

"Dressy jeans or casual jeans?"

He chuckled and kissed me again before standing straight. "Dressy jeans."

I sighed and plopped back on the couch, my heart skipping as he walked away. I fell asleep watching Amelie, and when I woke up, completely disoriented, I switched it off and sprinted upstairs. I showered, dressed, applied my makeup, did my hair, and then walked around the house once more. His house was huge. Too massive for one person to live in, with wide corridors and ample living spaces that I'd only seen on episodes of MTV Cribs. I contemplated going outside, but thought better of it. If Warren came home and couldn't find me, he'd flip. Finally, after I got tired of walking, I went back up to the master bedroom and called my sister.

"You're not using a calling card?" she asked, shocked.

I rolled my eyes. "Very funny."

"What? I'm surprised."

I looked at the phone screen. "Since you refuse to get an iPhone and I'm wasting my roaming, you have five minutes, so talk about something real and stop wasting my time."

She laughed. "Okay. Dad came over last night. It went well. He likes Adam. Adam likes him. Johnny is still being a huge asshole. He called me the Hispanic version of Martha Stewart."

"So basically Doña Florinda."

Vanessa laughed loudly. "I really hate you for saying that. When do you get back again?"

"Two days."

"Are you having fun? I bet Warren is ecstatic you're there."

I'd been thinking about that all day while I was home alone, walking around aimlessly. I couldn't even keep busy by cleaning since everything was spotless. I mean, the guy was barely home. I guess that was the secret to keeping clean floors and neat cabinets. I looked around and sighed, wishing he was here, wondering if he really was happy I was or if he was beginning to realize bringing me had been a mistake.

"He's so busy. I don't even know."

"You don't know what?" she asked. I could practically see her frown. "What's wrong?"

"This thing between him and I will never work," I whispered as I looked at the dark gray walls of his large bedroom.

"Why would you say that? He's obviously really into you if he invited you over there and look at how he was at Mom's house. Stop being pessimistic."

"This isn't me being pessimistic. This is real life. It's so lonely over here. So, so lonely," I said feeling tears building.

She stayed quiet for a long time and finally exhaled. "I'm sorry. Have you met any of his friends?"

"Yeah. They're nice. Their wives . . . not so much."

"Really?"

"Well, only two or three are mean, the rest seem okay. That's not what bugs me, though."

"What bugs you?"

My shoulders slumped. "He's always busy. I've been alone more than I've been with him, which is fine, I get it, he came here to work and I get it, but why ask me to come? Why bring me? And then . . ."

"And then?"

"It's stupid."

"Just say it."

"And I don't know. It's like the Warren his friends know and the Warren I know are completely different people."

"He's acting differently?"

"No. He's acting the same," I said. "It's the way they describe him like . . . I don't know. I just don't know. Some snobby rich kid."

"Um . . ."

"No. You know he's not like that."

"Um . . . "

I looked at my phone screen again. "Shit. Time's up. I gotta go, Vee. Say hi to everyone and tell Mom I'm not drinking the water."

She laughed. "You're in the UK, not DR, you idiot."

"Well, I'm being cautious."

"I love you. See you soon and have fun. Even if you have to go out and explore without him, do it, Peach. Maybe you'll find that you love it over there and it'll be great when you go back and see him again. Who knows, maybe we'll all have to move to England soon."

I smiled at that. "Love you. See you soon."

One hour turned into two. Finally, I sent him a text. Data plans be damned, I couldn't just sit there without knowing what the status of our date was. Thing was, my text wouldn't go through. Shit. Shit. Shit. Was I supposed to call the cellphone company and let them know I'd be traveling abroad? I groaned and threw myself back onto the bed. These were things that well-traveled people knew the answer to.

I ended up falling asleep and waking up with a jolt. I blinked and yawned as I sat up in bed, still wearing my heels, jeans, and the cute black leotard I'd acquired for the trip. When I'd fallen asleep the light was still shining in the room, but now it was completely black. I turned and looked at the time on the nightstand. It read twelve thirteen. I took my heels off and tossed them to the side before getting out of bed and going in search of Warren.

I walked downstairs to the living room, where the light was on, expecting to find him there, but it was empty. The kitchen, his office, the game room, the movie theatre room, it was all empty. Did he not come back? The thought came with a wave of anger. Had he really just left me there? My stomach growled and I headed to the kitchen to eat some of the cheese and grapes I'd put away from earlier. That was when I saw the lights on outside.

The cold wind hit me hard as I stepped outside and closed the door behind me. I wrapped my arms around myself and walked toward the lights. As I approached, I realized it was a soccer field and saw Warren bouncing the ball on the tip of his foot. He'd obviously come home and changed at some point and didn't bother to wake me up so I could do the same. He was wearing sweatpants and a long-sleeved T-shirt with the number ten on the back, as he kicked the ball up and caught it with both hands. For a moment he looked down at it like it was some kind of crystal ball that would answer his questions.

Then, just as quickly, his trance was over and he tossed the ball back on the ground and started to kick it to the other side of the field. His movements were slow, graceful, almost like a figure skater on a rink as he went from one side of the field to the other. His gaze was steady on the goal ahead as he did this. It made me wonder if he was picturing himself playing a real game against real opponents. His expression was serene as he looked at the net and did some fancy footwork on the ball. And maybe it was because it was him, or because I didn't know jack about soccer, but I was definitely impressed.

I padded the length of the yard quietly, trying to contain a shiver each time my bare feet hit the cold turf beneath me. When I reached the sideline, I sat down slowly, not taking my eyes off him even though his back was facing me and he hadn't noticed I was there. Maybe it was the calming wind, or the peace and quiet, or that it was just the two of us again, but my anger seemed to dissipate a bit as I sat there and watched. With both feet, he kicked the ball up behind him and somehow it ended up in the front part of his body. He hiked his knee up just before it landed, bounced it up, then let it drop to the tip of his foot and kicked it in. My eyes widened.

He practiced the same move once, twice, three times, and nailed it every time. I shook my head in amazement. It wasn't until he started to run toward the opposite goal that he noticed me, and when he did he stopped dead in his tracks, the ball rolling slowly out of reach. He pulled the hem of his shirt up and wiped his face as he walked over to me, giving me a peep show. He walked to the right and pulled out two bottles of water from a cooler and downed one as he walked over to me. He crushed it in his hand and tossed it aside as he sat down in front of me with a heavy sigh.

"How long have you been out here?" he asked, reaching out for my bare feet and placing them on his lap.

"A while."

"Your feet are freezing," he said as he massaged them gently. I closed my eyes and felt myself relax.

"I'm mad at you."

Warren's hands stopped moving. My eyes popped open and were met by his cloudy gaze. He sighed heavily, using a hand to comb through his hair before moving forward, spreading his legs apart, and lifting me up to place me on top of him. The movement made my legs wrap around his waist and I put my hands on either side of his shoulders to keep from tipping over.

"Why, baby?" he asked, kissing my lips, my cheek, my jaw.

"You told me you'd be back in a couple of hours, so I got dressed and put on my makeup and then . . . nothing." I searched his eyes.

"I'm going to be honest." He closed his eyes and let out a breath before looking at me again. "I forgot you were up there."

"You . . ." I started, but took a moment to swallow and regroup. "You forgot I was there?" I paused again, this time unable to hide my frustration. "I took a seven-hour red-eye, was picked up by a complete stranger who didn't even try to act as though he was pleased to see me, then put up with some stupid bitches acting like they were better than me to come see you for a few days . . . and you *forgot* I was here?"

He flinched. "I know. I'm sorry."

I shook my head and glanced away, dropping my hands from his shoulders to cross my arms as I looked out into the field.

"I'm sorry." He leaned into me and put his mouth on my neck. "Please don't be mad at me," he said, his voice a murmur beside my ear.

I rolled my eyes, though he couldn't see me with his face in my neck. He moved slightly, the light hair on his face sending a tickle down my spine, but still, I refused to move. He kissed my collarbone lightly and moved his mouth in open-mouthed kisses all the way up my neck, my jaw, until he reached my ear. I closed my eyes, trying to ignore the way my breathing picked up and my heart fell into my stomach.

"I'm really sorry, baby." His voice was a hoarse whisper in the shell of my ear. "I don't know what it's like to have somebody waiting for me."

"I don't know what it's like to travel thousands of miles just to see somebody for a few days," I whispered. "But I came. For you."

Our eyes met briefly, and in his I saw a flash of pain I didn't understand or have time to question before his lips crashed against mine. He kissed me deeply, his tongue taking away some of my doubts and replacing them with a wave of desire. His arm circled around me as he moved onto his knees, lying me down on my back as he hovered above me. Our eyes met as he shrugged off his shirt. My gaze left his momentarily to admire his tattoos, the piercings on his nipples, his completely shredded body.

"Are you cold?" he whispered. I shook my head, feeling dizzy from the way he was looking at me. He lowered his hand to the button of my jeans. "I want you naked."

"Then get me naked," I whispered back.

His heated gaze raked over the length of my body slowly as he peeled off my jeans, taking in my bare legs and the leotard I had on. His hands made their way up my calves, to my thighs, squeezing as they came up to the bottom of the leotard. He undid the buttons and pulled it over my head, his chest expanding in a heavy pant as he took in my naked form. His lips parted slightly.

"You're the most perfect thing I've ever seen."

"Me?" I said, smiling. "Have you looked in the mirror lately?"

He lowered himself onto me, his hard chest pressing against my soft breasts as his lips met mine in a soft, languid kiss. He broke the kiss and undressed quickly, tossing articles of clothing aside without bothering to see where they fell, and was right back on top of me, kissing me again, his hands threading into the hair over the nape of my neck as his tongue danced along with mine.

I pressed against him, moaning at the feel of his large erection digging into my lower belly when he rocked against me. His lips made their way down my body, to my left breast, his tongue swirling and tugging. One of his hands made its way down my side, digging into the flesh of my thigh as he pulled my legs farther apart to bring his hand between my legs, stroking, probing. I moaned out his name and grasped on to his hair with a force that made his eyes snap to mine.

"I don't have a condom," he whispered.

"I don't care."

He knew I was on the pill. He'd seen me take it every morning while I was here and commented about it and even though I knew his track record with women, I only cared about two things: that he was clean and that I needed him to get inside me right this instant. I rocked against the hand he had between my legs and moaned.

"Warren."

"You're going to kill me, pretty girl," he said, a groan against my other breast. He readjusted himself on top of me and I swallowed through my panting breath as the tip of his erection slid against my slick folds. "You're going to be the fucking death of me."

I wanted to tell him the feeling was mutual, but couldn't find my voice in time before he slid inside me completely. I gasped loudly, my back arching instead. A whispered, "Warren," escaped me as he continued to move slowly, giving me breath and taking it away once again with each deep thrust. Our gazes met and locked and he lowered his lips to kiss mine once more, my cheek, then my nose. He brushed his nose against mine once before carrying his weight on his hands again as he continued to thrust and look at me, his lips parting as he looked at me with an adoration I'd grown accustomed to seeing in his eyes when he looked at me. He picked up my hand and put it over his rapidly beating heart.

"Nothing is better than this," he said, groaning when I lifted my hips and met his thrust, causing him to sink in deeper. I held my breath for a second as I let my body acclimate to how deep he felt inside me from this angle.

"Not even soccer?" I managed to whisper.

He brought his mouth down on mine again, his lips molding against mine. He broke the kiss momentarily, his chest heaving against mine, mine against his as I felt the tension spike inside of me.

"Nothing, Camila," he whispered. "Nothing."

He kissed me again, my fingernails dug into his broad back as he moved deeper, harder, his fingers gripped the bottom of my ass as if he was carrying me into him, pushing himself deeper inside, harder. He echoed inside me. I felt him between every beat of my heart, marking me, taking me, the emotion in his eyes giving me answers I didn't dare ask questions to, and I returned them. "I feel the same," I said with my mouth on his neck. *I can't stop thinking about you when you're not around,* my hands said as they moved up his muscular frame and tugged on the tips of his hair. *And I can't get enough of you when you are. This is real,* his eyes said. *I know. I feel it too,* mine responded in a kiss.

Chapter
TWENTY-NINE

Warren

Before Camila, I thought most women were the same. Sure, they differed in physical features, but I'd always been attracted to the same type of woman: sure of herself, sexy, trophy-wife material. Camila was the kind of woman you couldn't try to categorize, and that was what drew me to her more and more with each passing day. Somehow over the course of just a few weeks, she'd managed to demand a spot in my heart. One that couldn't be filled by anybody else or erased by her absence. *That* thought scared me, because I knew what I was hiding from her would change things. I just didn't know to what extent, and I was afraid to find out. As I stroked her hair and watched her take soft, deep breaths in her sleep, a dreadful feeling spread through me. She was going home soon and I already missed her presence.

From the moment I laid eyes on her, I knew she'd be different. From the first conversation, I knew she'd be worth it. From the moment I had her, I knew I'd never get enough. And now that I had her I couldn't figure out where to go from here. The only thing I knew for sure was that the thought of losing her made me feel panicky.

Chapter
THIRTY

Camila

I was making breakfast for Warren and myself when I heard him come up behind me. I smiled and flipped the sausage I was frying as he wrapped his arms around my middle.

"It smells so good," he said, squeezing me and tucking his face into my neck.

"It'll be ready in about two seconds," I said. "If you stop moving your hands down my body."

"You love my hands on your body." He moved them lower, tucking one into the front of my shorts. I held my breath, my heartbeat quickening.

"I'm going to burn this if you don't stop."

"I can go without eating."

His hand snuck into my panties, his long fingers moving

along my folds. I threw my head back with a moan. The man definitely knew how to use his fingers. And his tongue. And his dick. I shivered against him.

"You should really stop," I whispered, gasping when he flicked my sensitive spot.

Though after the last two days, everything was sensitive. He continued moving his mouth along my neck, his fingers over my clit, his other hand coming up to cup my breasts, naked beneath the cotton shirt he'd lent me to wear to bed last night. I felt the build up coming before I could form another protest. The spatula dropped from my hand in a loud clatter against the frying pan and I moaned out his name, my knees going weak with pleasure. Warren held me up and leaned over my shoulder to move the pan and turn off the stove before pulling my cotton shorts all the way down and turning me around to face the living room. My hands splayed over the counter as he bent me over and spread my legs farther apart. He gave no warning before sliding into me in a slow, long stroke. I felt the length of him all the way to my chest, the girth of him taking up the rest of the space inside me, and I gasped loudly. He dropped a kiss on my shoulder, and then he started to really move.

"Don't leave me," he said, his voice a groan beside my ear. He groaned deeply when I clenched around him. "God. Don't fucking leave me, Camila."

My eyes shut heavily as the wave of my second orgasm began to flood through me, making me tingle from the tips of my toes to the top of my head. I met his thrusts deeper, faster, harder, and moaned again as I felt another wave coming over me. He bit down on my shoulder, his fingers digging into my hips as he pulled me to him roughly, meeting me in two final thrusts before emptying himself inside me with a loud, guttural moan of my name.

"I wasn't supposed to have sex before practice," he breathed out, resting his forehead on top of my shoulder.

He put a paper towel between my legs and I moved my hand to hold it as I walked to the bathroom.

"Why? Your knees go weak when you run?" I asked as I walked back over. Warren was tucking his jersey into his shorts. His eyes snapped up to mine and he chuckled.

"You have a serious obsession with my knees."

I smiled. "For purely selfish reasons."

"Well, in that case," he reached out to me, wrapping an arm around me and pulling me to him to kiss me again, "I'll make sure my knees are healthy for your sexual appetite."

I pulled away from him and turned toward the stove to hide my blush, but his chuckle told me he saw it anyway. We ate breakfast—burnt sausage included—before he headed out.

"If you think you can handle driving on the left side of the road, take one of the cars out. They all have navigation," he said as I walked him to the garage.

"I don't have a license, remember?"

"Ah." He grinned. "Want me to drop you off at Miriam's house? She's dying for one-on-one time with you."

I smiled. I'd met her briefly when she came over with her daughter Penelope yesterday, but we hadn't really gotten a chance to talk. I liked her. She was probably one of the only people I actually liked in Manchester thus far, so I agreed to that. Warren was on the phone when I finished getting dressed and walked toward the garage, and instead of going over to the driver's seat, he walked to the passenger and dangled the keys in front of me. I balked.

"I can't drive."

He grinned. "Humor me."

I looked around the garage, at the four luxury cars he had in there. "Which one of these wouldn't cost a fortune to fix if I break?"

"Break?" he asked, eyes wide. The smile slipped from his face. "Shit."

"I told you, I can't drive."

"You've never driven before? Ever?" he asked, shooting me a look of disbelief.

"You think I'd lie to you about something so . . . weird?"

"I would hope you wouldn't lie to me at all, but I don't know," he said with a shrug.

I rolled my eyes. "The only thing I've driven is a Vespa and that was in DR when I was fourteen years old. That doesn't even count since I was going about five miles per hour and my grandma was sitting behind me practically steering for me the entire time because she was so afraid for her safety."

Warren laughed loudly, throwing his head back. I smiled at the sight, though it was in my expense . . . or my grandmother's. Either way, I loved the way his face lit up when he laughed unabashedly like that. He looked at me, amusement glimmering in his eyes when he did.

"Just pick a car."

"You pick a car," I said sternly, eyes wide. "I don't want you to hate me if I crash one of them."

His gaze softened as he walked up to me and pulled me into his chest. I inhaled his scent as he massaged the back of my head. "I could never hate you, baby."

"You said you didn't let anybody drive your cars," I said, a muffle against his chest. He leaned back to look into my eyes.

"You're not just anybody," he said.

His eyes held a seriousness that made my stomach dip. I wanted to ask him what that meant, who I was, why he said it, why he seemed to be adamant in making me feel the way he did—like I was the most important thing in the world to him. I was too afraid to ask, so instead, I got up on the tips of my toes and kissed him. He groaned and pushed into me, making me stumble back onto the side of the black car behind me. We pulled away in a heavy breath.

"You're going to make me late."

"You're going to make yourself late."

He smiled. "Pick a car."

I swallowed and took the hand he offered me to stand back up. I turned around and looked at the cars again, finally pointing at the black SUV. I couldn't go wrong in an SUV, right? And if I did crash it, we wouldn't die . . . right? I groaned as we walked up to it. Warren chuckled behind me.

"And to top it off, I have to drive on the wrong side of the road," I said as we climbed into the car.

"But you've never driven before," he said, chuckling as he buckled his seatbelt.

"So?"

"So, you won't notice the difference."

I took a really deep breath and exhaled as I turned the car on and watched in the rearview as the garage door opened behind us. I gripped the steering wheel.

"You have to take it off the P and put it in the little R," he said.

My eyes cut to his. "I know that."

He shrugged. If he wasn't so damn good-looking, I would've wanted to slap the playful smile on his lips.

After a few seconds, I put the car in reverse and pushed down on the pedal. My heart climbed into my throat as the car moved back and out of the garage. I was going slow and there was nothing behind me, so I was still okay. I managed to drive it all the way to the gate and pause there as it opened, and when I turned out of the driveway, I looked over at him again.

"Oh my God. I can't believe I'm going to drive on the actual street," I said loudly. "Are you freaking insane?"

Warren laughed. "And here I was feeling lucky I knew the secret to get you to yell."

Heat rose in my cheeks. "Technically you're still the only one who makes me yell."

I couldn't take my eyes off the road out of fear I would do something wrong, but I could feel his eyes on my face. Warren told me the direction to drive in, and it turned out I didn't need to drive on any major streets in order to get to Miriam and Sergio's house. It was three winding roads and one turn away from his. When I pulled up to the house and into the driveway, I put the car in park and pressed my back against the seat, closing my eyes and letting out a heavy relieved breath.

"You drove," Warren said, his voice low. His hand found mine, still on the steering wheel, and he unclasped it to bring it up to his mouth. He kissed it softly. "You drove, baby."

I opened my eyes and turned my face toward him slowly. I smiled. "I drove."

His smile widened. "I knew you could."

"Thank you for letting me," I said, taking one more deep breath.

I felt my anxiety calming with each passing second. Our fingers threaded through each other's and we shifted in our seats to face one another. I hated the thing in the middle that separated us.

"Are you happy?" he asked. From the way his voice dropped an octave and he looked at me, I wasn't sure if he was talking about the drive or something else. I nodded and smiled.

"Very."

"Me too."

We moved toward each other at the same time, our lips meeting in a soft kiss that soon turned crazed. There was a loud knock on the window that made us break apart quickly. Sergio was outside with a smile on his face. Warren lowered the window.

"Any news for me?" he asked.

Warren sighed. "Not yet."

Sergio shook his head, and looked at me with a smile. "Hey, Camila. Miriam's been going on and on about your shopping trip. Come on inside when you're ready."

"Thanks," I said, grateful that he dropped his assholeness . . . at least for the moment.

Warren gave me his house key, explained his alarm system, his gate system, and went off to his practice and I went inside to wait for Miriam. We went to the biggest mall I'd ever seen in my life called the Manchester Arndale so she could get a swimsuit for an upcoming holiday trip she was taking with Sergio.

"Will Penelope stay by herself when you're gone?" I asked.

Miriam sighed. "Regretfully. She turns eighteen next week and wants to make her own decisions."

"She's a good girl," I said, based on the impression I had from meeting her.

"It's not her I worry about," Miriam said, cutting her gaze to mine as we walked into another store. "It's the boys we house."

I nodded slowly. "Soccer players seem to be an issue."

She laughed. "You would know."

"Warren's not bad," I said, smiling.

"He's not," she said with a kind smile. "He seems smitten with you. I've never seen him this . . . calm."

"Calm?"

Despite myself, my heart ceased for a beat. I instantly thought about the photos I'd seen of him and his past womanizing ways. I hated myself for having those thoughts after he'd shown me otherwise.

"Not in the way you're thinking. Just calm in general. He hasn't gone out drinking since he's been back . . . it's a good change."

I looked through the swimsuits absentmindedly as we spoke. "Not a good thing if it's a sudden change, or if he changed for me. That never works."

"I think it's been a long time coming. He needed to slow down. Even when he was with—" She stopped short, her eyes widening as she caught herself from continuing the statement. I wanted to know more about his life and how he was before, so I smiled and encouraged her to continue.

"I don't mind. When he was with Elena?" I said.

"With Elena," she said, shaking her head and sucking her teeth. "That relationship was a mess."

"I know she cheated with his teammate."

"One of his teammates. Who knows how many players from other football clubs," she said.

I raised my eyebrows. "How did he react?"

Miriam laughed once. "He went barmy."

"Crazy?" I asked, frowning.

"Yes. Absolutely nuts."

"I don't blame him," I said.

"Neither do I, not that he was a saint." She paused, offering me a kind smile. "I'm not saying he would ever do that to you. You have to realize you and Elena are night and day and you seem to bring out his best qualities." She laughed. "Qualities I had no idea he had before he met you."

"He seems to be busy a lot," I said, changing gears a bit. I didn't want to be the center of the reason he'd supposedly changed. "His life is pretty daunting."

"It's not for the weak," she offered. "You have to really want it if you want your relationship to survive the scrutiny."

I nodded. That was the big question, but to me it wasn't a question at all. Of course I wanted it. I knew I'd have to share my time with the world, and I was okay with that because at the end of the day, I got him. It was a scary realization, and one that made me question my own sanity because how would this work? I was going back to New York. He was staying here, or going to Barcelona. Either way, far, far away from me. Would I move and leave it all behind for him? Would I move away from my dad? I'd just gotten him back. Was that a change I was willing to make? Away from my sister? From my neighborhood and everything I'd ever known?

The look on my face must have been as cloudy as my thoughts, because Miriam squeezed my shoulder gently and beckoned my attention. "Everything will work out."

I smiled gratefully and changed the subject to the Almalfi Coast, her upcoming destination.

Chapter
THIRTY-ONE

Camila

At night when Warren got home, he told me to get ready because we were going dancing. I put on a short red dress Vanessa had packed for me and tall black heels she'd let me borrow. Warren was stepping out of the shower as I finished applying my makeup and fixed my hair in front of the steamy mirror. I kept wiping away the fog to make sure I looked presentable.

"That's what you're wearing?" he asked behind me, his voice catching me off guard.

I whipped around quickly, my gaze making its way down his body and stopping over the towel wrapped around his waist, below the V his muscles grooved. He gave me a full, slow once-over and I nodded, swallowing thickly. He shook

263

his head, his lust-filled eyes meeting mine.

"It's going to be a long fucking night."

"We could just skip it," I offered, smiling.

"The whole team is going to celebrate Stephen's birthday. Otherwise, I'd skip it." He walked toward me slowly, each step careful and measured and stopped directly in front of me.

"Okay," I whispered, tilting my head to look into his eyes.

He brought his thumb to my mouth and dragged it down my lips, my chin, the length of my neck, and when he stopped on the valley of my breasts, right above the scoop of my dress. The heat in his gaze was barely contained as he looked at me, and I could feel myself unraveling for him, my limbs softening, my breath picking up.

"The things I want to do to you, pretty girl," he said, finally, his voice thick.

I swallowed. "I'd let you."

"I know you would," he said, his gaze darkening as he slid his fingers between my breasts, teasing me, in and out before his phone rang and pulled us apart.

He cursed regretfully as he walked over to answer it and I sat on the bed watching him as he juggled his conversation and got dressed. When we finally got to the club, flashes of photographers' lights outside the club greeted us, and once again I wondered how he handled the persistent attention and scrutiny. They asked more questions about Barcelona and me and again we kept our faces down and walked inside quietly. One of the girls inside led us to a separate VIP section, where a large group of people were already drinking, dancing, talking, laughing. I recognized the ones I'd met and was introduced to the rest, and this time, unlike the last, all the women were friendly to me—even Evelyn, the former bitch. I ended up sitting beside one of the wives I hadn't met yet.

"I love your dress," she said.

"Thanks."

"You look like a doll. Has anybody ever told you that?" she asked. "Like a pretty, porcelain doll."

I didn't confirm that in fact I had heard that before, but thanked her for the compliment. She went on to talk about the other women who were there and paused dramatically when she pointed at a busty blonde sitting on the opposite side of us.

"That's Elena," she whispered loudly.

My eyes widened as I looked at the woman. She caught me staring and smirked at me when our eyes met. It was something I fully expected from her after everything I'd heard, so I ignored her.

"Don't worry. He'd never get back with her after everything she did," she whispered.

"I'm not worried." I smiled.

I wasn't. Not about her, anyway. There was very little I could do about the distance in our relationship and my ever-growing feelings for him, though. We spent the rest of the time we were there talking until her husband pulled her away and Warren put a protective arm around me as he spoke to another one of the guys. As he spoke, another guy came and sat beside me. I couldn't remember his name because there were so many of them, but he introduced himself as Pablo.

Warren told me he'd be back in two seconds and I watched him walk off as Pablo asked me questions about New York and what I did over there. I answered, though I wasn't really paying much attention to our conversation because my eyes were glued to Warren. I watched as Elena seized an opportunity to go up to him, and as soon as she said hello, they seemed to be in an argument.

"She's such a shite," Pablo said beside me. My gaze snapped to his. "Elena. She has a lot of nerve showing up here tonight."

Warren's gaze found mine and from his narrowed eyes and squared stance, I could feel the anger brewing inside him. Before I could stop myself, I stood up and made my way over to him. As if he sensed my presence, his hand reached out for mine without even looking to confirm it was me. Elena's gaze traveled the length of me slowly, a smirk splayed on her face.

"You could have at least upgraded," she said to him.

"Trust me, I did," he responded.

She turned her attention to him again. "I heard you couldn't use Warren Silva to get this one so you had to resort to your family name. Either way, it seems to work for you."

My eyes bounced between the two of them. I wasn't sure how much longer I could watch wordlessly as they bickered back and forth. Seeing her standing this close to him gave me a flash of what their relationship must have been like and that alone made me uncomfortable. They seemed volatile. Worse than Eric and I, and I always thought we were pretty bad.

"Shut up, Elena," Warren said. I looked up at him and saw the veins on his neck straining, as he seethed. "Shut the fuck up."

"Oh, I hit a nerve. How is your dad doing, by the way? Did he ask you to change your last name on your jersey again?" She looked at me. "Is that why you're with him? You're from New York, right? You know he's been written out of the family will? You won't see that money in your lifetime even if you marry him. Even if you have his child."

I stared at her, horrified. She thought I was using him? "I don't care about his will or his money or his fame."

Elena laughed, raising her eyebrows. "Sure you don't."

Warren's face looked like it was about to explode as he stood there. I squeezed his hand to let him know I was there, but he squeezed it back twice as hard until I yelped from the sting. He looked at me suddenly.

"Careful," Elena said, though neither one of us was looking at her. "He'll hurt you. One way or another. Didn't you get my warning package? You should have done yourself a favor and ended things when you had the chance."

My mouth fell open. Warren dropped his hand from mine and reared forward so quickly and with such a force that Elena stumbled back.

"You fucking bitch," he said.

Her eyes widened. She backed away a little more, but hit the back of one of the couches. Two of Warren's teammates were at his side before I could blink. They stood at either side of him, holding both his arms while I watched, completely glued to the spot, wanting to scream, wanting to shout, to move forward, but unable to do anything at all.

"Elena, leave," one of the teammates said to her.

She sidestepped them, and Warren went with her, blocking her path. The guys tried to plead with him, "Let it go. There are cameras here. You don't need this. The season is about to start."

But Warren looked like he was about to explode, his face reddening, the vein on his neck pulsing, his hands clenched in tight fists by his side. My heart was pounding hard against my chest as I finally stepped forward and went in between him and Elena to try to block her from his vision. Maybe if he saw me he'd calm down. Maybe. I stood there and felt a nervous tingle go down my spine as I glanced up at him and saw the angry look on his face. He looked murderous.

"Hey, it's okay. She's an idiot. Forget about her," I said, hoping my voice was loud enough to get through to him.

He tore his eyes from her and looked at me, his gaze softening for a beat before he glanced at her again. The expression on his face hardened once more.

"Don't ever fucking contact her again," he shouted. "Don't look at her, don't talk to her, don't come anywhere near her. If I leave this club it'll be because of you and your *Sadim* touch."

He jerked away from his teammates' hold and pulled my arm, growling a, "Let's go," that I wouldn't have argued against. As we walked away, I could hear Elena shouting behind us and the guys shouting back. She was calling me a plaything, saying Warren was an asshole, that I'd never keep him satisfied, and surprisingly, none of it bothered me.

"I hope you leave this club and go back to your bloody castle, Warren Belmonte!"

I jerked to a stop and listened for her next words.

"You and your father deserve each other!"

Warren, who had stopped walking when I did, continued to look forward, his jaw set, nostrils flaring. I knew he could feel me staring at him. I knew he could. Why wouldn't he look at me?

"Let's go," he said, his deep voice directed at the door we'd come in through.

I took a deep breath and soldiered on, following him outside, slinking into the low seat of his car as he put on his seatbelt, biting my lip and looking outside as I waited for an explanation from him as we drove off. Because there had to be an explanation for her words. Warren's body was still shaking, the aftershocks of his anger still radiating off him. I could hear the long, deep breaths he took, presumably to calm himself, and I wanted to wait a little longer, but couldn't.

"What was that about?" I whispered. "Why was she saying that stuff?

Warren's gaze finally cut to mine for a beat, and in it I saw a turmoil of emotions brewing, none of which did anything to relieve the coiling formed in my stomach. He looked at the street just as quickly, and I held on to my seatbelt over my chest. We waited for the gate of his house to slide open and drove into the driveway, straight into the garage.

"We need to talk," Warren said as we climbed out of the car.

His words sent a dreadful, empty feeling through me. Those words were never followed with positive news. I swallowed and watched as he dropped the keys on the dish beside the door and began to pace the length of the kitchen with his face in his hands. When he came up for air, it was only to give a quick explanation.

"I'd rather you hear it from me, than find out through the media or women like Elena."

I blinked rapidly, dread curling deep in my stomach, the feeling making me instinctually place a hand over it to ease it from spreading, from consuming me.

"Did you cheat on me?"

My voice was barely a whisper.

He stopped pacing, his head snapping up. "What?"

"Did you cheat on me?" I repeated, louder.

"No," he said, frowning, then lowered his voice. "No. Of course not. I would never do that to you."

I swallowed, suddenly feeling cold and terrified. I crossed my arms over my chest. I should have felt a wave of satisfaction at his confirmation, of relief, but I didn't. It just worsened my paranoia because if he hadn't cheated, then what? Then what? Then *what*?

"So tell me. What was she talking about? What did she mean?" I asked. He began pacing once more, and stopped suddenly again. "Warren. Stop. Just tell me. It's me. You can tell me anything."

With the way my throat was closing in on me, I was surprised the words even left my mouth.

"I've been keeping something from you," he said, swallowing visibly. My heart stopped beating. I'd never seen him this nervous. This was Warren. Sure-of-himself Warren Silva. The man that didn't hesitate to speak his mind. Warren, who didn't even blink when he asked me out and I turned him down all those times before I said yes.

"You're scaring me," I whispered.

"Fuck. What she said . . ." He exhaled harshly and brought his gaze to mine. "My birth name is Warren Belmonte."

"W . . . What do you mean?"

"My father is—"

"Not Javier," I said, feeling a wave of heat spread through me. "Not Javier Belmonte."

Angry tears burned my eyes and started trickling down before I could stop them. He tore his gaze away from mine and nodded slowly. I opened my mouth again to say something, to argue, to demand something from him, but closed it quickly. Warren picked his head up again and looked at me, regret filling his dark green eyes. Regret that I didn't want. Regret that I damn well didn't need from him. I wiped my face quickly.

"I'm sorry," he said.

"You're sorry?" I blinked rapidly. "Do you remember the first thing you told me before I finally agreed to go out with you?" He stayed quiet, so I continued, "You said you'd never lie to me."

"I'm sorry," he repeated, closing his eyes briefly.

"I . . ." A sob escaped me. I pressed my hand over my mouth. "Oh my God. I've been dating a stranger. This whole time. This whole time I didn't even know you."

"That's not true, Camila. You know that's not true." He took a step toward me. I backed away. "You know me better than anybody. You know me better than—"

"I don't even know your last name!"

"My last name is Silva," he said, his gaze softening, voice pleading. "I didn't lie about that."

"You just said—"

"Belmonte is the name I was born with. It's not my name now."

I stared at him, wiping my cheeks. "You're still a Belmonte."

"I'm a Silva!"

"Your blood," I said. "The man who made you, the mother that birthed you, the company you . . ." I sobbed again. "How many times did I tell you I hated them?"

He flinched, stepping forward once more, trying to bring his hand to the side of my face. I slapped it away, glaring through my tears.

"Camila, please. This doesn't change anything. You know me."

"This changes everything," I said, unable to even recognize my own voice.

"Please don't do this."

I jerked my arm away and faced him. "You did this. You. You lied to me. You kept this from me when you had a chance to come clean time and time again. You made me fall in love with you, brought me all the way over here, far away from my family, put me in situations that made me uncomfortable. I didn't complain because I knew they came with the territory, and now you tell me that all of this was a lie? That I didn't even know your true identity all this time? After everything I shared with you? After everything I told you your father did to my family. After I made it clear how much I hated the Belmontes."

His eyes widened. I could see the panic written all over his face, but for once I couldn't bring myself to put his feelings before mine. I turned around and rushed upstairs, taking my bag out of the closet and stuffing everything I could in it, not bothering to fold any of it.

"Please, Rocky," he said behind me. At the sound of the raw emotion in his voice, my hands stopped moving.

"Don't call me that," I said, my voice hushed. "Don't call me that."

"I couldn't bring myself to tell you after you made it so clear you hated my family. I was trying to save you some heartache."

I whipped around and glared at him. "You were trying to buy *yourself* time."

Pain flashed in his eyes before he shut them and nodded. "I didn't mean to hurt you—"

"Too late."

"Stop. Just. Stop."

"The first time I laid eyes on you was at your grandfather's funeral. You looked so lonely, so sad," he said. My heart plummeted into my stomach.

"What?" I said and then shouted, "What?"

I played back memories of that day, of me sitting in a foldable chair in front of the hole in the floor as I watched the casket lower into the ground. I couldn't even remember who was there. I couldn't remember who said anything to me, or what they said. I just felt empty. And sad. And lonely, despite being surrounded by my entire family.

"My father went to pay his respects and I went with him. I asked him who you were." He paused, looking at me, his eyes sad, his face crestfallen. Something that somehow managed to make my heart break more, despite what he was saying. "He said he didn't know, and we left minutes after I saw you, and then you showed up at Belmonte."

I held a hand over my mouth, feeling like I was going to be sick. I closed my eyes, unable to look at him any longer. He'd known who I was before he even went to the bar. He'd known.

"Did you know about my father?" I whispered, feeling another tear roll down my face.

"No," he said firmly. "I swear I didn't know it was your father. Everything I knew about you I learned from you. I didn't even know your name when I met you at the meeting. You have to believe me, Camila."

My gaze snapped to his. I could barely make out his eyes through my tears. "You see why I can't, right? You understand that now I'm going to question anything you've ever said to me."

"Please don't," he whispered. "Please."

I shook my head, wiping tears from my cheeks. He saw me at a funeral, felt bad, saw me at the meeting, felt bad.

"I was a charity case to you," I said finally.

"Never." His eyes widened. "Never, Camila. How can you say that when you were the one who taught me so much about life?"

I shook my head and wiped my face again. I could feel a headache building in the back of my neck and spreading.

"I need to finish packing. I can't even . . . I can't even look at you right now. As soon as I'm done packing I'm out."

"Please stay."

My head snapped up. "Are you insane?"

"Your flight is early in the morning. You don't need to rush out of here now."

"I'm not staying."

"I'll sleep in the guest room. Just . . . please. Please don't leave like this."

I stayed quiet. What could I do? Call a taxi and stay where? At a hotel? Which hotel? I knew nothing about this country or where I was. I could ask them to take me somewhere close to the airport but then what? Currency exchange, money I didn't necessarily have to spend after buying my family jerseys and things I'd promised to bring back. I had to stay. I knew I had to stay. It was only a couple of hours. After mulling it over, I nodded once and hoped that was enough for him to know I'd agree to that. He gave me one more nod and held the doorknob beside him.

"We'll talk in the morning."

I lowered my face and looked at the dark wood floors beneath us. "I don't talk to liars."

"I deserve that."

"You deserve worse," I whispered, bringing my gaze to his again.

"I couldn't stay away from you. I tried, but I couldn't."

"You tried?" I scoffed. "When did you try? When you showed up at Charlie's bar knowing I'd be there? When you showed up outside my apartment and begged me to go out with you? When the fuck did you try?"

He ran a hand over his hair, shutting his eyes again. "I'm sorry. I'm so sorry."

"Stop apologizing. Just leave me alone."

He turned around and stepped out of the room. "For what it's worth, I'm in love with you too."

His words made me recoil. I took a step back and hit the edge of the bed. A new wave of tears flooding my eyes.

"It's not worth anything," I said.

He turned around once more, not bothering to contain the pain in his expression.

"It's my birth name, it's not who I am. I changed my last name when he disowned me. I know we share blood, but we don't share the same beliefs. We're different people, Camila, just like you and your dad are different people. I understand that you're upset right now, but if you want me—"

"I don't." My voice was eerily calm and put together. I shook my head. "Tomorrow, I'm going back home. Back to New York, back to my normal life, and I'm going to forget any of this ever happened."

Warren blinked, staggering back. "You don't mean that."

"I wouldn't say it if I didn't." I turned around and faced the bed again. "I need to finish packing."

They were the last words I said to him.

Chapter
THIRTY-TWO

Warren

I'd been playing my entire life and had only missed a handful of practices. All had been when I was too ill to practice, but still, I went. I went and sat in the sidelines and did the workouts I could manage. Today, I was violently ill. I'd woken up to find every trace of Camila gone from my house, and I lost it. I took it out on everything in sight, from the two Ballon D'Ors I'd earned to the crystal vases of flowers Camila had dusted off and refilled for me the day she'd gone out with Miriam. Everywhere I looked, I saw her face. In the kitchen, I smelled her cooking. In the theatre room, I saw her on the lounge. In my bedroom, I smelled her scent on my sheets.

I was sitting on the cold marble floor, my foot not far from the broken pieces of the crystal vases I'd slammed into the ground, when there was a knock on my door. I ignored it. I glanced up and through the glass panel, saw Sergio standing on the other side. I looked back at the floor. After more loud knocking, he finally unlocked the door. My head snapped up.

"How the fuck did you—"

"Who do you think took Camila to the airport this morning?" he asked, his eyes wide as they swept over the living room. "This looks like a fucking war zone. No pun intended."

"So she called you?" I asked, my voice sounding as detached as I felt.

"She called Miriam."

"Did you see her?" I asked, swallowing past the knot forming in my throat.

"I did."

"How did she look?"

"Not much better than you," he answered, walking up to me and taking a seat on the floor beside me. "So I guess I should prepare a press release about you missing practice today?"

"I feel sick."

"Yeah, I was planning on using that excuse."

"No, I feel really fucking sick."

I'd thrown up twice earlier, and I couldn't tell if I was coming down with something or if it was a way of my body purging itself from myself. I wouldn't blame it if that were the case. Sergio stayed quiet.

"Do you think I lost her for good?" I whispered.

A wave of emotion came over me as I spoke the words. I knew I wouldn't cry, but I felt like I could. I looked at the door as if at any moment she was going to step through it and run into my arms again, though I knew she wouldn't.

"I don't know, mate. I hope not. She's good for you."

"She's the best thing that's ever happened to me."

Sergio sighed heavily. "I was an arse to her."

"I heard. I know you meant well, but I would have fired you if you'd kept at it," I said, glancing over at him. He smiled.

"Warren Silva falls in love. That's a great title to a news article," he mused.

"Fuck you."

He chuckled. "You'll be okay. Just give her time."

My heart jarred at that idea. Time. "How much time?"

"As much as she needs."

I sighed. I could sit there and blame Elena for being the cunt that she was, but I didn't, because it was my mistake to begin with. I should have come clean sooner. I should never have kept my identity from her.

"I've been around for thirty-one years, and it took me that long to really live," I said to no one in particular. "And it took Camila to show me how to do it."

"You'll be okay." Sergio stood up and patted me on the knee. "Clean up this mess, mate. I expect you back on the field tomorrow."

With that, he left. I knew Camila was still flying, so I waited, checking my phone every two seconds until I knew she'd landed. Finally, I did. I fully expected her to let the call go to voicemail, so when she picked up and I heard her hoarse voice say hello, my heart lurched into my throat and I could barely respond.

"Did you make it back?" I asked. My own voice sounded hoarse. I wasn't sure if it was the vomiting or the fact that my heart was throbbing in my throat.

"Yes."

I sighed, hating the way she was talking to me, like I was

a stranger. What could I do to make it better? What could I say? I went with the only thing I could think of.

"I love you, Camila. I love you so much."

She was silent for a beat, two, three. I looked at the screen to make sure she was still there. When I called out for her, I heard her sniffle.

"You don't know what love is, Warren," she whispered. "To love is to put your own feelings aside for the benefit of another."

I sat back against my headboard, the impact of her words searing right through my heart. I opened my mouth to say something, but she spoke up before I could.

"I have to go. Take care of yourself."

And just like that, she ended the call, effectively shutting me out.

Chapter
THIRTY-THREE

Camila

"You've been holed up in here for days, Peach," Vanessa said as she barged into my room and drew open the blackout curtains Warren had put up for me before he left.

Warren. Every memory I had seemed to suddenly include him one way or another. Every song I heard, every sign I read, everything. Which was exactly why I'd been holed up in my room for days. I didn't want to hear him, see him, breathe him every time I stepped outside. I was tired of him. I was tired of expecting to see him every time I stepped out of my building. Even worse, I was tired of expecting to see him and feeling like an idiot for actually wanting to.

"We're supposed to have lunch with Dad, remember?"

Vanessa added.

I turned over in bed and buried my face in my pillow. "Tell him I'm sick."

"You're not."

"I feel sick."

My sister sighed heavily and sat on the edge of the bed, running a hand over my hair. "Honey, you're not sick, you're heartbroken."

"Sick. Heartbroken. Same difference."

She sighed again. I turned over to look at her. Her eyes widened as I finally let her catch a glimpse of my face—puffy, red eyes, swollen lips. I was sure I still had spots beneath my eyes from when I vomited violently at some point in the middle of the night just thinking about him. About us. About his deceit.

"Camila," she whispered.

"More people die of broken hearts than they do of a common cold," I said. "Did you know that?"

She shook her head, brown eyes filled with pity. "I didn't know that."

"Well, they do."

"Charlie called asking for you today," she said, changing the subject. "He said he's come by a handful of times and you never answer the door."

I covered my face with my arm. "I'll call him later."

I felt her stand up from the bed and heard her walking around my room. "I completely understand why you're mad at Warren. Trust me, I get it. He lied. He knew about Dad and how you feel about Belmonte, and he kept that from you, but you would've never given him a chance if he'd have told you from the get-go. You would have blown him off and wouldn't have gotten to know him. Can you really blame the guy?"

"Yes. I can."

I uncovered my face and threw the covers off me as I stood up and walked to the bathroom. I brushed my teeth, washed my face, looked at myself in the mirror and flinched at what I saw. Even after Eric and I had broken up, I hadn't looked this bad. But I hadn't cried six out of a seven-hour flight, and then again when I got home, and then replayed everything on loop until I physically made myself sick thinking about it all. I'd lived with Eric for years. Shared a life with him. And when we finally broke up I felt sad, but I also felt relief. Warren seemed to have this hold on me that made it impossible to breathe without feeling a stab of pain every time I thought about his absence.

It wasn't rocket science. I'd given myself to him so completely, that now it was over I felt like I was falling apart. I showered, hoping to shed some of my sadness. When I stepped out of the shower, I opened up my bathroom cabinet in search of something for my rapidly growing headache, and what I found was a note from Warren. A note. My heart stopped at the sight of his handwriting.

I miss you already. – Warren.

How had I overlooked that before I went on my trip? I picked it up and smelled it. It didn't smell like him. I squeezed it in my hand and tossed it in the basket beside the toilet and stared at the paper, crumpled and alone. I dressed quickly and headed out with my sister. We were both quiet as we walked down the street. Each step felt heavier than the last, especially when I got near where my old building stood. They'd wrapped a temporary fence around it with big Belmonte signs that warned of a near-future demolition.

"That's what they do," I said, feeling tears burn my eyes. "They demolish everything."

Vanessa's hand found mine and squeezed. I was grateful she didn't talk or make a comment. We walked past the building and toward Charlie's bar, where my dad stood outside smoking a cigarette. Seeing him made me smile until all of the ugly memories came back and crashed through me all at once and the smile slipped off my face. *His* lies. *Warren's* lies. *Javier's* lies.

"There's my girl," he said.

He gave Vanessa a hug and a kiss before turning to me with a smile. As if he'd been in my life for the past ten years. As if he hadn't fucked everything up for our family, as if suddenly coming back made everything right again. He must have seen the sentiment written on my face, because he also stopped smiling.

"What's wrong?"

"Nothing."

I gave him a kiss on the cheek and brushed past him, walking into the bar and finding Charlie inside. He walked right over and wrapped his arms around me, holding me tight. I inhaled the smell of his cologne and cigarettes and tried hard not to cry.

"I heard about Warren," he said against my hair. "I'm sorry you're hurting."

That made tears form in my eyes. Hurting seemed like such a simple word for what I was feeling. I was hurt, sad, angry, and really confused because despite all of those things, I still longed for him. I backed out of Charlie's arms and smiled up at him.

"I heard you got food from Malecon. How'd you order it?"

He laughed. "My broken-up Spanish goes a long way, you know. Besides, they already know my order by heart."

"They didn't bully you when you picked it up?" I asked, feeling myself smile genuinely for the first time in days.

The girls in Malecon were obsessed with Charlie. He wasn't necessarily the best looking guy on the block, but he was different, and that was enough for the attraction to bloom.

"Not much. Cecilia practically begged me to ask her out," he said.

"Why don't you?"

He shrugged. "The girls in this neighborhood gossip too damn much. You should hear the things I hear around here."

"Trust me, I know," I said, shooting him a look.

Vanessa walked into the bar and Dad followed closely behind, closing the door and locking it as Charlie instructed. "We don't want anybody coming in and interrupting our meal," he said. We sat around the tables he'd set together and started eating. Charlie got up to get our drinks and switched on the television while he was over there before joining us at the table again. I looked up at my dad, who was staring at me while he ate his rice and beans.

"I understand if you're still mad at me," he said, taking a sip of his Coke. "I don't blame you. I know it's going to take getting used to having me around again and I appreciate you giving me a chance to prove my worth."

Why was it that men fucked up and thought that a simple apology could make it all go away? My leg started bouncing up and down on its own accord, the nervous twitch I hadn't experienced since I was back in high school setting in again. I blinked away from him and looked at Vanessa, who was sitting beside him. She shrugged and mouthed, "Just try." I felt my shoulders sag. This wasn't Warren. Or Eric. Or any other man who'd come in and out of my life and let me down.

This was my dad. My eyes met his again. Sure, he'd been the first man to fuck up in my life. And despite the strides we made that weekend at my mom's house, I was still upset, but he had been locked up—his fault for making a stupid, careless, selfish mistake—with no family around him. Which was also his fault for taking our visitation rights from us . . . the accusations rung out louder than my rationality. I closed my eyes briefly before meeting his gaze again. His dark brows were drawn in, and the lines on his forehead looked clearer than they had a couple of weeks ago. He looked completely exhausted and vulnerable. I wondered how much sleep he'd lost over this, over *us*.

"I wish I could turn back time and make better choices, but the only thing I can do is be here in this moment."

I sighed and reached over the table to put my hand over his. "I know. I promise I'll try harder. Most days I'm excited that you're here, but others . . . I'm just angry that you were gone at all."

There was a loud knock on the door. Followed by banging.

"Shit. That's Johnny," Vanessa said, getting out of her chair and walking over there quickly.

"You invited Johnny?" I asked, eyes wide, turning around to see her shrug as she unlocked the door.

My brother took off his Yankees cap as he walked into the bar and fanned himself with it. "It's hotter than the devil's nut sack out there."

Mom walked in closely behind him and glared at him. "Johnny!"

I wanted to keep a straight face, but I couldn't not laugh at the outrage on her face and the amusement on his. Charlie got up to greet him in a bear hug.

"Gringo, I haven't seen you in a minute. You look more and more like that dude from *Sons of Anarchy* every time I see you," Johnny said.

Charlie laughed. "I look nothing like him. We share a name, that's it."

"And the leather jacket," Johnny responded. "And the beard, and the white-dude thing."

Vanessa and I looked at each other and giggled like kids. We'd talked about that in the past. Our Charlie looked absolutely nothing like Hunnam. Maybe if you drank five beers and squinted and turned your face the right way in a dimly lit room.

My brother and Mom joined us with a plate of food in one hand and the remote control in the other. He started flipping through channels as we ate and talked about our newest show obsession: *Stranger Things*. Dad just watched us in awe as we explained what Netflix was.

"Is that the scary show you were watching last night?" Mom asked.

My brother nodded. "Mom thinks we're crazy for watching it."

"I just think it's wrong," she said. "Un show asi con niños!"

I laughed. "The kids are what makes it scary."

"They're the best part," Vanessa agreed.

"I thought they were DVDs that you watched and mailed back," he said.

"They used to be," I responded. "It's grown into a whole other thing."

Johnny took over the conversation and started talking about the way they were able to grow the company from DVDs to what they were now and we listened in awe. As annoying as he could be, my brother was smart as hell and had some really good ideas for companies and apps that weren't circulating yet.

"Pops, we could start a company," Johnny suggested.

Dad chuckled, amusement lighting up in his eyes. "It's not that simple."

"I know, but I'm willing to work, and if you're willing to work . . . " He shrugged. "We can do it."

Dad looked at me. "How's Winsor? Adam and his parents speak very highly of you."

"I love it," I said, smiling.

"You don't counsel kids anymore though. I thought that was your thing."

"It was. It is. I mean, I love the kids, but I think what I'm doing now helps them just as much. In a different way, of course."

"You're giving them places to learn and grow," Johnny said, glancing at me with a smile. "That's pretty major."

I smiled. "Thanks."

"You have to go to one of her events, Ruben. You'll be impressed," Mom said.

"She's kind of like a big deal there," Vanessa added with a wink.

"You know what the number-one thing you do in prison is?" Dad asked suddenly.

All of us looked at him. Charlie excused himself for a moment to receive a shipment out back.

"Work out?" Johnny responded.

"Think," my sister and I responded unanimously with a laugh.

Dad nodded, rolling his eyes at my brother. "Think about things. You think about things so much that you feel like either you'll end up going crazy or you'll come out of there with a higher understanding than everybody else in the world."

"I'm sure it's hard not to let hateful feelings fester," I said.

"Extremely hard, but once you let go of the anger, you begin to realize what's important, and I know I shouldn't have thought that a phone call a week would be enough for you guys, but I didn't want you to see me in there. I didn't want you to see the other guys in there. It's not a pretty place."

"We didn't care," I whispered, blinking away tears. "I'm so tired of people hiding things from us to shield us from pain. We could have dealt with it. We could have gone in there and supported you through the ugly. We would have happily done it."

Dad smiled sadly, wiping his wet eyes. "I know. I'm sorry. I shouldn't have undermined your ability to adapt."

I took a deep breath and nodded. Johnny wrapped an arm around me, finally sticking to one channel and putting the volume up loud. I shut my eyes when I heard the clear voices of soccer announcers. I knew it was soccer because they were the only ones who screamed that way over every single thing. I didn't want to look up, but then I heard the chant, "War Zone. War Zone. War Zone!" and couldn't help myself. Sure enough, there he was, in his zone with the ball between his feet.

The expression on his face was one of complete concentration as he dribbled it out of the reach of the opposing team and past the players. He kicked it in and scored a goal. His team jumped up, the commentators went ballistic. Johnny stood quickly, throwing his arms up in celebration, but then caught the tears rolling down my cheeks and dropped his arms quickly.

I glanced back at the screen and saw Warren running down the field and hugging his teammates—Felix, Stephen, and then lifted his shirt as he ran down the field again. He was wearing a shirt under with the words, *Chase moments* on it. I blinked, swallowed, blinked again to will the tears away, but couldn't hold them back and soon they were rolling down my face. He stood in front of the camera and mouthed the words, "I'm sorry."

I buried my face in my hands and continued to cry. My brother switched off the television. I felt him sit down beside me and wrap an arm around me, then felt another arm wrap around me and knew my sister had come around to do the same. I cried harder. When I heard a squeak of a chair against the hardwood floor and felt my dad come up behind me and wrap his arms around all of us, I cried even harder.

"It's going to be okay," Vanessa said against my hair.

That only made me cry even harder. They all dropped their arms and let me pull myself together.

"Sorry, sis," Johnny said when I wiped my face.

"You guys will be okay," Mom offered.

I smiled and shrugged. "It is what it is."

"I'm sure he's hating himself right now." He paused when I glanced up at him. "I know I was hard on you about him, but he really did seem like he was in love with you."

I tore my gaze away from him and looked at the half-eaten fried plantain on my plate. "I'm just a poor Dominican girl from Washington Heights, remember?"

"Ah, I'm an asshole."

"You are," I said, smiling. "But you're still my best brother."

"And you're still my Peach."

"And you're still not Mario," Vanessa added, looking at

him.

We all laughed and changed the subject, and despite the pain I felt and the tears that had fallen, that hot afternoon I found my antidote in my family.

Chapter
THIRTY-FOUR

Warren

I asked for more time to think about whether or not I wanted to go to Barcelona. The season had already started, and I didn't necessarily want to switch teams mid-season, but I would do it if that's what it took. After the scene at the club, the media caught wind of what Elena had said and tore her apart so viciously she fled the country. I wished I felt bad for her, but I didn't. She hurt Camila, she forced my hand and made me tell her something that while I should have told her before, I wanted to tell her at a better time. And she'd caused a rift in our club, which was unacceptable. Despite that, she wasn't the reason I was still considering Barcelona. Really considering Barcelona. I just didn't want to rush into anything. I agreed to meet with the owner and the manager of the club, though. I owed them that much.

Sergio couldn't understand why I would turn down what they were offering. It was almost twice as much as I was being paid now, which would make me one of the top-five highest-paid football players in the world. But for once, it wasn't about the money or fame it would bring. It was about peace. In Barcelona I could live near my grandparents, whom I was lucky to still have. I could live in the countryside, away from the flashes of the cameras and the flocks of people chasing me down. I could escape everything that came with the territory of being this sought after, until I needed to go to work and smile and pretend all of it meant everything to me. *It once had.* I tried to think about when the shift had happened. When had I stopped wanting the fame? When had I stopped caring about the cars and the sponsorships? Every question led to the same answer: when that poor little girl from Washington Heights walked into that meeting at Belmonte and stole my breath away.

When I spoke to her for the first time, I knew I had to have her. And once I started following her around, I became addicted to her. Out of every woman I'd ever met, Camila was the easiest one for me to fall for. She didn't make false promises or hide beneath materialistic things. She made no excuses for who she was or why she did the things she did. She was just real, with a body that would drive any man wild, and a heart of gold that would make any man lucky if they ever managed to catch her and keep her. And for a moment, she'd been mine.

With that thought, I got out of the bed I'd once slept in at my grandparents' house and joined them for dinner. They refused to let me stay in a hotel while I was in town, and I was grateful for their persistence, because in times like these

I needed family. My grandmother gave me pitiful glances as we ate dinner, throwing in an, "Eres un idiota, Warren," wherever she could fit it.

She said I was an idiot and she hadn't even met Camila. If she had, there was no doubt in my mind that she would've hit me over the head with my grandfather's walking cane. I couldn't bother to disagree with her. I was a complete idiot, but it was something I couldn't worry about. Not right now. I needed to figure out this loan situation. I was surprised to find out that my team actually wanted to loan me to Barcelona for three years, mainly because I was the second-best player on the roster. When I met with the owners in Barcelona I understood it, though. They were willing to pay me and my team millions of euros for the three years, and when they told me the powerhouse team they were trying to put together they almost had me convinced to sign. I just couldn't bring myself to do it. Not without consulting Camila.

"She's not your wife," my grandfather said over dinner. "You don't need to consult her."

"Manuel, por favor," my grandmother responded. "You're just saying that because you're bitter."

"Bitter about what?"

"Bitter because he went to play for your rival team."

"I didn't have a choice," I reminded them.

My grandfather sucked his teeth. "You always have a choice."

My grandmother rolled her eyes.

I grinned. "What was I supposed to do? Break my leg?"

"There's one option," he said, raising a bushy eyebrow.

I could only laugh at the ridiculousness, though it tapered off when I remembered Camila and my knee. I missed her. I missed her voice, and her eyes, and the animated way in which she spoke. I missed the comfort she brought me when she was around. Most of all, I missed her.

Chapter
THIRTY-FIVE

Camila

Three days later, I had bouquets of red roses waiting for me when I arrived home from work. Not two bouquets. Or three. There were more than I knew what to do with. I stood there, gaping at the roses, tears stinging my eyes as I pictured him picking up the phone to order them and tell them what to write on each card. I wondered when they'd delivered them and how they'd brought all of them up here. How many guys did it take to deliver them all? I was surprised building security had allowed the delivery guy to leave them all in the hallway like this. I was sure it was a fire hazard. Then I remembered that Warren was the owner of the building and my shoulders sagged. He'd really done this. My thought process was chaotic. I'd moved from flattered to upset in under thirty seconds.

He was inescapable. Unless I moved, which I couldn't do yet since I'd signed a lease. On top of that, what I was paying was a steal since Belmonte had the same effect on Harlem as they did on Brooklyn, which meant every playwright and every singer and every actor was now flooding our housing and hiking our rental prices.

I was still standing outside my door trying to figure out what I was going to do with all of them when the elevator door opened and an impressed whistle rang out behind me. I turned around to see Charlie walking up to me. I hadn't seen him since we had lunch at the bar the other day, though he had text messaged to make sure I was okay. And it was Charlie. He knew me well enough to let me have time to myself.

"Somebody's . . . sorry. Need help taking them inside?" he asked, brows raised as his eyes swept over the flowers. I sighed, looking at the flowers, and he spoke up again, with a smile on his face, "Or are we throwing them down the chute?"

That made me laugh. I considered that option, but each bouquet had a card attached to them and I loved the smell too much to just toss them. What could he possibly have to say? It had been over a week and he hadn't even called. Hadn't even sent a text. The only inclination of an apology I'd gotten was when I saw him score that goal on television and for all he knew I wouldn't have been watching. I mean, how the hell did he know I even saw that? Maybe he was apologizing to somebody else. Maybe he'd screwed over more than one woman at the same time. Anger ripped through me as I thought about that. Every time I thought I would get over it or at least be less upset, memories crashed through me and I felt the betrayal once more.

Charlie helped me bring all the flowers inside and stayed over for dinner. Unlike Vanessa, he didn't ask about Warren, which I appreciated. Unlike my mother, he didn't probe about issues with my dad. He just stayed. We watched TV as we ate and when he saw I'd yawned one too many times, he went downstairs to his apartment and left me alone with my thoughts and my flowers. I went to my bedroom with the full intention of leaving the cards unread until tomorrow, but the sweet rosy scent brought me back to my living room.

I opened up a bottle of white wine my sister had given me two years ago when I was hired at my new job and prayed I wouldn't die of alcohol poisoning if the bottle was expired by now. Google eased my worry and I started drinking away my sorrows as I stared at the cards clipped to the bouquets. After downing my second glass, I reached for one of the cards and read it. "I'm sorry. Love always, Warren."

That was it?

I opened a third, a fourth, a fifth. They all said the exact same thing. I drank some more. After my fourth glass, I started to get frustrated and instead of leaving it alone, I picked up my phone and did what all idiots around the world do when they have alcohol in their system . . . I called him.

More accurately: I FaceTimed him because my thumbs were working faster than my brain. Thankfully, I was able to shut it down before he answered, and once my adrenaline died down, I decided to forget about the whole thing. I didn't have to thank him. I didn't have anything to say to him that didn't involve insults. My phone vibrated in my hand, the little FaceTime alert making my heart lurch into my throat. I pressed end. It vibrated again. And again. Finally, I answered.

"Camila?" he said, eyes adjusting to the light in my living room.

297

My heart skipped at the sight of him. I opened my mouth and closed it. Maybe if I hung up he wouldn't remember any of this. I should hang up, but I couldn't stop looking at his bare chest and arms and those lips and . . . oh my God why was I on FaceTime with him?

"What's wrong? Did you get my flowers?"

Flowers. Right. "Yes, and you apologized in twenty-six notecards after I told you I didn't want a damn apology."

He blinked again, sitting up in bed. The sheet moved farther down his bare chest. "Are you drunk?"

"No," I scoffed.

He smiled, though it was small. "I can see the empty bottle of wine behind you."

"Oh." I reached behind me and clumsily moved it out of sight.

"I miss you, baby."

"You lost the right to call me that," I whispered, willing away the tears I felt building.

"I'm sorry, Camila. I know I sound like a broken record, but I don't know what else to say."

"I have to go."

He closed his eyes and shifted in the bed. I could hear the sheets beneath him and tried hard not to remember what they felt like on my fingertips. Had it really been over a week? It felt like I was just there.

"I'll be in town soon."

My heart leaped. I turned my face away from the phone.

"My dad isn't doing so well," he said. I kept my mouth shut, my teeth ground. "Is there any way I'd be able to see you while I'm there?"

I kept my face turned away and focused on breathing because I felt like at any given moment I would start to cry.

"I have to go."

I pressed end on the call before he could protest. I couldn't bear to hear him protest or to talk to me about his father or see me when he was in town. I switched off my phone, got into bed, and cried myself to sleep. The next morning, I woke up with a headache the size of Texas. Stupid wine. Stupid me. Stupid everything. Images of my call with Warren flashed through my head and I cringed. Had I really done that? I'd really done that. What was worse was that I knew with every fiber of me that there was no way I'd be able to erase him from my mind. Or my heart.

Chapter
THIRTY-SIX

Warren

The first thing I did when I landed late last night was to ask Antoine to drive me by her building. We parked across the street and I got out of the car and leaned against it and just stared at her window wondering what she'd do if I went up there and knocked on her door. Instead, I went to my brother's empty apartment on Park Avenue, which felt like a world away from Camila. Against my better judgment, when I woke up the next morning, I went to the grand opening of the soccer park knowing she would be there. I knew she wouldn't be pleased to see me, but I'd take a scowl on her face over not seeing her at all. And really, I couldn't stop myself from going. Even Antoine warned me that it might not be the best idea, and still, I soldiered on.

Vanessa spotted me when I got there and did a triple take, as if she couldn't believe I was really there. Then she marched over to me.

"What the hell are you doing here?"

"I need to see her."

She gaped at me. "Here? Do you know how much pressure she's feeling right now?"

I looked around the park, which had turned out really nicely. The field was perfectly manicured, the bleachers were brand new and the crowd of kids that had gathered was impressive for a soccer field.

"It looks like a good turn out. How could she feel pressure right now?" I asked, looking back at Vanessa who was still looking at me like I'd lost my mind. Maybe I had. "Listen, I'm not here to cause any issues. I just want to see her."

"I get it," she said, shaking her head. "But if she throws something at you, don't say I didn't warn you."

She walked away and went up to Adam, who lifted his head as she said something. He looked at me and nodded with a smile and a wave that I returned. I looked around the field once more, trying to find Camila. When I finally spotted her, I felt my heart plummet into the pit of my stomach. She was standing beside Quinn the band guy smiling at something he was saying to her. I watched them as he turned to a woman standing nearby and say something to her as he wrapped an arm around Camila's shoulder, squeezing her into his side. I swallowed past the knot forming in my throat and tugged down on the collar of my shirt. I wasn't jealous of him. It was Quinn, the guy with the amateur band, the one who frequented the movies with her, the one who wanted nothing more than to get in her pants.

"Well, you saw her." The voice startled me. I blinked

away from Camila and Quinn and looked at Vanessa beside me again. "She's happy. Just leave her alone."

"She's happy?" I asked, my gaze cutting to Camila again. "It's been two weeks. She hasn't . . ." *Moved on*, I wanted to say, but couldn't.

"What does it matter to you?" she asked. "You don't live here, you lied to her about the one thing she can't stand to even think about, and I still don't think you get it."

"She hates my father, I get it. I had nothing to do with his poor decisions. I wasn't even here for any of that."

"It's not about that. Are you that dense? You should have been upfront with her from the beginning. My sister is one of the most forgiving people I know, but you really fucked with her emotions."

"I know."

I felt horrible about it, but I sucked at apologizing. *I'm sorry* was the only way I knew how to apologize and even though I knew that wouldn't be enough for Camila, I didn't know what else to do about it. Vanessa walked away again and started talking to somebody else, and I watched Camila and Quinn a little longer before I walked away. Maybe she was right. Maybe Camila needed to find happiness elsewhere. I looked back one last time when I reached the sidewalk and caught Camila's eyes on me. She frowned a bit before realizing it was me and not her mind playing tricks on her, but once she did, her expression fell and she ran the opposite way, through the crowd. I tried to follow her, but couldn't see where she went. It was as if she disappeared completely. I stuck around a few more minutes before leaving for good.

In the car, I sent her a text message.

I'm proud of you. It's an excellent park. I hope you're truly happy.

She didn't respond. Not that I'd expected her to, and just like that I started to feel angry.

Chapter
THIRTY-SEVEN

Camila

I sat down in front of the TV with a plate of hot food on my lap. I'd gone to my mom's house the night before and took leftovers with me so I wouldn't have to cook. After what felt like an eternity of flipping through channels, I landed on one. My fingers freezing on the remote as Warren's face appeared on the screen. This was why I didn't watch sports channels (aside from the fact I didn't care to keep up with sports news). Warren's trade, or "loan" as they kept referring to it kept popping up everywhere. Soccer kept popping up everywhere or maybe I was just noticing more now. I couldn't bring myself to switch the channel.

Reporter: "Your one constant has always remained that soccer is the number-one love of your life. That you'd never trade it for anything or anyone. Does that still stand?"

I inhaled a heavy breath when I heard the question. I set down my fork and knife on my plate. I'd promised myself I wasn't going to look at him, listen to him, talk to him, have absolutely anything to do with him once he left. After catching sight of him last week at the park I realized this wasn't a normal situation, where I would move on and pretend I was okay with everything. I wasn't okay with anything.

Yet there I was, like I was sure countless of other females were, waiting on bated breath for his answer to that question. When he came into the screen, my breath left me altogether. God. I missed him. I hated him. Couldn't stand him. But seeing him on the screen, the way he sat back on the seat with his ankle crossed over his knee, looking completely relaxed as he was being drilled with questions . . . the way his chiseled jaw moved when he gave the reporter that lopsided smile that hinted at legions of pleasure that would make any sane woman blush furiously, those arms, roped in muscle and etched in art that I'd touched, clung to during so many sleepless nights . . .

"Of course it still stands. What do you think?" he asked, tilting his head, green eyes twinkling in flirtation. I groaned. What an asshole.

Reporter: "So the rumors about a woman you left behind in the US during holiday—"

"I think we both know how many rumors are spread about me." He tore his gaze away from her and looked directly into the camera. Directly at me. "If there was a woman that special, I would never leave her behind."

Reporter: "I understand that this mysterious woman came to see you recently. There is a lot of speculation that she may be the reason you haven't solidified your decision on whether you want to go to Barcelona or stay in Manchester?"

Warren shook his head. "That is completely false."

Reporter: "Fair enough. In closing, would you be willing to make your career number two for the right woman? Even if that means moving to another . . . country and giving all of this up?"

He stayed quiet for a long moment and finally looked at the camera again, his face sobering, all traces of humor gone. "I'd give up everything to chase moments with the right woman."

I was too stunned to move.

Chapter
THIRTY-EIGHT

Warren

'd asked Antoine to check up on Camila—in the most non-creepy, stalker way he could manage—and the news hadn't done anything to lighten my already damp mood. He'd seen her three times, and all those times she'd been with Quinn.

"Were they holding hands? Kissing?" I asked.

"No. They were just talking."

"Was he touching her?" I asked, my teeth gritting. I needed to stop asking questions I didn't really want the answers to, but I couldn't. I needed to know.

"He had his arm around her."

I bit my tongue so hard I tasted iron. I couldn't seem to shake the images that flashed through my head. All I did was think about her, dream about her, wish for her to pick up the phone when I called or answer one of my texts. Even as my name roared through the stadium I couldn't drown out thoughts of her. Somehow, I focused on the game. Kicking the ball toward the goal when it came to me, pushing my way through opponents, passing it to my teammates, running. I was setting up for a penalty kick, standing with the ball under one of my feet as I looked at the goal. Often during a game, this was the only time I had to clear my mind, and today was no different.

As I stood there, I took a moment to look around at all the red jerseys, to listen to all of the people screaming the unified chant they'd come up with during my first season there: "*War Zone! War Zone!*" Men wanted to be me, kids pretended they were me, and women wanted to be with me. Normally, I got high on the feeling. Today I felt empty. The woman I wanted, the one I still considered to be mine, was in a different country, spending time with another man, and as non-romantic as she may have found it, I knew he was just waiting for the right moment to make his move. What would happen when he did? Would I lose her for good? I took a deep breath and set the ball up in front of me again. I kicked it with as much force as I had, putting all of my anger into it.

The crowd went wild. My teammates ran up to me screaming and cheering.

And I just stood there, waiting for the feeling of elation that normally came with the adrenaline to crash through me. It never came.

Chapter
THIRTY-NINE

Camila

Through my sleepy haze I could hear my phone ringing. I rubbed my eyes and yawned as I sat up in bed, blindly reaching for it on my nightstand and missing with each attempt. When it stopped ringing and started to ring a second time, I managed to fully wake up and look at the screen – Nancy. I frowned and looked outside. I didn't have fancy blinds like Warren – or his brother – I had regular plastic blinds that kept getting caught every time I tried to open and close them and one of them always remained twisted open despite my attempt to keep it shut. Therefore, I knew that it wasn't even six in the morning yet. I answered the call quickly and braced myself for the news because I knew that no good news came this early. Not from a woman like Nancy who was

309

proper enough to call you after eight and only before nine at night.

"It's Treyvon."

My heart stopped. I closed my eyes. "Oh God. What happened?"

"He was shot last night."

"What?" I gasped so loud I coughed and then squeaked out, "Oh my God. What?"

"He's okay. He's not . . . " She let out a breath. "He's going to be okay. I got a call from his mother. Luckily he was grazed in the shoulder. I just wanted you to hear it from me. I already called his counselor to let him know."

"Where is he?"

"Brooklyn Hospital."

I got dressed in a hurry and rushed over there. The waiting room was a disaster— people waiting everywhere. Children, adults, elderly people all packed into a small space as they waited to be attended to and for loved ones and now I was one of them. I stood off to a corner where I couldn't disturb anybody and sent a text message to my sister letting her know where I was and what had happened. After what felt like an eternity, the nurse gave me the okay that visiting hours were underway and I could visit with Trey.

As I walked over I tried to picture what I was going to see. He was in the pediatric unit, where the walls and décor were meant for children. For some reason it struck me as odd. I met Trey when he was fourteen, he was seventeen now, and I couldn't think of a time that he reminded me of a child. Maybe it was because he'd been independent and had been looking out for himself and helping his mother for so long. Maybe it was because he was over six feet tall and I somehow associated that with a person of age. Either way, all of this reminded me that it wasn't the case. He was a child. An underage kid forced to do things for himself and his parent that no kid should be held accountable for.

Emotion gripped my throat as I held the doorknob to his room. I swallowed thickly and willed it away. I needed to be as strong as he was. For him. I owed the kid that much. Pushing the door open, I snuck a glance and saw him lying down in the middle of his bed with his phone in his hand. His head snapped up when he saw me, a huge smile breaking over his face.

"Miss. A!"

I shook my head, smiling as I walked toward him, blinking the tears I knew were impossible to hold back away a little longer. He looked like regular Treyvon, despite the wrapping on his left arm.

"T, what in the world?" I said, dropping a kiss on his forehead and placing a little blue bag on his food tray as I sat down.

"What'd you bring me?" he asked, ignoring my question.

"Nothing exciting. I got it from the shop downstairs." I gave him a pointed look. "What the fuck happened?"

His brows rose and he let out a heavy sigh. "You know how it is."

"No, I don't know how it is, so why don't you tell me?"

"I was playing ball and some guy started a fight with me because he saw me talking to his girl at school." He shrugged with his good arm. "We had words, I walked away and he pulled out a gun."

I closed my eyes, thinking about the scenario. It was one I saw often, but never had somebody I loved ever been shot like that. Never would I have thought anybody would get involved with Trey. He was one of the good kids. One of the best kids that came through Winsor. He was a great student and had a real future in basketball. I shook my head and opened my eyes again.

"You could have been killed, Trey," I whispered, reaching out for his hand.

"I know."

"Trey," I said, waiting for him to meet my gaze. "You could have died."

"I know." He swallowed. I could tell he was holding back tears.

"How am I ever supposed to sit courtside at a Knicks game if you die?"

That made him smile. We looked at each other for a beat and shared a laugh.

"You really think I'm gonna make it, huh?" he said.

How many of us go through life without anybody giving us an ounce of validity? Without anybody telling us, "You can do it." Or, "Keep going. You're going to be great someday." I knew what it meant to Trey, because even though he had family, none of them knew what it was like to step twenty miles outside of the neighborhood they grew up in. And that's okay. My maternal grandmother had never left the farm she grew up in before she turned twenty-five and she lived a happy life. To them, going to high school was impressive enough. But this wasn't DR or Haiti, where Trey's grandparents came from. This was America. And dammit, we had opportunities here. I held his gaze.

"Treyvon, I know you're going to make it." I squeezed his hand. "I never want to visit you in the hospital again, unless you're over twenty-five and your wife is having a baby."

He laughed and cringed. "Fuck, Miss. A, you're hurting me. How's the new boyfriend?"

I let out a long, harsh breath. "Old."

"Oh shit. You got rid of him?"

I shrugged.

"Is it because of the distance?"

I shook my head with a smile. "Why don't you worry about getting better and stop listening to all the gossip in Winsor?"

I left with the promise that I'd see him next week when he got out. As soon as I got to work, I called his mother and begged her to move to the Winsor housing unit. It was one way to keep Trey off the streets and make sure that he stayed on the right path. Thankfully, she didn't argue.

I knew I couldn't solve everybody's problems or make everyone happy. If I could, Warren wouldn't have lied to me, he'd have a stupid nine-to-five job, and live in New York. I was glad through work I could at least help others have a chance at one of those things.

Chapter
FORTY

Camila

The morning Javier Belmonte died, we were flooded by the news. Most outlets said the same thing: Real estate mogul dies. Unexpected death. Leaves behind a wife, two sons, and a grandson. As usual, Warren's name was not attached to any of it. Thomas Belmonte's name was everywhere. I wondered why that was. I wondered if it upset Warren at all. I wasn't sure if I should send him a text telling him I was sorry for his loss, send flowers, or let it be. I decided to do the one thing I never in my life expected to do: call my dad and ask him.

"The burial is tomorrow," he said.

I swallowed. "Are you going?"

"Of course. He went to your grandfather's funeral to pay

his respects. I need to go pay mine."

I looked around my small office in Winsor. My door was slightly ajar and I caught sight of Trey walking down the hall, his arm still bandaged. I stood up with the phone in my hand. "I want to go with you."

"To the funeral?" He couldn't have sounded any more surprised if he tried.

"Yes."

"They're having an open casket tonight. The burial is tomorrow."

I took a deep breath. "Are you going tonight?"

"Yes."

Dad and I had spoken at length about Warren and his father and the whole Belmonte fiasco. He didn't go into specific details as to who had done what, and it didn't really matter. I knew I would never completely understand how somebody could choose to give up their freedom and their family, but I knew Dad did it with the understanding that Javier would take care of us. Which he did, according to Mom. I knew about the money we were sent monthly and when I turned eighteen I refused any help offered by my mom because I knew where it was coming from. That was my cross to bear and I was fine with it. If I could turn back time, I'd do it all again, despite the student loans that were kicking my ass each month. No amount of money was enough payment for lost time with my father.

I wondered if Warren would be at his father's funeral all night. My heart squeezed at the thought. The cloud of sadness I didn't think I'd feel shadowed over me anyway. Not because I was sad that Javier had died. I never met the guy and even now I despised him, but because it made me think of my grandfather's funeral and our loss. I remembered the numb feeling I had during the burial and the loss that gripped me as they lowered his casket to the ground. I pushed the thoughts away.

"Do you think I should go tonight or tomorrow?"

"I'm sure Warren will appreciate you going to either one, sweetie," he said in a soft voice that made me close my eyes.

"Okay. I'll let you know," I whispered. "I have to go."

I caught up with Trey and talked to him about his arm and his move to the Winsor apartments. He told me about the college scout that went to visit him at the hospital and his plans for college.

"I have to do at least one year before I go to the NBA," he said, laughing at the glare I shot him. He knew damn well how I felt about people skipping college to go straight into sports.

"As long as you go," I said nonetheless, because let's face it, guys like Trey would be drafted and there was nobody on earth who would turn down millions of dollars to stay in school.

On my way home, I mentally prepared myself to see Warren. I thought about what it felt like to see him the other day, even if it was just for a second, even if it was from the complete opposite side of the field. As if somebody had taken my heart out and stomped on it—twice, for good measure. I wasn't sure how I would handle seeing him up close at the funeral, but I had to do it. When I left work, I received a call from Quinn asking me if I wanted to go to the movies that night. I politely declined. I'd been spending a lot of time with him, and while I appreciated the distraction, the only thing it offered me was a reminder of the man I actually wanted in my life and how he was no longer there.

I didn't end up going to the open casket. I felt like that

was more for family and friends, and I wouldn't have felt right going given I'd hated the man. The next morning, I put on a black dress and went to the burial with my dad. When we got to the cemetery, the first person I spotted was Warren's mom. The second person I spotted was Thomas, who looked surprised to see me there but didn't say anything to me. The third, not far from them, was Cayden, who was with a pretty woman I assumed was his mom. Lastly, I saw Warren. My heart lurched into my throat when I saw him. He was wearing a dark suit with a black tie, a white shirt, and sunglasses. He had a hard expression on his face, with a set jaw and his lips drawn into a thin line.

Dad walked around, saying hello to people while I stayed behind. It seemed like he knew everybody there and suddenly I felt out of place. Still, I stayed. I looked at Warren again. Each time I did, my heart squeezed in my chest. It physically ached from the pain. Finally, I grabbed hold of the little courage I had and walked over to him. I sat down in the empty foldable chair beside him. He didn't look up to acknowledge me. I focused on breathing, in, out, in, out . . . and on that last one, I put my hand on his knee.

"I'm sorry," I whispered.

His leg jerked up at the feel of my hand there and his face whipped to mine. His lips parted first, then his hand came up to take the sunglasses off his face. It was then I saw that the whites of his eyes were bloodshot, his lower lids swollen from crying. His father had just died. Of course he'd cried. I just hadn't expected to see him that way, and I definitely hadn't expected for it to affect me the way it did, as if it were my own family suffering. That's what I felt as I saw the raw pain in his eyes. I wished more than anything that I could take it all away, that I could feel it for him so he didn't have to. He blinked, and blinked again, then blinked faster as if willing away tears.

Before I could blink, his arms were around me and my face was against his chest. I had no option but to wrap my arms around him and let him hold me. He tucked his face into my neck and breathed deeply. We sat like that for so long, my arms got tired of being gripped around him like that. When he finally let go, he held my face in his hands and searched my eyes. Our faces were so close I was sure he was going to kiss me, and even though I was giving him this moment of peace out of respect, I couldn't bear for him to do that. He must have seen the panic on my face, because he placed his forehead against mine and breathed out instead. I closed my eyes.

"God, Camila," he whispered hoarsely, still holding my face, "I need you so much."

I felt the lump in my throat rise again and swallowed to hold back tears. I couldn't bring myself to talk. What would I say? Probably the wrong thing. I felt somebody tap my on the arm, and I moved to see Cayden standing there with a shy smile on his face.

"Hey, my favorite superhero," I said, backing away from Warren to give him a hug. "How are you?"

"I'm good. Grandpa went to heaven. He's not coming back," he said in a small voice, his brown eyes losing a little bit of light as he spoke the words.

Funerals were so damn heartbreaking. I didn't even like Javier, but I felt horrible for those who loved him. I kissed Cayden on the head and smiled.

"He's right here," I said, putting my hand over his heart. "He'll always be right here."

"That's what my mom said."

"You should listen to her."

He nodded slowly and glanced at Warren momentarily. "Uncle War thinks you're really pretty."

"I said beautiful," Warren said beside me, his voice still hoarse. "I said she's the most beautiful girl in the world."

I couldn't bring myself to look at him right now, so I kept looking at Cayden.

"Yeah, he said that," Cayden said with a blush. I smiled because I'd been blushing and was glad I wasn't alone in that now.

"Are you coming to my grandma's house after?"

"Oh, no." I shook my head. "I'm sorry, sweetie. I have to go to work."

"That's okay. Maybe you can come another day and see my comic books?"

"I'd love that."

He looked behind me and smiled. "I have to go."

We gave each other a quick hug and when he walked away, my eyes were on the hole in the ground. I sighed. Warren put his arm around me and moved closer to me again.

"Do you really have to go to work?" he asked.

"I just wanted to come by to . . . my dad was coming to pay his respects and I thought . . ." I paused to take a breath and closed my eyes. "I just—"

"Shhh," he said, kissing my cheek, my jaw. Every time I felt his lips against me, I shivered.

"Warren," I whispered.

"Baby, look at me."

My stomach dipped. I kept my eyes shut. "Please don't. I just came to . . ."

He grabbed my face and turned it toward him. I opened

my eyes and looked at him. "You're here for me, despite hating my father, despite the bad memories my last name brings up, you're here for me, and that's just one more reason why I love you."

"Warren, don't," I pleaded.

"I have to. If I don't do this now, I'll never get the chance." He brought his other hand to cup the other side of my face. "It was wrong of me to lie to you. If I could go back and do it all over again, I would have told you who I was. I'm sorry. Please forgive me. Please come back to me."

I shook my head slowly, closing my eyes but leaning into him, relishing the way his warm touch felt against me. I opened my eyes again just as a tear slipped down his cheek. The sight of it made me hurt all over again.

"I'm sorry about your dad. I really am, but I need time," I whispered.

"How do I make this better, Camila? How can I make you love me again?"

I smiled, though it was a sad smile, and lifted my hand to his face, brushing the path his tear had trickled down. "I never fell out of love with you, Warren. How could I? Love is easy to rekindle, but once you lose trust . . . it's hard to go back to the way things used to be."

He swallowed and nodded. "I understand."

"I have to go."

We both stood at the same time. I started walking toward my dad and stopped short when I saw he was talking to Thomas and his mom. Warren stopped walking beside me. For a moment I just stood there, willing my legs to move forward. I would pay my respects and excuse myself. But then I remembered the clear disapproval on Thomas's face at the cocktail party. Warren's hand closed over mine. I tilted my face to look at him.

"I want you to meet my mom."

My eyes widened. "I don't think that's—"

He tugged my arm and before I knew it, we were in front of them.

"I'm so sorry for your loss," I said before Warren could open his mouth.

His mom offered a small smile. "Thank you."

Thomas said the same.

"This is Camila," Warren said, looking at his mom. "She's the woman I'm going to marry."

I gasped, my eyes widening. I felt the rush of heat spread through my face as I looked up at him. He gave me a small smile. My eyes widened even more.

"It's nice to meet you, Camila," his mom said. I glanced back at her.

"I wish it were under different circumstances," I replied, still wishing the earth would swallow me up.

Thomas looked at me. "Cayden speaks highly about you."

"He's a great kid," I said, smiling, a real smile. He smiled back.

"Thank you."

Dad jumped in, looking amused. "Camila's my youngest daughter."

Neither of them looked surprised by this information. I wondered if they'd known all along. I wondered if Thomas knew who I was when he cast judgment on me. Maybe it was why he'd done it. Whatever the case, it wasn't the time or place to question any of it. I said my goodbyes and left on a good note.

Chapter
FORTY-ONE

Warren

I showed up at her door at eleven o'clock that night. I'd been
drinking, but not drunk, and sadness seemed to envelop
me every time I closed my eyes. After my father cut me
off when I was a teenager, I said I'd never cry at his funeral.
Then, somehow I managed to convince myself I didn't need
anybody. That I could survive the ruthless world alone. My
grandparents, who cooked for me and made sure I wasn't
too out of line, quickly proved me wrong. As did the press,
constantly on my back, scrutinizing my every move. My
nephew, who made me smile harder than anybody I knew.
And then by Camila, who taught me that there was much
more to life than aesthetics and material things. She opened
the door after my fifth knock, her eyes heavily lidded from

sleep, her hair all messy from tossing and turning, her mouth dropped in surprised when she saw me.

"It's almost midnight," she said.

"I know. I'm sorry. I didn't want to be alone." I held my breath and let it out slowly, relieved when she held the door open for me and shut it behind me.

"When do you go back home?"

"Tomorrow morning," I said, turning around to face her.

"How early is your flight?"

"I have to be at the airport at seven in the morning."

She stayed quiet for a long moment. I looked around the apartment.

"Do you want to stay over?" she whispered.

My eyes snapped to hers. "What?"

"You can just . . . I mean you don't have to and I'm not saying I'm going to have sex with you or anything."

"I won't try anything." I cleared my throat. "Not that I don't want to, but . . . I won't try anything."

She nodded, yawning as she brushed past me and walked into the bedroom. I followed her. She got back in bed and pulled the cover over her and I went to the other side of it, taking my clothes off as I walked. My back was facing her as I tossed my jeans to the side and I wondered if she was watching me undress. She'd said no sex. I needed to remind myself not to take it there. She said she needed to regain my trust and for once I needed to respect that without pushing. When I got into bed and pulled the covers over me, she switched off the lamp beside her. I breathed in deeply, taking in the smell of her sheets, the smell of her. All I wanted to do was scoot over and wrap my arms around her, but I was afraid she'd turn me away. I cleared my throat as I moved closer until we were side to side, her arm against mine.

"You said I needed to regain your trust. How do I do that?"

She sighed. "I don't know. Honestly. I wish there was a formula to the heart."

I turned on my side. She turned on hers. I couldn't see her in the darkness, but I could feel her and that was enough. "I changed my last name, legally, to Silva when I turned eighteen. My dad had disowned me, so I figured what the hell? I might as well, right? So I changed my name." I swallowed. "I don't think he ever forgave me for that. He looked at me like I was a stranger."

"Did he finally talk to you?" she asked tentatively, whispered.

"Yeah." I felt myself smile. "I started talking to him after you and I . . . when I came back. I figured I couldn't just sit there and keep scrolling my Instagram and Twitter feed. So I started talking to him. I told him about us. I told him what I'd done and who you were and how I'd met your dad. He let me talk for what felt like hours and didn't say a word. When I stood up to leave and he finally spoke, it was to tell me I was a complete idiot if I let you go."

I heard her sharp intake of breath.

"And that I didn't deserve you." I paused. "I don't. I know I don't. I'm sorry I kept that from you. It was wrong and I shouldn't have, but once I got to know you I was too afraid to lose you. You're the best person I've ever met, Camila, and I don't deserve you, but I need you. Even in your absence, my love for you grows."

She didn't talk, but she sniffled and that was enough for me. I brought my hand to her face and brushed her wet cheek with my thumb. "Take me back, baby. I'm homesick without you."

"God, Warren," she whispered, sniffling as she leaned into me. "I hate you, you know that?"

"You love me. That's why this hurts so much."

She shook her face and I pulled her closer, brushing my lips along her wet cheeks, her nose, her lips.

"Tell me you love me," I whispered.

"Love isn't enough. Not for us." She sniffled again, and this time her shoulders shook with her cry. "I'm sorry."

I pulled her into my chest and closed my eyes as I held her there for a long moment. I spoke against her hair. "What would make it enough?"

"I don't think even we have the power to change that," she whispered. "Your life is elsewhere. Mine is here."

"Would you move for me, if I asked you to?" I asked, leaning back slightly to make out her soft features.

"I . . . I don't know." She paused. "I just got my dad back, War. My life is here. I don't know."

"I understand." I didn't like it, but I understood it.

It wouldn't be fair for me to ask her to change her entire life for me. I needed to work for that right again, and even if I hadn't lost it, it wouldn't have been fair to her. I brushed my thumb against her cheek again, my face coming closer to hers until the tips of our noses touched.

"I miss you so fucking much," I whispered.

"You're not playing fair."

"I know." I smiled against her lips. "I can't seem to think with fair terms when it comes to you."

She didn't respond, but her breath picked up.

"What are you thinking about right now?"

"You touching me," she whispered.

My breath hitched. My heart started pounding at a speed it normally only used on the pitch. "Touching you how?"

"You know how."

"Where?"

"Anywhere," she said, pressing her chest against mine. "Everywhere."

My hand traveled down her face, her soft neck, her slender shoulder. I cupped her breast over her shirt and closed my eyes, holding back a groan at how it felt in my palm.

"I have to ask you something," I said, eyes still closed.

"Ask," she whispered.

"Have you . . . I saw you with Quinn."

I felt her hand on the side of my face and opened my eyes to meet hers. "Never, Warren. Never."

I let out a relieved breath and dipped my head to press my lips against hers. I licked the seam of her bottom lip, probing until my tongue met hers. She moaned into my mouth, deepening the kiss, and I molded myself against her, pulling one of her legs over my hip and pushing my erection against her pussy. She moaned louder.

"Warren," she said, a pant as she broke the kiss.

"Where do you need me? Tell me."

She leaned up and took her shirt off. Her underwear came off next. She tossed both away from the bed before tugging on the elastic of my briefs. I chuckled.

"Patience, baby. We have all night," I said, taking off my briefs and tossing them aside.

"Tonight is all we have," she whispered, throwing her leg over me and climbing on top of me.

She leaned down, her hair grazing the sides of my face as she pressed her lips against me. With one hand, she reached between us and closed a hand around me, stroking me slowly as she continued to kiss me. My hips jerked up. Her words replayed in my head. *Tonight is all we have.* I refused to believe that. I refused to accept that. I fought the urge to take the lead and flip her on her back and claim her right there, hard and fast, just for saying that, just for doubting what we had. I reached between her legs and stroked her. The moment my fingers slipped through her folds, she threw her head back with a moan.

"Camila," I groaned. "You're so wet for me."

She spread her legs farther apart and held her breath as she took me in, pausing to adjust herself on top of me as I gripped her hips and guided her. My breath was coming in short spurts as I waited for her to start moving. I swallowed, taking a moment to calm down, and when she placed the palms of her hands on my chest and finally began to rock against me, I thought I would lose the little reserve I had left. Each time she gyrated her hips and met my thrusts, a spike of adrenaline rushed straight into my heart. Every time she said my name, like a plea, a part of me felt like it was breaking. I lifted her and turned us over so that she was on her back and thrust deep inside her, deeper still. She gasped loudly.

"I want you to feel me everywhere," I said against her lips, thrusting again. "I want you to remember what we're like together." Her hands came up to my arms, her nails digging into my triceps. "I want you to feel what you're letting go of."

"I'm not," she gasped. "I'm not letting go of you."

I stopped moving and looked into her eyes, they were wild and wide. "You're not?"

"I just don't see how this could work," she said, tears filling her eyes. "I don't see how me being here and you being in England could work."

"We'll make it work." I slammed into her again. She gasped, her back arching, her nails digging deeper.

"How?"

"We'll figure it out." I cupped her breast and tweaked her nipple while kissing her lips, her cheek, her eyelids, her chin, her neck.

"Soccer is your life," she whispered.

I stopped moving again and stared down at her. At this beautiful, selfless woman who was willing to do anything for anybody without question. At this beautiful woman who showed up at my father's funeral, even though she hated him, just to see me. I leaned down and kissed her again, wishing that was enough to wipe all her cares away. I wished I could show her, not just tell her, that she was my life. Instead, I made love to her until we were both sated and out of breath, and then I held her in my arms and kissed her shoulders, her face, her lips, her head, until I had to wake up to make my flight.

Chapter
FORTY-TWO

Warren

The season started two weeks ago and out in the field I felt like a god every time the crowd screamed my name, but at home, when alone in bed, my emotions felt like a war zone. I felt Camila's pull from three thousand miles away. I missed her smile, longed to see her face, and ached whenever I thought about having her in my arms again.

The show went on.

Life didn't stop for us or our grievances. She refused to give up her job because she didn't want to become like her mother, a woman who needed a man to survive in the world, and even though I didn't understand it, I respected her enough not to continue to hassle her about it. I'd become so accustomed to not having days off, that when I finally arrived back from New York for good, I missed it. That alone was odd. Missing a city that I'd tried my best to stay away from for the majority of my life. But it had grown on me. The bustle, the loud music playing at night around Camila's neighborhood, the laughter as people told stories of their home countries. Those were things I had never experienced when I lived there, and things I never thought had the ability to make me feel at home.

Now every time I stood on that field, I wondered whether or not she was watching me. Every movement I made was second nature to me. Every dribble, every pass, every kick and block. Those were things I didn't have to over-think, but when Camila was on my mind and I was out there, I found my brain working harder to catch up with my movements. A couple of my passes didn't transfer faster and got blocked by the opposing team. Dribbles were kicked away. Things that were on point just months ago were suddenly questionable. Had she submerged herself so deeply in my thoughts that I couldn't even untangle her long enough to focus on one task without thinking of her as well? After one spectacularly awful game, my coach pulled me aside to tell me to get my head out of my ass.

"I know you just lost your father, but you have a whole bloody team depending on you."

He was right, of course. And yet, his words didn't spark the ammunition in me that they normally did.

Chapter
FORTY-THREE

Camila

Warren had been gone a week and with each passing day, I missed him more. We talked every day sometimes twice a day at ridiculous hours because of the time difference, but each time I heard his voice I forgot about the time. In my heart, I think I forgave him before I saw him at his father's funeral, but after that day, it just felt like a petty thing to hold on to. Yes, he kept something from me, but he treated me the way I'd only dreamed of being treated. That night, after a trying day at Winsor, he called me on FaceTime while I was making myself dinner, as he did most days around five o'clock. I put the phone up against the cookbook in my kitchen as I tossed the stir fry.

"I wish I was there," he said.

I glanced over my shoulder and smiled at the screen. "Me too."

"Are you making chicken or shrimp?"

"Shrimp."

"I *really* wish I was there."

I covered the wok and went back to the phone, leaning my elbows on the table as I looked at him. "I'm sorry you lost your game."

"Were you watching?"

I nodded.

"Were you bored?"

I laughed. "Surprisingly, I wasn't. Charlie kind of walked me through what we were watching. He kept asking if I knew what you were going to do about Barcelona."

"What'd you tell him?"

"That I didn't know." I paused, searching his eyes. "I don't even think *you* know."

He grinned, folding an arm behind his head and leaning back into the pillow as he brought his phone over his face. My eyes drifted down to his bare chest. I sighed.

"I wish I was there."

His eyes darkened. "You have no idea how much I wish you were here."

I pushed off my elbows and turned back to the stove, switching it off and uncovering the wok to serve my food. I settled into the barstool and waited for it to cool as I looked at him, his eyes kept closing and I hated that we had such a time difference between us.

"You should go to sleep," I said.

His eyes popped open. "No, no. I'm awake."

"You have another long day tomorrow."

He sighed and nodded. "Would you move with me? I

know you don't like the lifestyle, and I know some of the wives pissed you off, but if I take the deal in Barcelona we'd be near my family. We can live wherever you want, in the city, in the countryside."

My heart leaped. I pushed my plate aside. "That's—"

"I know. It's a big change. I know you're worried about losing your life and everything you've worked for, but you can do what you're doing now over here. There are so many children here that would benefit from your parks." He paused, letting out a breath. "You wouldn't be alone. I would make sure you wouldn't feel alone."

The fact that he'd been thinking about this so thoroughly warmed my heart and broke it a little. I wanted nothing more than to be with him, but being with him meant leaving everything behind. My sister, my parents, my brother, Charlie, my neighborhood.

"Warren," I whispered, blinking rapidly. "I need time. I already gave you the reasons as to why I can't just pick up and move."

"For a few years?" he asked, eyes pleading.

"You really are impossible to say no to." I sighed, smiling. He chuckled. "But, I still need time."

"How much time?"

I shrugged. "A few months?"

He yawned again. "I can do a few months."

"Hey, you coming to watch the game today?"

I laughed. Charlie's new favorite hobby was making me skip work so I could hang out at the bar in the middle of the afternoon and watch soccer with him. As much as I enjoyed the skipping work part, I was pretty sure Nancy was starting to catch on to what I was doing when I took those long lunch breaks.

"I'm not sure. I have to take some papers to Winsor."

"It's one day," he said.

"That's what we said yesterday."

"One more day. I'll feed you and give you alcohol. What more could you possibly want?"

"Fine. I'm going to be late, though."

"It's a ninety-minute game. How late will you be?"

I rolled my eyes. "It's a ninety-minute game and even if I get there eighty minutes late, chances are I won't miss anything."

He chuckled. "Your fucking boyfriend is always saying shit to you at the camera. I'm tired of recording that shit and showing you replays so you can pretend you saw it live. Next time he calls, I'm gonna tell him."

My eyes widened. "You wouldn't."

"Try me."

"Fine. I'll only be like five minutes late, since it's so vital I be there for the entire game."

I made it back from Brooklyn and was in Charlie's bar fifteen minutes after the game started. I looked up at the screen as I took a seat at the bar.

"Zero to zero. Shocker."

Charlie laughed. "Your boyfriend is playing his ass off, though."

I smiled and reached for the beer he was handing me. "Isn't that Barcelona?"

"Yeah, care to share any inside information with the class?" Charlie asked, leaning against the bar and looking up at the TV. "Because I for one am dying to know."

"Nope," I said, taking a sip of my beer. "If you were him,

would you stay or go?"

Charlie turned around to face me and shrugged. "Barcelona has a better team. All the playmakers are there, but Manchester is like the Yankees. Let's say the Mets got all your favorite players. Jeter—"

"That would never happen," I said, interrupting him. He laughed.

"Let's pretend. Jeter, Robinson Canó, Yasiel Puig, Clayton Kershaw are all on the Mets, and you play for the Yankees, and even though it's a good team with potential, and you grew up idolizing them—"

"He grew up idolizing Barcelona," I said, taking another sip of beer.

Charlie's brows rose. "Well, shit."

I shrugged and looked back up at the screen. I smiled when I spotted him. "He looks really good in a soccer uniform."

Charlie chuckled. "That's what your sister said when she was here yesterday."

"Of course she did," I said, smiling. "Did she also say Adam would look good in one? Because she loves to do that."

"She didn't and I don't think Adam would know what the fuck to do if the ball landed at his feet."

"He'd probably pick it up and throw it with his hands," I said. We both laughed. I flinched when I saw Warren jump up, get kicked in the shin, and land on his side. "You would think this sport would be less gruesome than American football, but it's equally as messed up."

"Have you ever asked War if they throw themselves on the floor to rest?"

"No, but I heard one of his teammates say that. I thought he was joking," I said, watching as Warren got up to complain to the referee. "But I'm starting to think there was something to it."

We kept watching the game. My eyes were glued to Warren as he made his way up the field with the ball at his feet. He wound around the opposing players with such skill, I avoided blinking to ensure I didn't miss any of it. He was right in front of the goal. Charlie started chanting under his breath *War Zone. War Zone.* I clutched on to the bar with both hands and held my breath as I watched him. The ball was under his right foot.

"Why is he just standing there?" I shouted, jumping out of the stool as I watched.

"He does that."

"But why?" I said. It sounded more like a whine.

"To build hype," Charlie said. "I don't fucking know but it makes my anxiety go through the roof every time, even though I know he's going to bend the shit out of the ball."

My heart lurched into my throat. I let out a strangled scream, still gripping on to the edge of the bar. "Jesus Christ, Warren. Kick the fucking ball!"

He tilted his face and smiled. It was a slow, seductive smile I'd become familiar with. My heart pounded faster. Then, he kicked the ball, his leg swinging, his body lifting with the motion, and just as it left him, an opposing player came up and tried to kick it away at the same time, but missed and kicked him instead, sending Warren straight into the ground.

"Goooooooooooooooaaaaaaaaaaal!" was shouted continuously.

Charlie jumped up screaming. I jumped up screaming. But once our adrenaline simmered, we looked back at the screen and realized that Warren was still on the ground, clutching his knee.

"Oh my God," I said, bringing my hand over my mouth. "Do you think . . ."

Charlie shook his.

My heart kept pounding. The commentators speculated about his status. Paramedics came on the field and lifted him onto a gurney. I took my phone out and started calling, even though I knew he wouldn't be able to pick up.

"Fuck," I said. "Fuck. Fuck. Fuck."

I called Miriam. She answered after the second ring. "Are you at the game?" I asked, looking at the screen as tears clouded my vision.

"No, I just saw what happened," she said. "Sergio's there. We'll hear back soon."

"Oh my God," I whispered.

"It'll be okay," she said. "It'll be okay. I'll call you as soon as I hear anything."

I blinked rapidly, nodding even though she couldn't see me, thanked her and hung up. Was this what helplessness felt like? The game went on and ended one to zero. Manchester won. I watched as Warren's teammates spoke after the game and wished him well before the cameras cut to the commentators, who were speculating what kind of injury he could have. They must have replayed the clip twenty times and each time, I cried harder.

"What is taking them so long to call back?" I said.

Charlie came around the bar and put a hand on my shoulder. "They'll call. He'll be okay. This happens all the time."

"I have to go," I said once patrons started to walk into the bar. I picked up my bag and my phone.

"Call me when you hear news," Charlie called out as I

walked out the door.

I was pacing my apartment for the hundredth time when Vanessa got there. She wrapped her arms around me and asked if I'd heard anything.

"Not yet."

I sat on the couch while she rummaged through my kitchen and popped open a bottle of wine. She came back and handed me a glass before settling down beside me. My phone buzzed beside me and I jumped up, setting down the glass and answering the unknown number.

"Camila, it's Sergio."

My heart stopped beating. "Is he okay?"

"He'll be fine. He's doing a live conference right now."

I picked up my remote and started flipping to the sports channels, sucking in a breath when I saw Warren walking, albeit limping a little. I let out a relieved sigh. He was standing on it with no help, which meant he probably hadn't torn anything.

"Are you watching?" Sergio asked.

I nodded and then realized he couldn't see me. "Yeah. Thank God he can walk."

"He should be out on the field in a few days," Sergio said. "Assuming it's just a bruised knee, which is what it looks like."

He also let out a relieved breath, but stayed on the phone with me as I watched, and I could hear the chaos on his end. I was sure he was holding his breath, as I was, waiting for the news on his knee. Warren glanced up at the first reporter, who was off camera. A man's voice rang through the room.

"How is your knee?"

"It's seen better days, but it will be fine."

"How many games will you have to miss?"

"Will this delay your decision on the loan?"

"Will you be staying in Manchester for good?"

All of the questions shot to him at once. Warren chuckled, smiling that charming yet measured smile he'd perfected. "One at a time," he said and took a deep breath. "My knee is only a part of the reason I'm here right now. I wanted you to hear from me that I'm taking a break from football."

"What is he talking about?" Vanessa said beside me.

"What is he talking about?" I said to Sergio on the phone.

"What the fuck is he talking about?" Sergio mumbled into the line. "I have to go."

I put the phone down as Sergio ended the call and continued to stare at the television with my mouth agape.

"As I said before, my knee will be fine. It needs ice and a little rest, I didn't tear or break anything." He paused, his eyes finding the camera, looking into it, at us. At me. "I've been playing football for as long as I can remember. I can't recall a time I took a break from it. I can't recall a time I wanted to. But if this incident is any indication of where my head is right now, I think it's safe to say I need one."

"But what will the team do?"

"What does your club manager, Josef say about your decision?"

"What do your teammates think of this?"

Warren made a movement with his hands telling the crowd to settle down. When they all stopped talking and the only thing you could hear were cameras snapping, he began to speak again.

"I understand this is a difficult thing to take in, but I'm a firm believer that your head should always be in the game and mine just isn't," he said. His face was solemn, the way he looked when he was sitting alone in his father's funeral watching the casket lower into the ground. As if this news was just as difficult as that one.

"I can't breathe," I whispered, placing a hand over my heart.

"He's quitting?" my sister whispered beside me.

"For the first time in my life, I'm putting something other than football first, and I hope you can respect my decision and accept it as well as my club did," he said, and stood up.

He walked out of the room and disappeared to the back while the reporters started to talk amongst themselves. The camera shot back to three ESPN commentators who looked as shell-shocked as I felt.

"That was unexpected," one said, letting out a laugh.

"I mean . . ." Another shook his head. "I'm floored. I was stunned when Messi announced he would no longer be playing for Argentina, but Silva? . . . I'm stunned."

The third still had his mouth hanging open. I wondered if this was something he hadn't learned to handle in journalism school. They recovered and started to talk about the many reasons Warren was taking time for himself. At the top of the list was his father's recent death. My sister switched off the television. I could feel her eyes on me, but I couldn't will myself to acknowledge her. All I could do was think about Warren and replay that conference. What was he thinking? Why hadn't he called me?

Chapter
FORTY-FOUR

Camila

It had been over forty-eight hours and I'd only heard from Warren once. He reassured me he was fine, that he had things he needed to take care of, that his father's death made him reassess some things, and he promised he'd call me once he had some things sorted. He said all of the right words to make me stop worrying, but I knew him. I could hear the pain in his voice. I could hear the frown and the sadness and it made my stomach tie up in knots. That morning, while I walked down the sidewalk, I looked up flights to Manchester.

"Holy shit," I said aloud as I looked at the price.

"You haven't been by the colmado, Rubia."

My head snapped up to look at Pedro from the corner store. I smiled. "I know. I've been busy. I'll go by this week, though. I'm running out of milk."

"Did your boyfriend go back to Europe?"

"Yeah. I was just looking up flights right now," I said with a sigh, putting my phone away.

"And?"

"And they're expensive as hell. I'd have to sell at least my kidneys."

Pedro chuckled, his eyes lighting up. "Hey, as long as you don't sell your liver."

"See you later," I called out, still smiling, as I walked down the steps to the train.

With something that must have been sheer luck, the doors were opening up as I stepped onto the platform. I picked up my pace and made it just in time and even found a seat right by the door. Closing my eyes, I let out a relieved breath. I could always ask for an extension on my rent. Or go a month without paying the full amount I sent in to pay for my student loans. I was calculating everything in my head when the person beside me nudged me.

"That you?" he asked.

My gaze cut to the old man beside me. I shot him a look that I hoped screamed *leave me the hell alone. I can't give you money right now because I'm trying to calculate every penny in my name to see if I can afford a trip to see my boyfriend.* He just looked at me and nodded up and asked once more, "That you?"

I followed his line of vision, my eyes widening when I saw the brand new advertisements above. I gripped the bar and took a step back, hitting the closed door behind me. Sure enough, it was me. More accurately, it was us. The picture we'd taken at the cocktail party, and beside it the words: "Love makes people do corny things."

My breath hitched in my throat. "Oh my God."

Beside it was a picture of one of the advertisements I'd seen in Manchester with the words, "Only for Camila." I began to laugh and took out my phone to snap pictures of it. I got up and walked the length of the train, making sure I documented them all. Another one, on a black background and white letters that read: "*I put everything aside for you.*"

That one in particular made me stop right there in the middle of the train. I could only stare at it. I felt the emotion building in my chest, in my eyes, and thankfully the train came to a screeching stop that jolted me as I crashed into the lady beside me. I apologized quickly and got off at my stop. As I stepped off, the billboard on the wall in front of me, the one the Housewives had ownership of until this moment, caught my attention. It was a picture of a soccer ball and the words, "This isn't my life. You are."

I stopped walking, my hands falling limp to my sides. I wiped more tears before I checked my phone. Still no reception. I looked around and didn't see any familiar faces, so I took the stairs two at a time to the surface in search of reception.

When I reached the landing, Warren was standing at the top. My heart fell so hard into my stomach I thought I'd lose balance. My mouth dropped and I managed to give him a quick once-over. He was wearing blue basketball shorts, a Yankees T-shirt, a wrap around his left knee, and a single crutch in front of him. His hair was brushed back neatly and although he wasn't smiling, his eyes were full of amusement as he looked at me. When my brain finally snapped back and I realized he was indeed standing in front of me, I ran up to him, throwing my arms around him, and burying my face in his neck as he leaned down and wrapped his arms around me and squeezed me to him. I started to cry again.

"I'm so sorry I wasn't there. I didn't know what to do with myself. I was looking up flights before I got on the train," I said against him. He stroked my back softly and hugged me tighter. When I collected myself, I pulled away from him. He brought both his hands to cup my face and brushed my tears with his thumbs.

"Hey, I got you."

"I saw your . . . announcements," I said, smiling. I brought my hands up to his, which were still on my face, and moved them one at a time to kiss his palms.

"Not too corny for you?"

I fought a laugh. "Just barely."

"Just barely," he said, grinning, eyes full of mischief. "You should've seen the other picture of us I was going to put up there."

Warmth flooded my cheeks. I slapped his arm playfully when he started to laugh.

"I thought you were going to be upset about it," he said, searching my eyes as he dropped his hands from my face.

I couldn't stop smiling. "It's not like you proposed on one of them."

He laughed loudly, throwing his head back and pulled me into another hug. He started to walk, leading me away from the spot we were standing in.

"You need a crutch to walk?" I asked. He let out a heavy breath, gripping on to the crutch on his other hand.

"Not really, but the doctor wants me to take it easy," he said, stopping and standing against the side of the wall of the McDonalds. I did the same and looked up at him.

"But you're not hurt?"

He smiled. "I'll be fine."

"Warren, in that sign," I whispered, feeling tears flooding back. I tore my gaze away from his momentarily. "At the conference..."

"You watched it?"

I nodded.

He turned his body into mine and cupped the side of my face, looking at me with an adoring expression in his eyes. "I've been playing my entire life and I've never been so out of a game than I was the other day. My head wasn't in it, my emotions weren't in it, my concentration was shit..."

My chest began to hurt again. "Because of me."

"Maybe," he said.

"Why aren't you upset about this?" I said. "Soccer is your life. I'm messing up an important part of your life."

His gaze searched mine. He brought up his crutch with his other hand and pointed them up, to the spot on the other side of the sidewalk, where the subway train was posted above a black background that read, "Will you marry me?" in white letters. I gasped, eyes wide. My eyes cut to his again.

"*You* are my life, Camila. *You.* I love football. I love my fans. I love running down that field every day, but none of that means anything if I can't enjoy it with you. And there's nothing I love more than you."

He dropped his hand and reached into his pocket, pulling out a ring and offering it to me. My mouth was still hanging open, tears trickling down my cheeks as I looked up at him.

"I'm taking a break to spend time with you, and there's nowhere else I'd rather be."

I shook my head, tears falling down my face. "You'll regret it. You'll get bored and start to hate me."

"No, baby," he said. I shook my head again. He put an

arm around me and pulled me into his chest. "There is nothing. Absolutely nothing I'd rather be doing than spending my days with you."

"What happens if you decide you want to go back and play next week?"

"That's something we can deal with then," he said against my hair.

"What if you wait too long and they don't take you back because you're too old and your knees are shitty?"

He looked at me with a mix of amusement and offense on his face. "Well then, I guess I'll have to get a job at Winsor."

That made me laugh. He grinned. "But—"

"Don't fight me on this, Rocky," he whispered, coming close, pressing his lips against mine in a soft, chaste kiss. "Marry me."

"Yes," I finally managed, my lip trembling. "Yes. Of course, yes."

His grin was so wide, it made me wish I'd said yes as soon as I spotted him waiting for me on the street. He slipped the ring on my finger—it was slightly too big.

"Fuck. I knew I shouldn't have trusted Vanessa."

"You told Vanessa?" I shouted.

He chuckled and lifted the crutch again, pointing to the other side of the street. I frowned, moving to see what he was pointing at now, and saw his black SUV, Antoine standing there with a phone pointed at us, my sister beside him doing the same. I could tell she was crying from here. My mom was beside her doing the same, also crying. My dad was beside them, also crying. My brother was just standing there smiling, as was Charlie. Adam lifted his arms in victory. I laughed loudly and looked back at Warren.

"I love you so much."

"Not as much as I love you," he said, kissing me again.

Chapter
FORTY-FIVE

Warren

"How does it feel to be a new resident of Washington Heights?" my brother asked as he walked through the door with a bottle of wine in one hand and his wife's in the other.

"It feels good," I said, grinning.

And I meant it. I moved in with Camila the day I proposed. I didn't give her much of a choice. I showed up with all my stuff and cleared some of her drawers to make room for my things. That was a few weeks ago, but between paperwork for Belmonte that my brother, Mom and I had to go through, my physical therapy, interviews, making sure my sponsors knew I would indeed be back soon, and everything else, I had barely got any sleep. That was until two days ago when Camila took my cellphone and said, "No more."

"We're having family over in two days. Get your stuff together, pick up the living room, take your sneakers to the closet, and stop taking calls for one day. One day, Warren," she said, her eyes forming a glare that she somehow managed to make look like a plea.

I couldn't argue with her. Camila didn't ask for much, but when she did want something, she made sure I knew it and didn't argue with her about it. She spent the day making rice, beans, fried chicken, fried plantains, and baked a cake which she decorated with Captain America figures for Cayden. He ran right up to the cake as soon as he saw it and gave her a huge hug. The smile on her face made the whole picking up after my shit and getting things prepared for the day worth it.

"Every time you look at her, you start drooling," my brother said as he served glasses of wine.

My gaze cut to his as I took one of the glasses from his hand. "Can you blame me?"

He smiled and looked over at her and his pregnant wife. "Nah. I just can't believe you're not bored living here and not playing pro."

I shrugged. I definitely missed it. I couldn't lie about that. Every day when Camila asked me, I responded a genuine yes, I missed it a lot. Would I trade her for that life, though? No. There was no comparison. Football taught me a lot about myself, about patience, winning, and losing. Camila taught me to look at things differently. To appreciate things in a way I probably never would have, had it not been for her. We started talking more seriously about moving so I could go back to playing and she seemed to be on board with the plan. I wouldn't push her on it. I'd wait until I knew she was ready to go with me.

"I'm good," I said.

Tom chuckled. "I can see that. Do you think you'll go back?"

"Yeah. I think she's ready to take the leap."

"Whatever happened with Elena? Did she say how she found out where Camila lived?"

I sighed heavily, my mood instantly dampened at the mention of her name. "She saw pictures of us online from the Winsor event and did some digging. I can't believe I ever thought I was in love with that parasite."

"I tried to warn you," he said.

I rolled my eyes.

Vanessa and Adam arrived shortly after, followed by her parents and Johnny. My mom showed up last and brought a spread of cheese with her. Once we were all there, Camila came around with a basket in her hands.

"Everybody needs to put their phones in here. You'll get them back when you leave."

Our jaws dropped.

"Baby," I said, but the look she gave me made me shut my mouth. I shrugged and looked around the room. "She's the boss."

Everybody laughed and shook their heads, but did as they were instructed. It was the best time I'd ever had with my family. My only regret was that my father wasn't there to share it with us. As the days passed, I found myself wishing I hadn't spent so many years holding on to the grudge I had against him. Wishing I'd tried harder to talk to him, to visit him, and that I hadn't waited until he'd become sick to turn that around. Yet, as I looked around the room and saw the people I loved sitting together, my heart swelled. I knew things had panned out exactly as they were supposed to.

Epilogue

Camila

Six months later

"It's weird to see him wearing that jersey," I said, glancing at Warren's grandfather, who was sitting beside me wearing the same one.

"That's the jersey he was born to wear," he responded gruffly.

I laughed at the grumpy old man beside me. After a couple months of being at home in New York, I surprised everybody by going into Winsor with my resignation. Nancy wasn't caught off guard by this and offered to let me work from home. I told her home would be Barcelona soon enough, and she insisted I keep my job anyway. At least temporarily, until I could find something else to do and she could find a replacement. Warren was shocked by the news. And elated. He'd stayed true to his word and hadn't brought up moving

351

once, but every now and then I'd come home for lunch and catch him pacing the living room while he watched a game. Whenever a bad play was made or a goal was missed the entire building heard him scream. I thought at any moment he'd dive into the television and appear on the other side of the screen.

We spent a lot of time with his mom, who was one of the sweetest women I'd ever met. She spoke a lot about being a soccer mom and being so proud of Warren when he decided to move in with her parents in Barcelona to follow his dreams. "Who has dreams that big at fourteen?" she'd said with tears in her eyes. When he wasn't around, she told me about the guilt she carried for not forcing Warren and his father to make amends sooner. "I tried, but they're both so stubborn."

Despite feeling a little guilty for keeping Warren off the pitch for so long, a part of me was happy he was in New York and away from everything that came with his demanding career. He needed time to heal and be with his family while they grieved. Just as I needed time to heal and completely accept my father back into my life. He'd been thrilled when I told him we were moving. *Just for a while*, I said. *We'll be back before you know it.* I wasn't sure how long it would take, but every time the crowd screamed *War Zone* and the camera panned to my face during the game—which much to my embarrassment was a lot—Warren looked up at the screen and blew me a kiss. Every time. And every time I felt myself melt a little more.

"You haven't eaten anything," his grandmother said as she joined us in the suite again.

"I'm okay."

"Are you sure?" Her gaze dropped to my stomach.

I laughed. I wasn't pregnant *yet,* but it was all she ever talked about. And his mom. And mine. And now my newly pregnant sister.

"I'm positive," I responded, smiling.

"Just checking," she said. "Do you think he'll score today?"

The old man shushed his wife. "You'll jinx him."

When Warren was in front of the goal and the crowd started chanting their *War Zone, War Zone, War Zone,* I jumped out of my seat and clasped my hands together, quietly chanting with them. My heart was in my throat as I watched him dribble to the right and escape his opponent, then to the left, and finally, with two guys on either side of him, he jumped up and kicked it.

The crowd went wild. My heart soared as I watched him run down the field with his arms up as his teammates ran to him and embraced him. I smiled broadly. I loved the new club, and even the old club had learned to accept me and welcomed me with open arms when we came back. The wives were nice, their kids were adorable, and their husbands had such great respect for mine that I couldn't help but love them as well. Warren glanced up to where he knew we were sitting and blew a kiss with his hand, mouthing the words, "That one was for you."

I blew a kiss back even though I knew he couldn't see me. The wide grin on his face made me wonder if he felt it.

Epilogue
PART DEUX

Reporter: "So the rumors were true after all?"

Warren chuckled, leaning back in his chair. "What? What rumors?"

Reporter: "Ah, no need to be coy. You're a married man with a spanking new contract in a brand-new city. The entire world has been following your story for months now."

Warren continued to smile as he looked at her. "What story would that be?"

Reporter, laughing: "Everything I just said. Barcelona seems to have taken her in with open arms, fans have dedicated several social media accounts to just the two of you. They're calling her their queen."

Warren tilted his head. "They'd be right to call her that. She's my queen."

Reporter: "They say it takes a special queen to tame a dragon. Tell us more about your New York girl."

"My New York girl," Warren said slowly with a smile on his face. "Well, if you believe the rumors, I guess you know that she's not my New York girl. She's my life, and the reason I'm back on the field."

Reporter: "Any plans on starting a family? I read somewhere that she wants to adopt."

"We do, actually. We're also exploring the possibility of having our own." He looked at the camera. "But for now, we're just chasing moments together. After all, isn't that what life is about?"

Acknowledgements

I always say that I'm not going to do these and in the end I cave and write them anyway. I think one of my greatest fears is that people will think I'm ungrateful, and I'm so not, so here I am ... again.

I have so many incredible people to be thankful for and I'm always afraid I'll forget a name (I always forget at least one name), but I'm going to try my best.

My family- I'd give up anything, everything for you. Thank you for not making me.

OTIS crew- I love you. Thanks for answering all of my soccer questions, making me get a stomach ache from laughing every day, and getting me drunk every weekend (well, not eeevveerrrryyyy weekend ;) . #Bathroomfight ... it'll make it into my next book. Just you wait. LOL)

Rachel- You put up with the worst of this process. Thank you so, so much for reading, rereading, and encouraging me to keep going.

Jenn Wolfel- Your encouragement means the world to me. I love you.

Clarissa LaFirst- I'm SO happy you told me that I was a hot mess and forced your help on me. It was the best thing that's happened to me this year (and I'm not just saying that). Your ideas, excitement, positive vibes, organizational skills, and reminders are always welcome and always appreciated. I love you. Thank you for putting up with my crazy.

The girls (and boys) in my FB group- You're my people. You make me laugh, cry, shake my head, and make me realize that maybe I'm not as crazy as I once thought I was. Your support is invaluable. I love you, I appreciate you, and have so much respect for you.

In NO particular order: Milasy Mugnolo, Happy Diggs, Sunny Borek, Julie Vaden, Lauren Blakely, Michelle Kannan, Yvette Vega, Christina Collie, Barbie Bohrman, Amanda Cantu, MJ Abraham, Tiffany (my favorite little psycho with the million last names), Lucia Franco, Ali Hymer, Debbie, Holly Malgieri, Katie Miller, Priscilla Perez, Teri Maxwell, Trish Brinkley, Sandra Cortez, Kayla Sunday, Julie, Sunny, Lisa Chamberlin, Sara Queen, Stephanie Brown, Christine Reiss, Kristy Bromberg, Natasha Minoso, Ursula Uriarte, Tarryn Fisher, Willow Aster, Corinne Michaels, Mia Asher, Jenn Sterling. — Your eyes, your time, and your friendship is everything.

Author friends: There are a LOT of you. Too many for me to sit here and name individually. I'm afraid that I'll forget one of you (and I WILL forget one of you), so I'll just say this— I count my blessings every day because you're in my life. We're in an industry where the majority of the CEOs are women, and I'm grateful that I have found so many bosses that I can genuinely call my friends. Women who root for my success as I root for theirs. Women who take the time to message each other, talk through problems, and figure out ways to

HELP one another. You are a dream to work with. I love you and champion for you every day.

Stacey Ryan at Champagne Formats- YOU deserve a gold medal. I need to call the Olympics and make them send you one.

Hang Le- I was so worried about having a "hot guy cover", but as soon as you agreed to take on the project, I let out a long, relieved breath (like a fictional character, but in real life). Thank you for making every single project your priority. THANK YOU for putting up with my shit.

Marion- Thank you for all of your help!

Ellie- I love you, you know that, right? Thank you so much for penciling me in and only freaking out (a little) about my timeline. You are a rockstar.

Bloggers- There are way too many of you for me to name, but that doesn't mean that I don't see and appreciate everything you do for me.

Other Books

THE HEARTS SERIES
Kaleidoscope Hearts
Paper Hearts
Elastic Hearts

Catch Me

THE DARKNESS SERIES
There is No Light in Darkness
Darkness Before Dawn

THE CONTRACTS & DECEPTIONS SERIES
The Devil's Contract
The Sinner's Bargain

Made in the USA
Middletown, DE
14 October 2018